HOT BUTTON

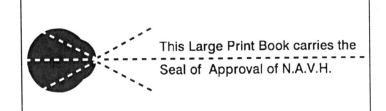

This Large Print Book carries the
Seal of Approval of N.A.V.H.

A BUTTON BOX MYSTERY

HOT BUTTON

KYLIE LOGAN

WHEELER PUBLISHING
A part of Gale, Cengage Learning

GALE
CENGAGE Learning

Detroit • New York • San Francisco • New Haven, Conn • Waterville, Maine • London

GALE
CENGAGE Learning·

LIBRARY OF CONGRESS CATALOGING-IN-PUBLICATION DATA

Logan, Kylie.
    Hot Button / by Kylie Logan. — Large Print edition.
        pages cm. — (A Button Box Mystery) (Wheeler Publishing Large Print
Cozy Mystery)
    ISBN-13: 978-1-4104-5425-6 (softcover)
    ISBN-10: 1-4104-5425-8 (softcover)
    1. Buttons—Fiction. 2. Murder—Investigation—Fiction. 3. Large type
books. I. Title.
PS3612.A944237H68 2013
813'.6—dc23   2012044645

Published in 2013 by arrangement with The Berkley Publishing Group,
a member of Penguin Group (USA) Inc.

Printed in the United States of America
1 2 3 4 5   17 16 15 14 13

For collectors everywhere who
understand the temptation of buttons!

ACKNOWLEDGMENTS

Readers often ask where story ideas come from. Honestly, it's hard to say. Each book is different and so is every author. Sometimes, a story idea might spring from something I see on the news. Or a scrap of conversation I overhear in a restaurant. Other times, I'll play with some obscure historical fact and see where my imagination might take it.

The idea for *Hot Button* originated back when I was first thinking about writing a mystery series about buttons. I was messing around online, doing research and indulging my interest in vintage buttons, when I came across the story about Geronimo and his buttons.

How could I resist!

As for the button enthusiasts portrayed within these pages . . .

When it comes to button collecting, I am the rawest of beginners. I am grateful for the advice and guidance given to me by all the collectors and dealers I've met. Their knowledge of not only buttons, but of their construction, their history, and their significance to fashion and society, is amazing. I am always impressed!

CHAPTER ONE

Within ten minutes of meeting Thad Wyant for the first time, there were two things I knew about him:

1. He was high maintenance.
2. He wasn't going to let me forget it.

On the five-minute walk from where I collected him at O'Hare over to the baggage carousel where we'd pick up the luggage he'd brought with him from Santa Fe, I added two more items to the list:

3. It was going to be a very long week; and
4. Thad liked scotch. A lot.

"That showed that varmint a thing or two!" Finished telling the story he'd been recounting loud enough for everyone in the airport bar to hear, Thad slapped his thigh, threw back his head, and laughed. No small feat, considering he managed to do it all while downing a glass of Johnny Walker Blue. Blue. That's the expensive stuff.

"One more for the road." He tapped the bar in front of my ice water. "And this young lady here, she'll be paying for it," he told the bartender. "Her and that cute little button club of hers."

"That cute little button club . . ." I didn't give the words the same sickeningly sweet twist Thad had. But then, that would have been tough since my teeth were clenched. It was no wonder why. The International Society of Antique and Vintage Button Collectors was a group near and dear to my heart. It better be. I was chairing this year's convention and — I glanced at the time on my cell phone — I still had a heck of a lot to do back at the hotel before this evening's opening festivities.

It was no easy thing to stifle my worries, but then, I reminded myself the delay was all for a good cause. The best of causes. Thad Wyant might be loud, pushy, and more worried about grabbing a drink than getting to the conference, but he was also reclusive — and legendary in the button business. The fact that I'd convinced him to come to Chicago at all was something of a coup. Now all I had to do was not murder him before we got over to the convention.

"Our membership is honored that you agreed to give our keynote address this year, Mr. Wyant." Oh yeah, that was me, sounding as professional as it was possible for a woman to sound when she knew the Blue Line train to downtown was set to arrive in exactly four and one-half minutes, and there were a million little details that needed her attention, details that couldn't be handled from O'Hare.

"Who you talkin' to, girl? My dear ol' daddy? He's the only Mr. Wyant I know." Another of his laughs rattled the glasses on the bar. "I wouldn'a agreed to come to this here conference at all if it wasn't for you sweet-talkin' me with your letters. You won me over, darlin', heart and soul." To prove this, he pressed one hand to his heart. "That means you can call me Thad, just like all my friends do. We are friends, ain't we?"

It's a delicate line a conference chair walks.

An older-than-middle-aged man in ratty jeans, a worn flannel shirt, dusty cowboy boots, and a seen-better-days Stetson. Scotch on his breath. A leering smile and a slow, deliberate look that took in everything from my black skirt and jacket to my tasteful white tank, and yeah, it did kind of make

11

my skin crawl.

Of course, all that was balanced by other attributes: keynote speaker at the most prestigious button event of the year. Expert extraordinaire on Western-themed buttons. Owner of the one-and-only-known-to-exist, coveted, and wonderfully historic Geronimo button.

Automatically, I glanced at the carry-on Thad had tossed on the floor beside his bar stool. Was the Geronimo button in there? Well, of course it was. I answered my own question because there really couldn't be any other answer. No collector in his right mind would dare put the button into checked baggage. Not the Geronimo button.

"So what d'you think?"

Thad's question snapped me back to reality, and once there, I heard that clock tick-tick-ticking away inside my head again.

"You think we'll get a chance to get some of that Italian beef? I've been reading about it online, Josie. They say Chicago is downright famous for them sandwiches."

Who uses words like *downright*? And *varmint,* for that matter?

Who couldn't point out that Thad talked like a bit player in an old TV Western? Not without offending the man hundreds of button collectors from all over the world had traveled to Chicago to finally meet.

"I'll make sure you get an Italian beef sandwich," I told him, deliberately leaving out the part about how there wouldn't be any money left in the conference budget for Italian beef — or anything else — if he didn't stop drinking the top-shelf stuff at the speed of light. "In fact . . ." I grabbed my purse. Subtle hint. "It's a forty-five-minute train ride back into town, but if we hurry, we'll still have plenty of time this afternoon. We can stop at one of the Italian beef places on our way over to the hotel. If there's time, that is."

OK, so that last bit was not quite as subtle. It might as well have been attached to a helium balloon and dangling up near the ceiling. That's how far over Thad's head it went.

He crooked one bushy gray eyebrow at me. "Shucks, little lady, I must have heard you wrong. I could have sworn you said *train*. Well, that for sure can't be true." Like a man who'd just been given a death sentence he didn't deserve, Thad shook his head sadly. "A man like me —"

I knew what he was going to say, and I didn't give him the chance. "You're used to being driven. Of course you are. It's just

13

that my friend, Stan, he was supposed to come pick you up this afternoon, and he couldn't make it. Just as he was about to leave to come over here, he got a call that his granddaughter was having her baby. And obviously, a great-grandchild has to take precedence over doing me a favor."

With thumb and forefinger, Thad snapped his cowboy hat further back on his head. "It surely does," he said. "But I gotta say, I don't see as how that has anything to do with me. And it sure, by gum, has nothing to do with a train. But then, I guess my ears is playin' tricks on me. On account of the plane ride and all. There's no way you said *train.* 'Cause if you did, that would mean you'd expect me to git on down there to baggage claim and pick up my own luggage and haul it down to this big, fancy conference on a train. And there's no way in hell a conference expects that of the guest of honor. Not a conference that's dragged a man all the way clear across the country from his home, where he's nice and comfortable and happy spending all these years just writin' about buttons and studyin' buttons and never comin' out to meet people because buttons . . . Well, shucks, buttons is enough. That man, he don't need people to make his life complete. And so he's doin'

14

you and all these other button folks a big ol' favor. And expectin' him to be treated like just an average sort of Joe . . ." With one thick-fingered hand, he waved away the very idea as preposterous. "It just don't make sense, does it?"

It did.

At least it had back at the hotel when I was going through the registration list one last time and I got that call from Stan. By that time, the other conference committee members were too busy to drop what they were doing and get out to O'Hare. And it would have taken me too long to go home, get my car, and get over to the airport. I would have been way late picking up Thad, and that, to me, was the height of rudeness.

Besides, it wasn't exactly like I was asking him to rough it. Thousands of people took the El every day. It was efficient and economical. The train made sense.

Yet there I was, with my tongue tied, unable to explain and afraid that whatever I said, I was about to offend the man I'd worked with for more than a year in order to make his appearance at the convention possible.

"You see, it's like this, Mr. Wyant —"

"Wyant? Thad Wyant? Well, isn't this lucky!"

The voice came from behind me, and I spun around on the bar stool and found myself face-to-face with a face I hadn't seen in six weeks.

Eyes the color of a shot of double espresso and hair to match. Shoulders that wouldn't quit.

That afternoon, they were encased in a black suit jacket that set off a blindingly white shirt, black pants, a killer silk tie in swirls of red and gray, and —

A chauffeur's cap and a hand-lettered sign that read "Giancola and Wyant" in fat Sharpie letters?

Bewildered, I sat back, the better to take stock of Mitchell Kazlowski. My ex acted like being there where he had no business was the most natural thing in the world. Which in Kaz's world, it usually is.

"You must be Ms. Giancola." His smile was wide and, yes, as seductive as a nibble of Godiva truffle. But then, Kaz knew that. In fact, I'd bet he was counting on it. He put two fingers to his hat. "I'm from the limo service, ma'am," he said. "Here to pick up you and Mr. Wyant."

"Well, that's more like it." At the same time Thad clapped Kaz on the back, he slipped off his bar stool. "I'll just head to the outhouse . . ." He tipped his head toward the back of the bar and the sign that indicated the restrooms were that way. "I'll be back in a jiffy. I knew it. I just knew it." When he looked my way, his grin revealed uneven teeth. "One look at you, little lady, and I knew you'd know how to treat your guest of honor right."

Lucky for Kaz, he waited until Thad walked away before he had the nerve to chuckle and say, "Little lady."

I swung his way. "What are you doing here?"

Kaz rolled back on his heels. "Looks like I'm saving your pretty little butt."

I ignored the "pretty little" comment. But only because I had more important things to worry about. "How did you —"

"Saw Stan." I guess he was taking his role as chauffeur seriously, because Kaz reached down and retrieved Thad's carry-on. I was tempted to tell him about the precious button inside and how — considering that Kaz doesn't care about buttons and I am one of the country's most respected experts on the subject — he really should let me handle the bag. Kaz didn't give me the chance.

"I was actually heading over to see you, and your apartment door was open, and I poked my head in and saw —"

"Chaos, right?" I am organized and tidy. I

couldn't stand the thought. "Since I'll be at the conference for the next seven days, I'm having the kitchen remodeled. And as long as they've got the place torn apart, I figured I'd have the rooms painted, too." I squeezed my eyes shut and shuddered. "How bad is it?"

"It actually looks like they're making good progress. You did want the living room painted purple and orange, right?" When my eyes flew open, Kaz laughed. "Just kidding," he said.

It was another one of his not-so-funny jokes — I hoped — and I ignored it and got back to the matter at hand. "And Stan . . ."

"Oh yeah, Stan. When I realized you weren't around, I left, and I met Stan at the elevator, and he told me about the new baby and how he was supposed to be here and how you were going to pick up Wyant and take him back to the hotel on the train. Jo, Jo, Jo." Kaz shook his head like Thad just had, only there was a spark in Kaz's eyes when he did it. "You've got to stop being so practical. This Wyant guy is some kind of button rock star, right? Then that's how you have to treat him. It's what he's expecting and what he deserves."

"I guess you're right." In the three years we'd been married, I don't think I'd ever spoken those words to Kaz. Right wasn't something Kaz usually was. With Kaz, it was more like in over his head. In trouble. Owing somebody money and showing up to see me because —

I narrowed my eyes and gave him the once-over. "What do you want?" I asked.

Kaz is delicious, and he knows it. That would explain why he thought he could get away with flashing a smokin'-hot smile and resting one hand on my arm in a very un-chauffeur-like way. "Just trying to help," he crooned.

"Yeah, like you were just trying to help when I was investigating that murder a while ago, and you practically scared me to death, hiding out in my car and hitching a ride to West Virginia with me."

He backed away a step, his hands up in a gesture I would have taken as surrender from anybody else. From Kaz, it was more like *Hey, not my fault.* "I helped you catch the bad guy, didn't I?" He knew I couldn't deny it, and — big points for him — he didn't make me embarrass myself and admit it. "How's that policeman boyfriend of yours?"

"I don't have a policeman boyfriend." This was mostly the truth. Though Nevin Riley and I had reconnected during the above-mentioned investigation (we'd had a disastrous blind date a few months before that, thanks to Stan, who is a retired cop), we hadn't exactly gone skipping off together down some primrose path. Nevin was committed to his work as a homicide detective. He was professional, busy. I was just getting the Button Box, my newly opened button shop, off the ground, and in my own way, just as committed and professional as Nevin was. Not to mention busy.

"He's been working nights," I said, only because I knew that Kaz would never leave the subject alone if I didn't give him some kind of answer.

"That means you haven't been seeing much of each other." He sounded way too pleased by this turn of events.

Exactly why I ignored Kaz.

I saw Thad step out of the men's room, so it was the perfect opportunity for me to climb off the bar stool. And change the subject, too. "You didn't really rent a limo, did you?"

Kaz didn't answer. Instead, he grinned and pointed. "Like the hat?"

"You rented a hat?"

"Nah. One of the other drivers parked outside took his off so he could comb his

hair. He set it on the hood of his car, and
—"

"You're wearing a stolen chauffeur's cap."

"I don't know if the guy stole it."

"But you sure did."

His expression brightened. "All for a good cause."

In Kaz's universe, *good cause* always means *Kaz's best interests.* It was one of the reasons I'd divorced him. That, and the fact that he couldn't pass up a card game, a bet on a horse race, or a Mega Millions lottery-ticket sales machine. Then again, with Kaz, I knew that what I saw was what I got. The trick was remembering that. And forgetting that for a few years of my life, I'd actually been naive enough to think he was my happily-ever-after.

"You might want to explain what that good cause is," I said, glancing toward where Thad was closing in on us. "Before I tell my guest of honor that you're really a phony."

"What, and make yourself look bad when he was just realizing how classy you and the rest of the button crowd are?" Kaz's grin said it all. He had me, and he knew it.

I watched as Thad stopped and chatted with a man seated down at the end of the bar. "He's sure not what I expected," I

21

mumbled. "He's so —"

"Noisy and obnoxious?"

I slid my ex a look. "I was going to say *outgoing*. Thad Wyant's the world's leading expert on Western-themed buttons. But he never goes to conferences or button shows. He's a recluse. He sits at home and writes articles for the collectors' magazines. He's even written a book on Western collecting. I thought . . ." Thad roared a laugh and slapped the back of the man he was talking to. "I guess I pictured someone a little more studious. You know, kind of quiet."

"Maybe he's loud because he doesn't get out enough." Kaz had an eye on Thad, too. "You know, like he's making up for lost time."

"Maybe." I glanced at the carry-on Kaz was holding. "I just wish we could get back to the hotel so I could take a look at that button."

I pretended not to notice when Kaz rolled his eyes.

"You can't deny the historical significance," I said.

"Sure I can. I saw your conference brochure, and it says something about some famous Geronimo button, and this guy's all into Western stuff, so I'm guessing he's the owner of the button. But I dunno, Jo; I just don't get it. What's so special about one little button?"

"Geronimo? The famous Native American warrior?" I figured he knew this much, so I didn't elaborate. "In the last years of his life, Geronimo was a prisoner of the American government. But talk about being a rock star!" Remembering all the stories I'd read, I couldn't help but smile. "Geronimo rode in President Theodore Roosevelt's inaugural parade. And he appeared in Wild West shows. And even though he was technically a prisoner and the government wouldn't let him return to his people in Arizona, he received dozens and dozens of visitors and admirers. When people came to see him, he sold them the buttons off his shirt."

I didn't need Kaz to open his mouth; his look said it all.

"Of course it sounds dumb to you," I said. "You don't care about buttons. Chances are, most of the people who bought Geronimo's buttons didn't, either. But the buttons gave them something to remember him by, some connection to history. And for Geronimo . . . Well, the story is that at the time of his death, he had more than ten thousand dollars in the bank. That was a lot of money for 1909. So he did pretty well for himself, selling his autograph and those buttons. And when he cut one button off his shirt and sold it, he just sewed another one on. The actual value of that little button might be minuscule, but the fact that it came from the shirt of the most famous Native American warrior in history . . ."

I guess Kaz actually got it, because he nodded. "And this Wyant guy is the one who owns one of those buttons."

"I'm pretty sure it's in that bag you're holding." My fingers itched to grab the carry-on and root through it. "Thad is going to talk about the button at dinner tomorrow night. He's going to display it throughout the conference. In the world of button collecting, Wyant might be a rock star, but the fact that I got him to agree to come to the convention and do all this for us, well . . ." I pulled back my shoulders and stood tall. No easy thing for a woman as short as I am. "In the button world, I'm a superhero."

"Wonder Woman. I always said so."

Thad was closing in on us, so I was forced to grumble under my breath, "I never heard you say that."

"I thought it."

"Not the same."

"So what are you two lollygagging around for?" Laughing at his own cleverness, Thad

24

grabbed my arm and dragged me out to the concourse. "We've got a convention to get to. Let's get a move on."

Get a move on, we did. Kaz retrieved Thad's two suitcases from the luggage carousel, and we headed out to where the car was parked.

Only the car wasn't Kaz's beat-up Jeep.

It was a limo. A long, black limo so shiny I could see my reflection in the door.

"Kaz . . ." I waited until the luggage was stowed in the trunk and Thad was in the backseat. "Please don't tell me you stole the car, too."

"Don't be silly. You know I'd never do anything like that. The limo is legit. Bought and paid for. Well, rented and paid for."

I breathed a sigh of relief.

At least until I remembered the state of Kaz's bank account. "But you —"

He didn't give me a chance to ask the question. He opened the door and stepped back to allow me to climb inside, and once I did, he bent down so that he could give me a thousand-watt smile and a wink while he whispered, "Not to worry. I told the rental company I was your assistant for the conference. The limo's on your charge."

Chapter Two

Limo charge notwithstanding, so far, so good.

Fifteen hours and counting until the official Monday-morning opening of the conference, and I took a deep breath to calm my clattering heartbeat and glanced around Navy Pier, a Chicago landmark that juts more than three thousand feet out into Lake Michigan and includes exhibition halls, amusement-park rides, and boat docks.

The clear evening skies promised a spectacular sunset, the lake waters were calm, and a hint of late summer warmth lingered in the evening air. In the downtown buildings that provided an elegant backdrop to the Pier, thousands of lights in thousands of windows winked at me, and directly across from where I waited, members of the International Society of Antique and Vintage Button Collectors, along with guests and spouses, were gathering for a dinner cruise.

Things back at the hotel were hectic, sure, and I knew I wouldn't get much sleep that night, but for now, all was right with the world.

"It's brilliant, dear." Helen Obermyer must have known what I was thinking because she put a hand on my arm and gave it a squeeze. "This cruise was such a good idea! It's certainly going to be an evening to remember. Look at our conference attendees! They're smiling and happy. You're making a very good first impression." I glanced at the people lining up near the canopy just outside the gangplank that led onto the boat, and I smiled, too. Organizing a conference of this size is never easy, but thanks to Helen, who'd chaired the conference in Pittsburgh the year before, it had gone more smoothly than I would have thought possible. Helen had years of experience with the group, and she was just as willing to share her knowledge as she was to pitch in and help. It was a winning combination.

"I couldn't have done it without you," I told her, and I swear, though she didn't need the reminder, she blushed as pink as the trim suit she was wearing. Helen was nearing seventy and petite, and her hair —

cut stylishly short — was as silvery as the puffy clouds that floated overhead.

"Oh, honey, when you've been involved in this group as long as I have, it's all just second nature," she said, slipping behind the table where she'd help me check in our guests. "You'll find that out once you've done this another decade or two. Or three!"

Laughing, I sat down beside her, and once we were in place, we signaled the line to start moving forward. After that, it was pretty much controlled chaos. Fun, controlled chaos. I greeted people I hadn't seen since Pittsburgh, met new faces to put to the names of people I'd bought buttons from and sold buttons to over the years, and was pleased to make the acquaintance of more than a few people new to the hobby of button collecting.

"Mrs. Winston, so nice to see you again!" I smiled up at the tall, broad woman standing in front of the registration table and handed her the nametag Helen had designed. It featured the name of each registrant along with a picture of an antique button.

"Oh, a moonglow!" Gloria Winston beamed at the picture of the glass button next to her name. "How perfect! And so clever since I specialize in collecting moonglow buttons. How ever did you remember, Josie?"

Rather than admit it was pure dumb luck, I smiled in a way that indicated conference chairs have inside information that just might be magical, and I handed Gloria off to Helen, who checked her name off our master list. I moved on to the next guest.

"Daryl Tucker," the man said, and practically before I had time to look up and register the fact that Daryl was in his midthirties and that he had dark hair, a bushy beard, and wore glasses with fat, black frames, I heard Helen nearly gag on the Starlight Mint she was sucking.

"Tucker! Oh my gracious." I was glad when Helen spoke — at least I knew she wasn't choking. She pinned the man with a look and softened it by fluttering her eyes in her little-old-lady way. "No relation to that horrible Donovan Tucker, I hope. Oh good heavens, wouldn't that be terrible?"

I took pity on Daryl. But then, it was hard not to, considering he looked totally bewildered.

"Donovan Tucker," I explained. "He's a filmmaker."

"And a monster with no scruples." As if just thinking about Donovan Tucker caused her temperature to climb, Helen fanned her face with one hand. "He makes these silly films — he calls them documentaries — about collectors. He's done one on brick collectors and one on PEZ dispenser collectors, and he makes terrible fun of them all. He sneaks into their conferences, and he takes the least flattering pictures he possibly can, and he films things that really aren't relevant. In other words, he does anything he can to make these people look like laughingstocks when, really, they are just people with eclectic interests. Oh my . . ." Helen's face went ashen, and her delicate hands curled into fists. "If he showed up here to film our convention and made fun of us . . . Well, I don't know what I might do . . . I might . . . I might . . . Well, good gracious, I might have to resort to murder."

"She's just kidding, of course." I made sure I added a little laugh to my disclaimer. Partly because I was afraid Helen meant it. Mostly because it was my duty as conference chair to put Daryl at ease. And poor Daryl, shifting from foot to foot, his left eye twitching behind his Coke-bottle glasses . . . Poor Daryl looked anything but at ease. "It's just that Helen is a serious collector, you see, and —"

"You don't have to apologize." From somewhere in that bushy beard, a shy smile emerged. "I know how you all feel. About the buttons, I mean." It was hard to say if Daryl kept his smile in place. That's because he took one look at me, turned the color of the setting sun, and fixed his gaze on his sneakers. "I'm new to collecting, and this is my first convention, but I really like my buttons, too." He took the nametag I handed him and stepped to his left and in front of Helen. "Don't you worry, ma'am," he told her. "I don't know this Donovan guy, and if I did, well, I guess I wouldn't like him very much, either."

"What a nice young man," Helen crooned once Daryl walked away. "He looks to be about your age, Josie."

I didn't wait for her to get any farther. "No," was all I said.

"But why not? He's a button collector. Wouldn't that be refreshing? You getting together with a button collector? It wouldn't be like it was with that what's-his-name, Karl."

"Kaz," I corrected her.

"Yes, just what I said. It wouldn't be like that at all. You'd have so much in common with a man like Daryl."

"I don't want to have anything in common with Daryl Tucker." I made sure I said this in a whisper just loud enough for Helen to hear. "I've got enough to worry about for the next week. I don't need to add romance into the mix."

"But there's always a place for romance."

I guess my whisper wasn't soft enough. That would explain why Kaz heard what I said.

It didn't explain what he was doing standing in front of the registration table in that dapper black suit of his, the last rays of the setting sun glinting against his smile.

In answer to my questioning look, he raised his eyebrows.

"What? Get with the program." Kaz bent backward to look down the Pier. "I brought Wyant over from the hotel."

"You mean he didn't come on the shuttle buses with everyone else?" Silly question. At least that's what the look on Kaz's face said. "Yes, you're right." I said it before he could remind me I should. "Wyant expects to be treated like a rock star. Absolutely. Sure. Thanks for taking care of him. The boat is supposed to leave in about fifteen minutes, and it's a three-and-a-half-hour cruise. You can wait around here or go back to the hotel or —"

"No worries," Kaz said, and he strolled onto the boat. "I'll be here whenever you need me." Over his shoulder, he threw me one last smile. "Whatever you need me for."

"Oh dear." This time when Helen fanned her face, I was pretty sure it had nothing to do with being aggravated about Donovan Tucker. "He is charming, isn't he?"

"He's a pain in the —" I bit off my words. But that was because Thad Wyant sauntered to the front of the line, and I was afraid somebody might think I was talking about him instead of Kaz.

Maybe I was.

"Well, lookee you!" I was wearing black pants, a black cardigan, and a long-sleeved silk blouse the same shade of ivory as my grandmother's pearls looped around my neck, so really, Thad's long, ogling look was unwarranted. "You're as pretty as a picture, Josie." He tipped his cowboy hat to me before he glanced Helen's way. "And this young lady is . . ?"

Helen dithered. I made the introductions. Once she realized the man in the jeans (at least they were clean) and the black Western shirt with the red embroidery at the yoke and cuffs was our guest of honor, she only quivered more. We were nearly at the end of the check-in line, and the cruise would be starting in just a few minutes. I told her to go onto the boat with Thad and I would finish checking in the guests myself.

I would have, too, if the next man in line wasn't so busy glaring at Thad that he never stepped up to the table. I coughed delicately, and the man jumped and moved forward.

The middle-aged man had a face that looked familiar, and it didn't take me long to place him. I checked his name off the list. I'd done business with Chase Cadell over the years, mostly selling, not buying, since I wasn't all that interested in the Western cavalry buttons that were his specialty.

"Nerve of the guy." Chase still had his eyes on Thad, who already had a drink in his hand and a crowd of starry-eyed button collectors surrounding him. "Thinks he can just step ahead of everybody and go to the front of the line."

"I'm sorry." I was. For a couple reasons. For one thing, the timing couldn't have been worse. Over the years, Chase and Thad had developed a relationship that was legendary in button circles — for all the wrong reasons. Thad considered himself the be-all and end-all of Western-themed button experts. Chase thought he was king of the proverbial Western button hill. Over the years, their bitter back-and-forthing had been played out on the pages of every button-collecting magazine and online button forum there was. Thad would pose some theory on the development of buttons on cowboys' clothing or how buttons with pictures of horses' heads on them had evolved over the years. And the next month or the next day, Chase would write an article or post a message that claimed Thad was wrong. Thad would parry. Chase would thrust. I swear, one of the reasons I have a dislike of Western buttons (and disliking any button is major for me) is the bad taste these two left in my mouth.

Oh yeah, things were ugly between them. So ugly, in fact, that the organizing committee had recently spent a whole lot of time e-mailing back and forth, talking about the need to keep the men apart at this conference.

It was my bad luck that they'd just happened to converge on the registration table at the same time. The only saving grace was that Thad hadn't confronted Chase. In fact, he'd acted like Chase wasn't even there. That didn't keep me from making a mental note to myself: don't forget how pushy Thad can be. Get him his tickets for the keynote banquet and all the conference-sponsored breakfasts and luncheons early so he won't have the excuse to horn his way to the front of any more lines. I should have thought of that earlier.

"Sorry," I said again.

"Yeah. Sure." Chase held out his hand for his nametag.

And I would have been happy to give it to him — if only I could find it.

"Cadell, Cadell," I mumbled under my breath, glancing through the cards still on the table. They'd been laid out alphabetically, and I wondered how, after Helen and I had done a final count at the hotel and we had as many nametags as we did registered guests, I had managed to leave one behind.

Like grumbling and being embarrassed would actually make me locate the tag faster.

Didn't it figure, the one person who was already starting off the conference on the wrong foot, and there I was, scrambling around like a so-not-together conference chair. I finally gave up with a sigh, grabbed a nearby Sharpie and wrote out a tag for Chase.

"Sorry." I cringed when I said it — again.

Chase grabbed his nametag, and just as he marched onto the boat, I saw Kaz walk past the doorway. I waved him over.

"There are only a few more people in line," I told him, getting up from my seat so I could pilot him into it. "If you could just . . ."

"Sure, Jo." He took my place. "Something up?"

Kaz wouldn't understand — or care — about the Thad/Chase smackdown or the missing nametag, so I didn't even try to explain. "I need to buy one of our attendees a drink as an apology," I said, and hurried after Chase.

Within ten minutes, Chase was enjoying a glass of Syrah courtesy of my personal credit card and not the conference account, the ruffled feathers were smoothed, and all our guests were aboard. By the time we cast off and set sail on the beautiful blue waters of Lake Michigan, I was on the second deck, doing a last count of the seats around the round dinner tables with their white-linen tablecloths and the amazing center-pieces Helen and a dedicated subcommittee had put together — flowers cut from heavy paper in shades of ivory, brown, and pink, each with a button at its center. The center-pieces would be given away as door prizes at the end of the cruise, and already, I saw our guests eyeing them. I couldn't blame them; the arrangements were clever and adorable, and a couple of them included buttons I wouldn't mind getting my hands on. Too bad that, as conference chair, I wasn't eligible to win one.

When she swept past me and toward the buffet line, Helen grabbed my arm. "Don't argue," she said before I could. "I know what you're going to say. That you have one more thing to check. Or one more thing to do. Or one more person to get something for. If you remember, Josie, I told you that when you're in charge of a conference like this, you have to pace yourself. You'll never be standing at the end of the week if you try to do everything for everyone all the time. You need to look after yourself, too. That includes eating dinner. Now."

"But . . ." I held back. "There's a woman here all the way from Australia, and she doesn't know anyone and —"

"She'll make friends. Just like we all did at our first conference." Another tug.

"But I don't want anyone to feel neglected, and I want to make sure they're all mingling and having fun and —"

"Oh, honey!" Helen had a glass of white wine in her hands, and though I'd never known her to be much of a drinker, I wondered if it was her first. There were two spots of vivid color in Helen's cheeks and a spring to her step I'd never seen before. "You can't be all things to all people," she confided. "So don't even try. If you do,

38

you'll be useless by day two of the conference. Remember that. Come on."

She was right, and even if she wasn't, I owed it to Helen to follow her advice. We took our places at the end of the buffet line, right behind Langston Whitman, one of my favorite people in all the button world. Langston was a tall, handsome African American in his forties and probably one of the only people in the room who wasn't a collector. (Well, not counting Kaz, who I'd seen earlier charming the socks off a young fashion designer from New York who'd come to the conference to look at antique buttons because she was thinking about including some in her next year's fall line.) Langston, in fact, catered to the rest of us. He was one of the vendors who sold all the paraphernalia collectors depended on: the awls we used to punch the heavy paper stock we mount our buttons on, those heavy-card-stock pages, plastic sleeves, wire, cleaners. Always impeccably dressed and soft-spoken, he was a pleasure to do business with. After we exchanged greetings and hugs, he introduced me to his partner (business and personal), a younger man by the name of Elliot, who had the flair of an artist and the face of an angel.

"Wait until you see what Elliot has been

up to." Langston's eyes gleamed. He stepped forward and took white glass plates from the stack on the buffet table and passed them down to me and Helen before he grabbed his own. I followed him on one side of the buffet table, with Helen and Elliot on the other, and together, Langston and I piled our dishes with mixed green salad, lemon chicken, horseradish-encrusted grilled salmon, and roasted seasonal vegetables in all the glorious colors of the coming fall.

"He's not just a woodworker, you know," Langston said, with a quick smile at Elliot and one hand poised above slices of cheesecake and the sugar cookies shaped like buttons. "Elliot is an artist." He took two of the cookies and put them on his plate. "He's making awls with hand-carved handles. Cherry, mahogany, oak. They are magnificent. You are going to be so impressed, Josie. I'm going to make a prediction — before this week is over, you'll be carrying a full line of his tools in that sweet little shop of yours."

I had no doubt of it, and told Langston so. We crossed the room together chatting about the different woods Elliot was experimenting with and took our places at one of the tables near the window. I'd gotten exactly one bite of lemon chicken into my mouth when I heard Thad Wyant's voice rattle the chandeliers.

"You call that rare? Shucks, that little ol' piece of beef could be used fer a doorstop. I said rare. You know, as in red. Mooing."

That bite of chicken felt like a brick going down my throat, but I managed to choke out "Excuse me" to my fellow diners and got up from the table so I could hurry over to the buffet, where Thad was nose-to-nose with a man in a tall white toque.

Thad didn't miss a beat. He took one look at me and poked his chin in the direction of the server, who was shaving thin slices of beef from a prime rib the size of my button shop. "You see what this here fella is trying to pass off as rare? I told him rare. Josie, sweetie, you understand that, don't you? But this guy here —"

I took a look at the tag the server was wearing. "I'm sure Jorge is doing his best," I said, and tossed the server a smile that I hoped would count as enough of an apology until I had a chance to slip him a little extra tip. "You know how restaurants are these days, Thad. They even have that little disclaimer on their menus. About how they can't serve undercooked meat because of the risk of contaminants."

41

"Horse hockey!" Thad swept off his Stetson and ran a hand through his salt-and-pepper hair, which hung over his collar. "They don't want to take responsibility for how their food is cooked so I should eat meat that's better thrown out to the coyotes? I don't think so. And another thing —"

This was pretty much when I became aware of the fact that the gentle buzz of conversation that had filled the dining room earlier had pretty much come to a halt, and a couple hundred pairs of eyes were trained on us. I knew I couldn't waste another second. Over the last few months, I'd worked with Micah, the banquet manager, to put this dinner together, and I scanned the room, spotted him, and caught hold of Thad's arm. One more apologetic smile at Jorge, and I ushered our guest of honor over to where Micah was standing.

"We need a steak," I told Micah.

Thad stepped between me and Micah. "A filet."

Don't ask me how, but I managed to keep my best smile in place. "We need a filet for Thad, and we need it cooked as rare as rare can be." I looked at Thad for confirmation, and when he didn't contradict me, I turned back to Micah. "Mr. Wyant will be seated at my table. You can bring it over to him when it's done."

"Certainly, Ms. Giancola." Micah was young and eager to make his way in the dog-eat-dog (no pun intended) world of Chicago restaurateurs. His expression was as smooth as the filling in the key-lime pie on the table over to our left. "But you do realize that the per-person buffet cost you agreed to doesn't include individual dinners."

"Of course she does." Thad gave Micah a too-friendly slap on the back. "You sittin' over there, Josie?" he asked, with a glance at the table where my dinner was getting cold. "I'll be by in a jiffy, soon as I stop up at the bar and get this here drink refilled." He rattled the ice cubes in his glass. "A jiffy." He stepped away, his eyes on Micah. "That's how soon that filet is gonna be ready, right? I mean, after you stop standing there staring at me, son, and get to the kitchen and put the order in."

I swear I squeezed my eyes shut only for a second. Just long enough to pray for patience. When I opened them again, Thad was already at the bar, and Micah was waiting for me to give him the go-ahead. I did, and with a sigh, I went back to the table to sit down.

Helen was seated on my left, and just after I sat down, she dropped her napkin on the floor, bent to recover it, and crooned, "Well played," on her way back up.

It was, and I congratulated myself.

Crisis averted.

Dinner guests back to chatting and eating.

Guest of honor happy.

For now.

My fork and the roasted vegetables on it were halfway to my mouth when that last thought struck, and my stomach soured, but since Langston had just turned to me to ask about the setup in the vendor room at the conference, I had no choice but to pretend everything was A-OK and go on eating. Good thing, too. Though my meal was a tad on the chilly side, the food was delicious, and I chomped my way through it, the tension unwinding inside me with each delicious bite.

At least until Thad arrived. Lucky for all of us, so did his filet just a minute later, and wonder of wonders, he didn't have one word of complaint. Well, except to say that the meat was a tad underdone for his taste. Fortunately, that didn't seem to take the edge off his appetite. He wolfed down his steak, pointing around the table with the tip of his knife to whoever's attention he hoped to capture.

"And what's your specialty, sir?" He poked his knife in Langston's direction. "Let me guess: you look to me like one of them fellas who collects them cute little china buttons. What are they called, Josie?"

"Calicoes." I was amazed that a man whose knowledge of Western-themed buttons was encyclopedic could be that out of touch when it came to any other buttons. Then again, I supposed that was why Thad was considered to be the leading expert in his field (don't tell Chase Cadell). He was a specialist, not a generalist.

Langston had just finished the last of his grilled salmon, and he touched his napkin to his lips. "I'm afraid I'm not one of you," he said. "Supplies are my specialty. I'm Langston Whitman." He put out a hand to Thad.

Thad shook it readily enough, but his expression was clouded in confusion. "Supplies. Is that some kind of button?"

It wouldn't have been all that funny of a joke coming from anyone else, but Thad was the conference guest of honor, after all. We all laughed a little more than was called for, and when we were done, Helen scooted forward in her seat.

"How soon can we see it?" she asked, her eyes on Thad. "You're not going to make us wait until dinner tomorrow night, are you, Thad?"

He knew exactly what Helen was talking about, and his eyes lit up. I knew what she was talking about, too, and in spite of the fact that I told myself that it was nothing more than a button and that I had known for a while that it would be on display at this conference, a little tingle of excitement shot through me.

"You'd like me to say you can see it before then. I can see that in those pretty blue eyes of yours." Thad was done with his steak, so he wagged one finger at Helen. "You're figurin' I'll say somethin' like come on up to room 842 tonight at eleven and you'll get a look at it — the Geronimo button."

I may have been imagining it, but I swear, at the sound of those words being spoken, every person at the table caught his or her breath.

Everyone but Thad.

He slapped his knee. "Sure, you're gonna have to wait. Just like everyone else. Ain't that right, Josie?"

All eyes turned to me. "Thad and I have an agreement," I explained. "You know, so that none of his thunder gets stolen before tomorrow night's banquet. That's the first anyone here at the conference is supposed to get a look at the Geronimo button."

"I can't wait." Helen's cheeks flamed. At least for a second. Then it was as if someone had turned off a switch. She cocked her head and stared at Thad. "But how —"

"Lookee this, my glass is empty!" Thad jiggled the ice cubes in his glass and got up from the table. "Gonna pay a quick visit over to the bar. Be right back, folks."

Honestly, I thought about joining him. It had already been a long night, and officially, the conference hadn't even begun. I talked myself out of a trip to the bar and a well-deserved glass of wine, though, wishing my dinner companions a pleasant rest of the evening and staying right where I was as they rose and scattered, walking around the room to chat with other conference-goers, heading up to the open third deck to watch the Chicago skyline in all its glory.

I would have to go outside eventually, too, but for now, I savored the peace and quiet, the smooth whoosh of the boat in the serene waters, and the contentment that comes after a good meal in (mostly) good company.

"Wanna dance?"

I didn't even bother to look at him when Kaz flopped into the chair next to mine. "It's not a dancing cruise," I told him. I sat up and worked a kink out of my shoulders.

"I should know. I planned it. No music."

"We could hum and dance."

Like I said, I was feeling content. I laughed. "Actually . . ." I pushed my chair back from the table. "I've got to go mingle. There's a woman here from Australia —"

"Meghan Moran." Kaz nodded. "I hooked her up — in a button conference way, I mean — with a couple ladies from Indianapolis. They're hanging out like long-lost friends."

"Thank you." Had I actually said that to Kaz? Had he actually done me a favor? I eyed him carefully, but then, that wasn't exactly uncalled-for; when Kaz is in a giving mood, it's usually because he expects to receive something in return. "I don't suppose you took care of the contingent from Paris, too?"

"Sorry." He shrugged his broad shoulders. "Don't speak the language. But that guy from the Czech Republic . . ." He glanced over to where I saw Alexander Benes talking to some folks. "He speaks really good English. He was telling me about the glass buttons they make at that factory of his."

"And you were listening?" OK, call me cynical, but let's face it — in the three years we'd been married, Kaz had never listened to word one from me. Not when it came to buttons.

Another shrug. "I was sitting next to the guy at dinner. I didn't have a lot of choice but to listen. I had him on one side and some lady from L.A. on the other. She specializes in buttons with pornographic pictures on them. Jo, you never told me button collecting could be so interesting!"

"You wouldn't have listened if I'd tried." There was no use debating the point. Even when I was in a good mood, being reminded of how Kaz had always treated my "little hobby" as just that always had a way of rankling. I stood, ready to head up to the open deck. "I've got to go make sure everyone is happy," I told him.

"You could start with me."

Oh yeah, he was smiling, all right. In that devil-may-care way that used to make my blood boil. In a good sort of way. These days, the boil was usually because he was annoying me. This time . . .

I gave him a smile. "Thanks for helping out. For the rest of the week, Thad will be at the conference and at the hotel. You can take the limo back."

"And miss all the fun?" Kaz followed along behind me. "Hey, I'm just getting into all this button stuff."

"Right, and I just fell off a turnip truck." I

shook my head. Honestly, the man can be brazen. The fact that he still expected me to fall for his line never ceased to amaze me. "Good-bye, Kaz," I said, just as a man came up behind me.

"Oh, there you are!" I turned to see what he wanted from me and realized he was one of the waitstaff and was talking to Kaz. "We've got the tea you requested for that woman from Japan," he told Kaz. "It took some digging, but we found it in the kitchen." The waiter turned to me. "You're Josie, right? I saw you talking to Micah a little while ago. I've got to tell you, I don't know where you got this guy . . ." The look he gave Kaz was one of pure admiration. "But you've got an amazing assistant here."

"Assistant? I —"

There was no use trying to explain. Kaz and the waiter had already walked away.

And I told myself not to worry. If Kaz wanted to play the good guy for tonight, so be it. Once he took Thad back to the hotel, that would be that, and we could get on with our conference.

My conference.

I breathed a sigh of pure contentment.

Every program was organized and interesting.

Every speaker and panel was ready to go.

All was right with the world, Lake Michigan was as smooth as glass, and my guests were having the time of their lives.

"Oh, yeah?" The words — spoken by a woman — were loud and said with enough sarcasm to sour a lemon. They echoed down the metal stairway from the open third deck. "I can't believe you'd have the nerve to show up here, you son of a bitch. I'm warning you right now; you'd better step away from that railing, Thad Wyant, or you're going to find yourself in Lake Michigan — floating fish food!"

CHAPTER THREE

I scrambled up the stairway as fast as my less-than-long legs allowed, and got up onto the open deck just in time to see that every single person out there had gathered in a semicircle around the far railing. The fabulous Chicago skyline was at their backs. But the show was happening right in front of them. Eager to diffuse whatever time bomb they were watching and waiting to explode, I pushed myself to the front of the crowd (politely, of course) just in time to see Thad Wyant shake his head in a way that told me that woman's outraged voice I'd heard was nothing to him — nothing but pitiful.

My guest of honor had both his elbows propped against the railing. His lanky legs were stuck out in front of him, crossed at the ankle. With his Stetson far back on his head and those cowboy boots of his coated with enough dust to make it look as if he'd just come in off the range, he was the picture of serenity.

Not so the middle-aged woman who stood across from him, a woman I didn't remember checking in at the gangplank. She was no more than five feet tall and as thin as a stick of chewing gum. Tiny hands, bitty feet. She reminded me of a little gray mouse. Gray pantsuit, gray hair, sensible gray shoes. From where I stood, I could see her trembling like the flag that snapped at the back of the boat in the breeze we kicked up as we scooted through the water.

"You don't even care, do you?" Her voice — high-pitched and quivering — floated away on that same breeze. "How can you stand there and pretend like it doesn't matter?"

"Aw, shucks, lady." As if it was a monumental effort, Thad unfolded himself from the railing and scuffed his boots against the metal deck. "Why don't you just head on out of here? I told you; I don't know what in the tarnation you're talkin' about."

"You . . . don't . . . know . . . what . . ." The woman contained her aggravation, but just barely. And it cost her. Her hands curled into fists, she pressed her arms close to her sides, and she pulled in breath after uneven breath. "I'm not going to give you another chance. You hear me, Thad Wyant?

You've had every opportunity to come clean about this. Now —"

"Yer wasting your time! Git along. Git yourself outta here." Thad never touched her, but the shooing gesture he made toward her might as well have been a slap in the face. That's how violently she reacted.

Her shoulders so stiff that I swore they were going to snap, the woman backed away from Thad and whirled around. It was the first she realized there were a couple dozen people watching their confrontation, and when she did, all the color drained from her cheeks, leaving her grayer than ever. Her chin quivering, she dropped her face into her hands and raced to the stairway, sobbing.

I was torn between going after her and checking on my guest of honor. I'm pretty sure I would have opted for the woman if not for the fact that Thad, hands in the pockets of his jeans, ambled over like he didn't have a care in the world.

"Well, ain't that just the darndest thing." He looked toward the now-empty stairway, shaking his head.

I am not the dithering type. Still, I found it hard to get anything evenly vaguely coherent out of my mouth. I looked from the stairway to Thad and from Thad to the crowd that, now that the excitement had ended, was heading over to stand near the railing and watch the city skyline float by and — no doubt — go over a play-by-play of the knock-down, drag-out they'd just witnessed. By the time I did, my blood pressure was down and I'd regained some of my legendary composure. "I'm so sorry," I said. "Things like that shouldn't happen in public. It's bad enough that your friend was upset, but —"

"Friend?" Thad wrinkled his too-big-for-his-face nose. "Never seen that there lady before in my life."

"But how . . . Why?" I didn't want to get into an instant replay. I mean, really, Thad must have remembered everything the woman said just as clearly as I did. "Why was she so angry then? And who is she?"

He had a glass in one hand, and he looked down into its empty depths. "Darned if I know. Crazy, huh? Button folks, they're just darned crazy!" He threw back his head and laughed, then twitched his shoulders, tossing off the whole incident just like that. As if he didn't have a care in the world, he strolled downstairs.

That's exactly when I realized Daryl Tucker was standing next to me, looking where I was looking.

"I'm so sorry." There I was, saying it again. *Sorry* was quickly turning into the conference mantra. "That certainly isn't the best way to start off a conference."

"It's amazing." He didn't so much speak the words as let them escape on the end of a sigh. Behind his glasses, his eyes were thoughtful. "I can't believe it."

"Me, either." I tried for light and was afraid I sounded callous, so I figured it was as good a moment as any to try to put Daryl at ease. "No worries. The woman apparently mistook Thad for someone else."

Was that enough to reassure Daryl that he hadn't come to his first button convention and found himself in the midst of a bunch of loony people? I can't say. I do know that when he walked away, he was muttering to himself, "Didn't look that way to me."

"Chin up, Jo." Before I even knew he was in the vicinity, Kaz had an arm around my shoulders. He gave me a squeeze. "You can't control every minute of this conference. You do know that, don't you?"

I slipped out of his embrace. "It's my job. I should find that woman," I said, already moving toward the stairway where I'd last seen her. "Only I don't know who —"

"Beth Howell." He supplied the information before I could even ask, and I guess my openmouthed stare said it all, because Kaz added, "She was one of the people I checked in after you boarded the boat. Said it was her first conference."

"Beth Howell." I committed the name to memory. "I need to make sure she's all right."

I would have, too, if I'd been able to find Beth. I tried every ladies' room on the boat, glanced around the knots of people who were chatting, went to the bar — twice — and even checked the kitchen. Either I wasn't very good at picking out a tiny gray woman in a crowd or I had terrible timing and always ended up exactly where Beth wasn't exactly when she wasn't there.

Either that or Beth Howell's threat to Thad about ending up as fish food had gone awry, and she was the one who'd gone over the side of the boat and into the water.

I had already mingled my way through the rest of the cruise, the boat was docked, and I was standing at the gangplank wishing folks a good evening when that thought hit. It took my breath away.

"What is it, dear?" Helen was just walking by, and she took me aside. "You look as if you've seen a ghost."

"No. I was just thinking, that's all, about —" From over Helen's shoulder, I saw a wavering in the shadows, and the next thing I knew, a tiny gray figure slipped off the boat and hurried down the pier. I would have gone after Beth, right then and there, if not for the fact that the man who walked off after her was someone I had just sold an entire collection of Japanese satsuma buttons to. He couldn't wait to thank me for my excellent service as well as my good taste in buttons, and by the time he was done, Beth was long gone.

And I was breathing a sigh of relief.

Beth hadn't taken a header off the boat. Her argument with Thad hadn't escalated further or continued later. Mayhem and murder didn't happen at button conventions. By the time I was ready to head back to the hotel, my fears were calmed and I was smiling.

Little did I know that within twenty-four hours, I would welcome a little mayhem. Because mayhem isn't necessarily murder, and murder . . . Well, that was about to hit a little too close to home.

Adrenaline is a wonderful thing.

So is coffee.

Though I didn't get more than five hours of sleep that night, I was raring to go the next morning. I'd better be. I had to emcee the opening ceremony at ten, host a panel on scrimshaw buttons at eleven, introduce our luncheon speaker (a wonderful woman who knew everything there was to know about rubber buttons), and still be perky at six for the banquet and Thad's keynote address.

By eight in the morning, I was in the elevator and heading down to the hotel's conference rooms, and when the doors swished open and the first thing I saw was a life-size picture of Thad on the poster that featured the huge headline "Geronimo!" in heavy block letters, I didn't need to look at myself in the mirrored panels that lined the walls. I could feel my grin stretch from ear to ear.

Sure, there had been some bumps on the proverbial conference road. And yes, I was still on the lookout for Beth Howell so I could try to figure out what had happened on the boat the night before. But all in all, I was handling things with poise and assurance. And besides — I passed another poster advertising Thad's keynote — I had gone after and snagged the most coveted speaker on the button circuit.

"Josie Giancola . . ." I shifted the briefcase I was carrying from one hand to the other and tugged my sage-green suit jacket into place, marching across the lobby. "You are doing an excellent job."

"You really are!"

When I realized I'd spoken loud enough that the stranger standing nearby sipping a cup of coffee heard me, I blushed a thousand shades of red. She was kind enough not to point out that talking to yourself is one sure sign of mental instability and, instead, hurried forward. "My first national conference," she said. "And things are going so smoothly over at the registration table that it's a dream. Helen Obermyer . . . I've known Helen for years. She's got everything moving like clockwork. And that assistant of yours . . ." The woman's little shiver spoke volumes. "Talk about a dream!"

I didn't ask who she was talking about.

I didn't have to.

The way she shivered said a whole lot. It ought to. I myself had once been prone to those same kinds of shivers, and not that long ago. In fact, I was convinced it was that shiver-inducing charm that had robbed me of my senses and made me utter those fateful words, *I do.*

I hurried over to registration to find Kaz and get him the hell away from my conference, but that was not so easy considering when I finally spotted him in the crowd, he was in the middle of helping a man from Georgia — not the state — make sense of our conference booklet and which sessions were being held in which rooms.

I left my briefcase in the care of one of the conference volunteers and waited until they exchanged cordial goodbyes in English and whatever language it is they speak in Georgia before I closed in on him. "What, you're some kind of expert in foreign relations now? What are you doing —"

"He's as smart as a whip." A woman walking by patted Kaz's arm.

"And as cute as a button!" her companion said, and laughed.

"See?" Once they were gone, Kaz turned up the wattage on his smile and aimed it full at me. "I'm indispensable."

"But why?" I was tempted to throw my hands in the air and raise my voice while I was at it. Maybe then I could get through to Kaz. I controlled myself, but only because we were within feet of the registration table, and the area was abuzz with eager conference-goers. After the debacle onboard the boat the night before, I didn't need another scene. Especially one that featured me and my ex duking it out in front of button collectors from all over the world.

I grabbed onto the sleeve of Kaz's blue

61

blazer and dragged him further down the corridor, where things were quieter.

"You own a blue blazer?" When I realized what I was doing, I dropped my hand as if the cloth were on fire and looked over Kaz's outfit: blue blazer with shiny brass buttons, white Oxford cloth shirt, khakis. "You've never owned a blue blazer in your life. And khakis?" I had a rule about not getting within touching distance of Kaz's bare flesh, but I figured desperate times, desperate measures, and all that. I pressed a hand to his forehead. No fever.

"What's going on, Kaz?" I asked. "What are you up to and why aren't you working down at the port and why are you here?"

"Apparently, to help." When a group of elderly women walked by, grinned, and waved at him, Kaz waved back and called each and every one of them by their first names. "A conference chair can never have too many dedicated volunteers to do her bidding."

"Apparently, this one can." I crossed my arms over my chest and stepped back, my weight against one foot. I'd hoped for intimidating.

Kaz's smile never wavered. "Hey, I took some vacation time. Because I figured this was a big deal for you and you could use the extra help. Now, there is something you can do for me. You know, to show your appreciation."

"I knew it." The words popped out, along with a whoop that pretty much said *I knew you were up to something, buster, the moment you showed up at the airport.* When I realized how loud both had come out, I clamped one hand over my mouth, grabbed Kaz's sleeve, scooted a few feet further down the corridor toward the room where the vendors were set up, and hissed, "I knew it."

Kaz was less than repentant. "It's nothing like that!"

"Like what?"

"Like whatever you think it is. I was just thinking, that's all. Helen tells me you're staying in a suite and —"

"Josie?" Langston Whitman stuck his head out of the vendors' room, and the instant he saw me, a look of relief swept over his face. "Well, this is lucky. I thought I'd have to search all over for you. Could you . . ." He glanced from me to Kaz and back to me. "Could we talk somewhere? Privately?"

I didn't bother excusing myself. But then, I don't think Kaz noticed. A group of four middle-aged women came over and said they needed help figuring out where the ballroom was. Just for the record, it was about fifteen feet to our right, but rather than point that out, Kaz showed them the way. Kaz was in his glory, all right, playing the button hero the way he never had back when we were married.

Yes, I know. Sour grapes. And I refused to go there. Langston stepped out of the dealer room, looked around to make sure we were alone, and then, even though we were, beckoned me even further down the hallway and farther from the conference-goers.

I didn't like the little vee of worry creased between Langston's eyes any more than I liked the fact that though he looked calm enough, his fingers were tight around the handle of the awl he held in one hand.

Automatically, my stomach knotted. "What's up?" I asked him.

"We've got a . . . situation." He was as reluctant to say it as I was to hear it, and he rolled the awl between his palms, steeling himself. The awl must have been one of Elliot's. It was seven inches long with a warm mahogany handle that was carved in a series of hypnotic, undulating spirals. The steel tip . . . Well, if the way the overhead lights glinted off it meant anything, that was perfect, too. It was sharpened to a no-nonsense point that was just right for pierc-

64

ing the heavy card stock we used to display our buttons.

Langston's nostrils flared. "Thad Wyant stopped by last night after the dinner cruise. Here in the dealer room as we were setting up our booths."

I groaned. "And he said something stupid. I'm so sorry, Langston. When I invited him to the conference, I had no idea that a man so studious and with such a good reputation could be so —"

"Neanderthal?" Langston's eyes glittered. At least for a moment. The next second, he took pity on me. "No, no, don't worry about that. I saw Wyant in action on the boat last night. I knew I was in for trouble the moment he showed up. But I never expected . . ."

His hesitation made my heartbeat speed up.

Langston tightened his grip on the awl. "He said he'd be busy this morning, and he asked if I'd mind if he bought some things last night. I know, I know . . ." Even though I wasn't going to object, he held up the hand with the awl in it to stop me, just in case. "We aren't supposed to sell anything before the official opening of the vendor room this morning. But he is the guest of honor, after all, and I figured it wouldn't hurt to make one exception. Wyant has a stellar reputation, and frankly, I liked the idea of a little publicity. You know, when word got around that he was buying his supplies from me."

"Is that what he wanted? Supplies?" I wasn't sure why this sounded so odd to me; I only knew it did. I suppose I thought a man as well versed in the world of buttons as Wyant was would have all the supplies he needed. After all, he'd been building his collection for more years than I'd been alive.

"Oh, yes." Langston nodded. "Supplies were exactly what that son-of-a —" He remembered himself and took a deep breath. "Supplies were exactly what Wyant was looking for. He chose one of Elliot's awls, one much like this one but with a cherry handle. And he bought some plastic sleeves and card stock, too. Or at least he tried." Like he was as embarrassed now that he was telling me about it as he had been when it happened, Langston glanced away. "Wyant's credit card was declined."

I cringed. "And that's when things got ugly. I can only imagine."

"No, no. It wasn't like that at all. In fact, Wyant was barely fazed by the whole thing. He said there must have been some mix-up with his credit-card company. He said he was going back to his room to call them. And he left."

"No big blowup?" I was grateful but ambivalent.

"Not one unpleasant word," Langston assured me. "Elliot and I went about our business setting up our booth. Then this morning . . ." With the awl, Langston pointed back toward the vendor room. "You know how busy it can be, especially the first day of a conference. Everybody's so eager to see everything, especially the buttons some of the dealers are selling. Things were hectic, and just a little while ago . . . Well, Wyant came back. I figured he'd worked out his problems with the credit-card company. But I was with a customer and so was Elliot, and by the time we were finished, Wyant was gone."

No way that was the end of the story. I tipped my head, my eyes on Langston. "And?"

"And . . ." Like just saying it was distasteful, Langston made a face. He'd controlled himself long enough, and now the words rushed out of him, his voice rough with anger, the bones of his knuckles showing where he grabbed the awl. "And when I finally got around to catching my breath, I realized there were some things missing

67

from my booth. That cherry-handled awl, for one thing, and you see how fine Elliot's work is, Josie." He opened his palm to give me another look at the awl with the mahogany handle. "Beautiful and expensive. And besides the awl, some plastic sleeves and card stock. In fact, every single thing Wyant looked at last night was gone."

My breath caught. "Are you saying —"

"No, I'm not. Because I don't know for sure. And damn, I wish I did, because I'd like to take that egotistical bastard and —" Langston realized he'd lost control and sucked in a sharp breath. "I only know what Wyant looked at last night. And that he came back this morning when we were too busy to take care of him. I'm certain of what's missing. But I never saw him take any of it, Josie. As much as I don't like him, I can't accuse the man. I'm sorry." He put a hand on my shoulder, and honestly, I don't think it was as much to comfort me as it was to help him get a grip on himself. "It's a lousy way to start your morning. But I thought you should know that there just might be more to your guest of honor than meets the eye."

"Yes, of course. You're right. I'll contact hotel security and file a report."

"And we'll check the bastard's room, right?"

In spite of the fact that I had solved a murder a couple of months before, I'm definitely no expert when it comes to the law. I didn't want to make any promises I couldn't keep. "I suppose if the security finds some kind of evidence —"

"Evidence?" Langston rumbled. "The supplies that are missing are worth a couple hundred dollars," he said. "That makes it a felony, right? And even that isn't the most important thing. You've got a guest of honor who thinks he's better than everyone else. That he's above the law, and that he doesn't have to play by the rules. You've got to do something about it, Josie." He whirled around and strode off toward the lobby. "You've got to," he said, turning to me one last time. "Or I will."

When he disappeared into the crowd, I let go of a breath I hadn't even realized I was holding and sagged against the wall, waiting for my heartbeat to ratchet back before I dared to head out and do a last-minute sound check in the ballroom. I was almost there when Helen scurried by. She caught sight of me and made a beeline in my direction.

"Trouble in River City!" she said in a

singsong voice and stage whisper meant only for me. She waved me closer. "You need to see this, Josie, before anyone else does."

I didn't ask what she was talking about. But then, Helen didn't really give me a chance. She hurried around the perimeter of the lobby so quickly that I had to scurry to keep up. She didn't stop until we were right outside the elevators, and by then, she didn't have to say a word. I saw exactly what she was talking about.

It was the picture of Thad, the one I'd seen just a little while before, when I got off the elevator.

Only it didn't look like it had then. But then, that was because someone had taken a sharp object to the poster and gouged out Thad's eyes.

CHAPTER FOUR

Opening ceremony, and it went off without a hitch.

Well, except for the microphone that was working right before we started and somehow cut out just as I was giving my opening remarks.

Scrimshaw panel, and that went well, too — aside from the fact that the dozen antique whalebone buttons I'd brought from the shop for show-and-tell got misplaced. Not to worry. The buttons were located, but not until after the panel was over. Losing five hundred dollars in inventory before lunch is not my idea of a good time. Especially when the video company we'd hired to record each session so we could make the DVDs available to our membership had cameras rolling while I tried to bluff my way through a half-baked explanation of why my visual aids weren't there.

And then there was that lunch — the

rubber-button luncheon, to be exact.

That went fine.

Really.

Except that the hotel catering manager insisted I'd called him the week before and cancelled the salads. Believe me when I say I had not. Thank goodness Helen jumped to the forefront and agreed to go over the menus for the rest of the conference with him very carefully.

With all that going on, I didn't have a moment to myself, so it wasn't until after lunch that I was able to do a quick sweep to check out the rest of the Thad Wyant posters we'd placed around the hotel. On one, someone had drawn a thick, black mustache under Thad's too-big nose. On another, there was a trembling *X* scratched over his heart. Three more posters matched the first Helen had found, with Thad's eyes gouged out.

Doing my best to look inconspicuous and hoping no one noticed either the vandalized photos or me getting rid of them, I took down each of the posters, folded them in half, and tucked them under my arm.

Good thing, too, because when I finished with the last one and turned to head toward the hotel's security office with them, Daryl Tucker was right behind me.

"Sorry." He jumped back, which was a

good thing because when I spun around, we were practically nose to nose. It was the first I noticed that his eyes were hazel. He was wearing a green shirt the same color as the glint in his eyes. "I saw you standing over here and I wanted to tell you how much I enjoyed the scrimshaw panel this morning and . . ." Behind those thick glasses, his eyes flickered from my face to my arm. "You're taking down posters. Do you need some help?"

Sure, I was a theater major back in college, but I'd never done very well in my acting classes. I excelled at all the behind-the-scenes stuff, like costuming. Costumes. Buttons. To me, they were a natural go-together. But acting? Pretending I was something and someone I was not went against my nature.

Which made it all the more remarkable that I was able to play it cool, like nothing unusual was going on and finding those pictures of Thad with his eyes stabbed out didn't give me the royal creeps. "That's so kind of you, Daryl. But I'm fine. Really."

"He's not cancelling, is he?" I didn't have to ask who he was talking about. When he glanced toward the posters under my arm, Daryl's left eye twitched. "There are a lot of people here who are counting on hearing

73

Mr. Wyant speak. They'd be really disappointed if he didn't show up."

"Oh, he'll be here." My voice was perky even while inside my head it grumbled, *He better show up after all I've spent so far on plane fare, hotel accommodations, and those endless trips to the bar.* "Thad is as excited to be here as we are to be hosting him. No worries there." One of the posters slipped out from under my arm and floated to the floor.

I bent to retrieve it just as Daryl asked, "And that button of his? The Geronimo button?"

It wasn't until I stood up that I realized Daryl had bent over, too. He might have been trying to beat me to the poster. Maybe. To me, it looked more like he didn't want to miss a word of whatever I was going to say.

"Do you think it's real?" he asked.

"Of course it's real." Once again, I had the uneasy feeling that Daryl was encroaching on my personal space, and I shifted slightly to my left, putting a tad more distance between us and hoping it didn't look too obvious. "Thad has the provenance to prove it. Geronimo's autograph dated the same day the original owner purchased the button, a letter from the soldier in charge of the barracks the day the button was sold, a list of every person who's ever owned it. You know how it is with buttons, Daryl. Collectors are very particular."

"Sure. Yeah." Apparently, I looked like I was ready to leave, because Daryl moved back a step to let me by. "Only it seems like a whole lot of hoopla. You know, for one little button."

I forgave him — but only because he was new to the button game. "You'll want to hit the afternoon session," I told him with a smile. "The one called 'Collecting Mania.' We do a workshop on the topic every year at the conference. It's a good-natured look at what goes on inside button collectors' heads, and it's always a lot of fun."

"I wouldn't miss it." That bashful smile peeked out from behind the bush of his beard. "Will you be there, too?"

Was that a come-on?

I looked Daryl over and decided instantly that it was not. The guy was too nerdy to try a pickup line as lame as that.

Or too nerdy to know how lame it was and try it anyway.

"I'll be there," I promised. Only not in a way that made it sound like a date. "I'm trying to make it to every workshop, even if it's just for a couple minutes. You know, to make sure the presenters have what they need and that there are enough chairs for everyone. Stuff like that."

"So you won't be staying the whole time? I thought . . ." Daryl glanced down at the blue-and-green carpeting. "I thought maybe we could sit together."

"Not sure I'll have time for that," I said, and hurried away as fast as I possibly could. In a busy-conference-chair sort of way, of course. Not an oh-my-gosh-I-don't-know how-to-handle-this-so-I'm-outta-here way.

I hoped.

Still, when I rounded the corner to head over to hotel security to talk to them about the vandalism and about the items missing from Langston's display and realized Daryl hadn't followed me, I breathed a sigh of relief. Not so when I spoke to a security supervisor named Ralph. As far as he knew, no one had reported seeing anyone vandalize the posters, and sure, they had cameras around the hotel, he informed me, but not in all the areas. Ralph would look at the tapes — he said this with as much enthusiasm as noncollectors muster when the subject of buttons comes up — but he didn't hold out a lot of hope that we'd find the perpetrator, either of the vandalism or the theft.

"Kids," Ralph grumbled just as I was leaving his office. "Must have been kids. Who else would bother to steal any of that button stuff? Or do such a dumb thing to a button poster?"

Who else, indeed? The theft from Langston's booth, that was one thing, and apparently, Thad's work. But when it came to the posters, don't think I'd forgotten about Beth Howell and the fight she'd had with Thad on the boat. Or Chase Cadell, for that matter, who didn't seem above finding some way to get back at his rival, even if it did involve the childish destruction of Thad's pictures. Or even — as impossible as it sounded to me because I knew what a gentleman he was — Langston. After all, the last I'd seen him, he was heading off toward the lobby with an awl in his hands and the certainty in his heart that Thad had ripped him off.

These were the sorts of thoughts that swirled through my head the rest of the afternoon as I went through the paces. They were not necessarily what I was thinking about in the "Collecting Mania" workshop, where I was more concerned about staying in the back corner of the room and not even looking in the direction of the empty seat next to Daryl's.

By four o'clock, when the afternoon sessions were over, I had just enough time to race up to my room to shower and change into my clothes for the evening banquet. Things would have gone a bit smoother if I could have found my comb faster. I was sure I'd left it in the bathroom earlier that morning, but it wasn't there, and of all places, I found it finally on a shelf in the hallway closet.

"Weird," I told myself, not so much because of where I found the comb but because I didn't remember putting it there. Then again, with everything that had been happening and all the conference minutiae packing my head, it shouldn't have come as a surprise that I was forgetting details. And misplacing things, too.

By the time I was ready and on my way back downstairs, my head was spinning and my anticipation of the night's event was whirring through my bloodstream. I made sure everything inside and outside the ballroom was ready for our guests.

"Lookin' good, Button Babe!" There's only one person on the face of the earth who would have the nerve to call me that, so when I turned around, I wasn't surprised to see Kaz. I was surprised to see him wearing a tux.

"What?" Like a model on a Milan runway, he held out his arms and spun around to give me a better look. "You've never seen me in a tux before?"

"I have seen you in a tux. Once." I did not elaborate. We both knew the day we were talking about, and what's that saying about beating a dead horse? Well, there was no use beating a dead wedding. Or more precisely, a dead marriage.

"You look good," I told him, because it was true.

"And you look . . ." Kaz grabbed my hands and held me at arm's length. Thanks to a recent royalty check from a low-budget movie I'd once done costumes for that had turned into a cult favorite, I'd treated myself to a new dress for this special occasion. Three-quarter sleeves, scalloped neckline, black lace. It was fun without being too funky, elegant and romantic and still professional. When I bought it, I had absolutely no intention of impressing anyone but myself, but the way Kaz's eyes lit told me otherwise.

"You look amazing!" he said.

"And you're apparently still my assistant?" I was hoping he'd contradict me, but no such luck, and when I realized it, I breathed a sigh of surrender. "OK, assistant, what's on our agenda before dinner starts?"

"I was hoping for a glass of champagne and —" The look on my face told Kaz to stick to the subject, and the subject was the conference. "Everything's all set up for Helen and the people who will be checking the guest list," he said, pointing to the table near the door. "Only she's not here yet and . . ." He glanced at his Rolex, the one I'd bought him back in the day, after I'd received my very first royalty check. Honestly, I was surprised it hadn't gone the way of all of Kaz's other assets — to the pawn-shops, or the loan sharks, or his landlord to pay his back rent. "She told me she was go-ing to be down here by five, and it's nearly five thirty."

"Why don't you call her room?" I nudged Kaz in the direction of the nearest house phone. "She's not a spring chicken, and if something happened and she needs some help . . ."

"Done!" Kaz the Assistant got right on it.

And I hurried over to the sign-in table to get the volunteers waiting there for Helen organized and working. While I was at it, I checked the dinner list for Beth Howell's name. According to our guest list, she'd be there, and believe me, I was keeping an eye out for her. There was no sign of her yet. I wasn't sure if I wanted to offer her an apology or whether I was just looking for information on what happened the night before and why. I only knew that, as chair, my duty was to make sure no one had a bad experience at the conference. What had happened on the boat . . . Well, that was all about bad.

"So where's the almighty guest of honor? Not here, waiting for everyone to bow and scrape to him?"

When he walked up to me grumbling, I knew Chase Cadell was perfectly serious. Which is why I had no choice but to act as if he was joking. "Oh, I'm sure Thad will be down in just a few minutes," I said, and made sure I punctuated the statement with a laugh. "I have a feeling he likes to make grand entrances."

"Humph." Chase was dressed in a rumpled gray suit, and when he crossed his arms over his broad chest, the buttons on his white cotton shirt strained. "You know I love ya, Josie, but —"

"Yes, I know." I made sure I kept my smile in place. "I would have been far better off inviting you to be our banquet speaker."

"Damned straight."

"And I would have loved listening to you. You know that's true, too. But you, Chase, you do not own the Geronimo button."

He scanned the area where our guests were gathering, and whatever he was going to say, he waved it away as inconsequential. "Bah! Never mind. See you later, Josie. Maybe in the bar after this whole fiasco is over."

"You're not joining us for dinner?"

He threw a look over my shoulder into the ballroom and the podium that had been set up for Thad, along with the video screen, where we'd get our first look at the Geronimo button. "You don't think an old rattlesnake like me is going to pass up food I already paid for, do you? But I'm not staying for Wyant's talk. Geronimo button. Hah!"

By the time he walked away, Kaz was just returning. "Helen didn't answer her phone," he said. "You want me to —"

"There she is!" When the elevator doors whooshed open and Helen scurried out, what felt like the weight of the world lifted from my shoulders.

"Sorry!" Helen hurried past me with hardly a look. She was winded, and her cheeks were red. "Sorry, sorry, sorry! I fell asleep. Can you imagine? Went up to my room after the last session and fell sound asleep. By the time I woke up and got dressed and —"

"Not to worry!" Just like she would have done if our roles were reversed, I looped one arm through hers to force her to slow down and take a deep breath. "Everything is under control."

"Oh, don't tell me that." She looked positively stricken. "If you do, I'll think no one needs me."

By the time Helen was settled at the table, where the other members of her committee had efficiently checked in the dinner guests, most everybody was already in the ballroom, and it would have been rude of me to wait outside, even if I was waiting for our guest of honor. Instead, I went into the ballroom and went from table to table, welcoming people and telling them how excited I was about the evening's program. I did a last-minute sound check at the podium and then talked to the catering director to make sure the staff was ready to start serving and that the ice-cream cakes we'd ordered in the shape of buttons had arrived and looked perfect.

And Thad Wyant was still nowhere to be seen.

"You pacing from the front of the ball-room to the lobby and looking worried isn't helping things." From out of nowhere, Kaz showed up at my side. "The salads are be-

83

ing served. You're going to have to sit down."

"But I —"

"I already called his room." As smoothly as if we'd choreographed it, Kaz spun me in the direction of the table at the front of the room with the "Reserved" sign on it. "No answer."

"But I —"

"I checked the bar, too. He's not there."

Kaz deposited me in a chair between Helen and the empty spot where Thad was supposed to be sitting and went around to the other side of the table.

"You said Mr. Wyant would be here." Until Daryl spoke to me, I didn't realize my chair was back-to-back with his.

"Of course he will be." That was the perky me. And just to prove it, I glanced around both my table and his, a confident smile on my face. "Thad's just been delayed for a few minutes. You know how these things are."

"How?" Daryl's question was so sincere that I didn't have the heart to answer. Good thing I didn't have the opportunity. From the pocket of his orange-and-brown-plaid sport coat, his cell phone rang, and Daryl checked the caller ID, excused himself, and left the ballroom.

I turned back toward my table just as a

waitress deposited my salad in front of me, and honestly, it looked as delicious as the picture I saw when I went through the hotel catering menu and ordered tonight's dinner. Fresh field greens, diced pears, a sprinkling of blue cheese. Too bad my stomach was too jumpy for me to enjoy it. I did another quick scan of the ballroom. No Thad. I pushed my chair back from the table.

"Sit down." Kaz mouthed the words. "Calm." Like a baseball umpire signaling safe, he made a gesture over his salad and smiled.

I knew what that meant, too. Upbeat. I was supposed to remain upbeat. Even though the program was scheduled to start in exactly forty minutes and my speaker was nowhere to be seen.

Chase Cadell was walking back from the bar, a bottle of beer in one hand, and he leaned over and purred in my ear. "Told you you should have picked me. I'm actually here, Josie. And that son-of-a-gun Wyant —"

"Will be joining us in just a jiffy." I wasn't sure how my popping out of my chair and heading out to the lobby was supposed to help accomplish that, but I did it anyway, and it was a good thing I did. I was just in time to see a tiny woman in a black suit disappear around the corner toward the vendor room.

Beth Howell.

Yeah, the timing was bad, but this was the first time I'd caught up with Beth since the incident on the boat, and I wasn't going to let the moment pass me by. I took off down the hallway, and I would have caught up to her if the door to the vendor room hadn't swung open and stopped me in my tracks.

"Langston!" He stepped out of the room so quickly that he surprised me, and I pressed a hand to my heart at the same time I dodged to my left. "You just —"

"Need to get into the banquet." Langston stepped to his right.

"And I need . . ." I looked around him, but by then, the hallway was empty. Wherever Beth Howell was headed, she was nowhere in sight now. "I'll go back to the ballroom with you," I told Langston, and I hoped I didn't sound disappointed because of that, so I added, "You're late for the banquet. The salad's are already being served."

"Is it really that late?" He looked at his watch. "The time just got away from me. I was taking care of some last-minute details at the booth."

"And I . . ." I suppose I could have told him I was hotfooting it after Beth Howell, but I never had a chance. But then, that's because Ralph the security guard came racing across the lobby, caught sight of me, and headed my way.

"You've got to see this. I mean, you really don't have to, but you do. You know what I mean?"

I would have gladly told him I didn't if I could have gotten a word in edgewise. But then, with the way Ralph latched on to my arm and dragged me back across the lobby, I didn't exactly have a chance.

"You were asking about him and all," Ralph said, his voice high-pitched and panicky, the way I would hope a security guard's never would be. "And then Linda called. You know, from the laundry room, and I went down there and all, and I'm going to have to call somebody, only Zack, my boss, he's gone for the day and all, and —"

By this time, Ralph had already punched the button to call the service elevator at the end of a corridor off the lobby. The doors whooshed open, and he dragged me inside. "You're not going to believe it," he said. "I don't believe it. And I've seen it. And I've got to call somebody. Fast. Only I can't think straight; you know what I mean?

Because these kinds of things aren't supposed to happen. Not at a nice hotel like this."

The elevator bumped to a stop, the doors opened, and Ralph, who was still hanging on to me like a limpet on a rock, pulled me down a hallway with green-tiled floors and bare walls. Down here at basement level, there were no windows, and the overhead fluorescents buzzed and flickered. The air was heavy with steam and the scent of bleach.

Ralph veered to the left and into a room lined with metal shelves that were stacked with freshly laundered towels.

"Over there." One hand to the small of my back, he pushed me forward. "You're not going to believe it."

He was right. I didn't believe it. But then, I was having a little trouble believing my own eyes and the fact that Thad Wyant was slumped against the far wall of the linen room in a pool of blood. There was a gorgeous hand-carved cherry-handled awl plunged into his neck.

CHAPTER FIVE

Ralph the security guard did nothing to make me feel secure. Or guarded, for that matter. In fact, Ralph was so upset at finding Thad's body, he crumpled up in a corner and whimpered, and I was the one who called 911. I was also the first person Nevin Riley saw when he walked into the basement hallway, where Ralph (still trembling and crying) and I were waiting.

"Hey." OK, it doesn't sound like much, but for Nev, this is the equivalent of *Hello, how are you?* and *Boy, you're looking fine* all rolled into one. To say he's not much of a talker is something of an understatement. "You find the body?"

I hadn't, and I told Nev as much and pointed him toward Ralph, then got out of the way so he could calm Ralph down and so the crime-scene techs who streamed in behind Nev could get into the linen storage room.

That gave me a chance to pull out my cell, dial Helen's number, and whisper a silent prayer that the banquet wasn't so loud that she couldn't hear her phone ring.

"Josie?" I could tell she'd seen my name pop up on caller ID, and I imagined her giving the phone a quizzical look. "Where are you, honey? And what's going on? You were here, and now you're not, and they're already serving the entrée. And I hate to tell you this, honey, but Thad Wyant isn't here, either."

"I'll explain later about why I'm not there." Yes, that was my voice, rushed and breathless. But then, I wasn't exactly at my best. Sure, I'd once found the body of a famous actress at the Button Box, but truth be told, not even previous experience can prepare a person for this sort of thing. Nothing would ever make me immune to the blood, or the horrible thought that a life had been so violently cut short. I gulped, and rather than watch the techs examining Thad's body, I stepped down the hallway and into the cavernous room opposite, where row after row of industrial-size washers and dryers stood silent, waiting for the next morning's delivery of sheets and towels, and a couple of uniformed officers were checking above, below, and inside everything in sight to make sure no one was hiding there. "I need you to do me a favor, Helen."

"Of course, dear. Anything. What's that?" This question obviously wasn't meant for me because Helen's voice was suddenly muffled, as if she'd turned in a different direction. "It's Josie," I heard her say, and I wondered who she was talking to. "She's got some kind of problem and —"

"Helen!" Sure, I felt dopey standing there in the laundry room and yelling into my phone, but it was the only thing I could think to do to get her attention. "Helen, this is kind of important."

"Of course it is. You wouldn't have called during dinner otherwise."

She was back, and before she could get distracted again, I said all I had to say and said it fast. "Thad Wyant isn't going to be able to make the dinner tonight." Talk about understatements! Rather than dwell on it, I kept my focus. "I need you to rustle up a banquet speaker," I told Helen. "I was thinking . . ." I almost said Chase Cadell, then reconsidered. Things were bad enough; there was no use making Chase the center of attention and giving him the opportunity to say "I told you so."

I scrambled, furiously thinking about our

conference attendees. "How about Brenda Perry? You know, the woman who makes those really cool polymer-clay buttons and —"

The ladylike *tsk* on the other end of the phone was enough to stop me cold. "Lovely woman," Helen said. "Gifted artist."

"But . . ."

"Terrible public speaker. Oh my, yes. You haven't heard her, have you? Mumbles. Stumbles over her words. Simply terrible. When Brenda's speaking in front of a crowd, she's uncomfortable, and so is everyone who's in the room with her."

I scratched Brenda off what had been a very short list and tried for another idea. No easy thing, considering my gut was twisted in painful knots, my knees felt like they were made out of some of Brenda's uncured polymer clay, and my heart was pounding so hard, I was sure Nev and the other cops across the hall heard it and figured the thumping was coming from the washing machines. Fighting to steady myself, I waited until the cops were done with their sweep of that side of the basement and leaned against the cool, tiled wall. "Then how about Bob Johnson? He knows everything there is to know about cloisonné buttons."

"Just saw him at the bar." Helen's tone of voice told me she was shaking her head sadly when she said this. "One too many glasses of Jack Daniel's, I'm afraid. My goodness, and it's so early in the conference for him to misbehave like that. Bob usually waits until the last night to let it all hang out."

"Then what about —"

"Thad isn't just late. Is that what you're telling me? He's not going to make it at all?" I think the enormity of what I'd been trying to tell her finally sunk in. Poor Helen didn't know the half of it. That's why she didn't sound as worried as she did uncertain. "Are you sure, Josie? He's your guest of honor, after all. The conference paid for him to fly all the way here from New Mexico. And the conference is covering every single one of his expenses. Hotel and such, I mean. Are you telling me you've lost him?"

I drew in a long breath and let it out slowly even as I switched my phone from one sweaty hand to the other. "It's complicated."

"It must be, dear, for a conference not to have its guest of honor at the opening banquet."

Don't ask me how, but I somehow managed to sound as levelheaded and focused as I wasn't feeling. "You're right. It's unforgivable, but I'm afraid it's unavoidable. Still, we can't have people sitting there after dinner waiting for a speaker who's never going to show."

"Does that mean we're not going to see the Geronimo button tonight?"

Leave it to Helen to get to the heart of the matter. And for the heart of the matter to be all about buttons. I can't say I blamed her. Had I come all the way to Chicago from who-knows-where just to get a gander of the famous Geronimo button, I, too, would wonder what Thad's absence meant.

The Geronimo button.

The thought galvanized me, and I straightened up like a shot. A chill crawled through my bloodstream, and this time, it had nothing to do with Thad's death. What if Thad's death was somehow tied to the Geronimo button? What if something had happened to it? That button was a priceless historical object, a one-of-a-kind link with the past and a valiant warrior.

What if . . ?

Panic is so not a pretty thing, and make no mistake, I was toeing the edge of it.

I gulped down a breath to calm myself, and when that didn't work, I tried another. I paced and told myself it was too soon to worry. We would look for the Geronimo button as soon as possible.

Er . . . that is, Nev and the other cops would look for the button.

After all, it was their job, not mine. I would mention the button to Nev as soon as I was able, but other than that —

"Did you say something, dear?" Helen's voice on the other end of the phone snapped me back to reality. "About the Geronimo button and how there are lots of folks here who are eager to see it, and now, they might not get the chance? Because it's a little hard to hear. There are people nearby talking and chatting and having a good time. Of course, they don't realize the entire conference is about to crumble around them. They're counting on hearing Thad Wyant speak tonight. And on getting their first look at that button of his."

"I'm afraid that's going to have to wait. But don't tell them that. Don't tell them anything. Just that . . ." I imagined standing at the podium in the front of the ballroom and trying to explain away the inexplicable. "Just that Thad can't be there and that I can't be, either, and that I'm very sorry. Just find me someone who can stand up after dinner and talk about buttons for forty-five minutes. Any buttons. That shouldn't be hard in a conference full of button collectors."

"Well . . ." I had known Helen for a long time, and I could tell by the way she drew out the word that she was pink from chin to forehead. "My laptop is up in my room, and I might still have a PowerPoint presentation on it that I gave at a local button society meeting a couple years ago. It's about fop buttons. You know, buttons that depict French aristocratic fashions of the eighteenth century. That just might be enough to take people's minds off the fact that Thad Wyant is missing."

"He isn't. Not exactly."

The subtle distinction was lost on Helen. "I don't want to seem pushy," she said. "I mean, by suggesting I do the talk. There are plenty of other people here who might be willing to jump up and volunteer. You know, if we want to interrupt them and make them scramble to put together some kind of talk when they should be enjoying dinner. I don't want to come off looking like a publicity hound."

For the first time since Ralph dragged me into the basement, I felt some of the stress inside me uncurl. "You're not, Helen. You're a lifesaver, that's what you are."

"Then you'd like me to take over your duties? And Thad's?"

"Yes. Please. Thank you." From across the hall I saw Nev glance around, and I knew he was looking for me. "Sorry," I added, right before I clicked off the call.

I was just in time to watch Nev hand Ralph off to one of the uniformed cops standing near the service elevator, then head straight for me.

"Hey." He'd said that once already, but I didn't bother to point it out. I also didn't bother to mention that he was wearing almost exactly what he'd been wearing on our last date: rumpled khaki suit, wrinkled blue Oxford cloth shirt. That date was two weeks earlier, and we'd gone to a movie. Since buttons are just about the only thing I am capable of discussing for any length of time and police work is pretty much the only thing Nev can talk about, movies provide us a nice conversation-free environment. In the couple of months we'd known each other, we'd seen a lot of movies.

Not that we're complete morons when it comes to interpersonal skills. After all, we'd already worked together to solve one murder, and truth be told, I had figured it would be our last. Fortunately, there was no murder on the menu the night of our last date. Just that movie, and we'd gone for coffee afterward, and it was . . . nice. Just sitting there at Starbuck's enjoying each other's company, filling the long silences by talking about nothing more than the details of our daily lives. Yeah, it was nice. But then, Nev has that whole cute vibe going for him, so that helps. It's his shaggy, sandy hair, and the fact that he's tall and lanky.

His sense of fashion . . . That was another matter. At least I could be certain that sometime in the last two weeks he'd actually changed his clothes; he was wearing a different tie. This one was green-and-white stripes, and as ugly as any tie I'd ever seen.

Apparently, he was sizing up my fashion sense, too, because his gaze traveled from the scooped neckline of my black-lace dress to the hem, which skimmed my knees, and back up again. "You look amazing," he said. Exactly what Kaz had told me when he saw me in the lobby earlier in the evening. Only coming from Nev, the compliment was warmer and more sincere. Or at least that's how it felt when it curled around my heart. Before I had the chance to turn completely mushy, he tempered the compliment with, "What are you doing here?"

"At the hotel? Or here? Here in the laundry room?" I realized it didn't matter. "Conference," I explained. "You remember.

The International Society of Antique —"

"And Vintage Button Collectors." He nodded. "Of course I remember. Your annual meeting is the reason you've been so busy, and you've been so busy, we haven't had much of a chance to see each other."

It didn't seem fair to lay the whole blame on me. "And you're working nights."

"I would apologize if it was my fault." The smallest of smiles relieved an expression I knew he was obliged to wear at the scene of a crime. "But I'm only on the schedule for working nights for another month, and by then, you'll have this conference wrapped up. Maybe then . . ."

I guess the way my insides warmed even further was all the proof I needed that I hoped it was more than a maybe. "Dinner at my place. If the remodeling is finished."

"And it looks like we'll have plenty to talk about." Nev's expression twisted. He glanced over his shoulder toward the linen room. "The deceased —"

"Is . . . was . . . my guest of honor." I looked toward the linen room, too, but not for long. I'd seen enough blood for one evening. "Do you have any idea what happened?"

He didn't answer, but then, I really didn't expect him to. Like most cops, Nev is a ducks-in-a-row kind of guy. No way he was going to say anything until he had all the facts, and plenty of time to digest them. "What can you tell me about the victim?"

I shrugged and started with the fact I deemed most pertinent. "He's an expert on Western buttons."

This bit of information might have confused a lesser cop. I guess by now, Nev had come to expect that if I was involved, buttons had to be, too. He simply scribbled a line in the notebook he was holding.

"His name is Thad Wyant." I should have said this first, of course. "He's here from Santa Fe and . . ." I weighed the wisdom of gossiping against the sure knowledge that Nev couldn't do his job properly if he didn't have all the facts. "There's been plenty of trouble since he got here."

He raised his flaxen eyebrows. "Trouble because of Wyant?"

I shrugged. "It's hard to say. I mean, not having Chase Cadell's nametag, and misplacing my scrimshaw buttons . . . That kind of stuff can't possibly have anything to do with Thad. But there have been other things. Bigger things. And I don't know if Thad was the cause or just on the receiving end. Last night, he had a fight on the dinner cruise with a woman named Beth Howell. And this morning, one of our vendors accused Thad of stealing from his booth. Chase Cadell can't stand Thad, and Thad's posters were vandalized and . . ." I pulled in a deep breath and forced myself to let it out slowly. "I guess it's not so hard to say. Yeah, there's been trouble. And it's all because of Thad Wyant."

Nev made another note, glancing up only when he was done. "So I'm going to go out on a limb here and say people didn't like him."

"That's putting it mildly."

"And you know I need the names of all those people."

"Of course."

"And it would help if you came along when I talked to them and made the introductions. I mean, I know how button people can be . . ."

I wouldn't have been so defensive if he hadn't caught me at such a bad time, but the way it was, I couldn't help but bristle. "How?"

Nev wrinkled his nose. "Careful," he said. "Button people are careful. At least that's what I think. But then, there's only one button person I really know. And I'm thinking the fact that that particular button person is careful might have more to do with past

101

experience with a certain ex-husband than it does from working with buttons."

He'd picked an odd time to bring up a subject more personal than any we'd talked about before.

Or maybe not.

One of the uniformed cops called to Nev to come and have a look at something, and I saw right through his strategy: it was safe to discuss a topic so highly personal here at the scene of a murder because Nev knew we'd never have a chance to finish the conversation.

Another woman might have been miffed. Me? I was actually kind of grateful. I have never been known as a daredevil. I like the idea of wading more than I do of diving right in. That's true when it comes to swimming, and relationships. (Well, except for my relationship with Kaz, but then, that was never much like swimming; it was more like surfing a tidal wave.)

Wading into talking about Kaz and the damage he'd done to my heart and my ability to trust was far less shocking than closing my eyes and taking a plunge.

And I was surprised Nev realized it.

I guess that explained why I was smiling just a little bit as we walked back to the linen room side by side. Not to worry. I knew better, and I erased the expression the moment we walked through the door.

Good thing.

Otherwise, my smile would have been flash frozen when I stepped into the room and saw an officer wearing latex gloves holding up a blue blazer.

Yeah, one with shiny brass buttons on it that I would have recognized anywhere.

"You don't actually think I had something to do with some guy who got murdered, do you?"

Kaz looked at me when he asked the question. He would have been better served to keep his eyes on Nev. After all, Nev was the one leaning against the far wall of the hotel's security office, writing down every word Kaz said.

Nev's eagle-eye gaze didn't flicker away from Kaz for a second. "So you admit that's your suit jacket in the linen room with the victim?" Nevin asked.

Kaz ran his tongue over his lips. "Well, yeah. It was in the linen room, all right. But not in the linen room with the victim. At least last time I saw the jacket. Last I was in that room, there was no victim. Just towels and such."

Nev made note of this, too.

While Nev was busy, Kaz smoothed one hand through his hair. It was a gesture I'd seen him use before, mostly when he was nervous about telling me he'd lost some sure bet. I can't say I felt sorry for him. I can say I was glad Kaz had the sense to be worried. "This cop boyfriend of yours . . ." Kaz lowered his voice and tipped his head toward Nev. "He doesn't really think —"

"That it's pretty funny that your jacket just happened to be at the scene of a murder you claim you don't know anything about? He sure does." I made a mental note: Nev has really good hearing. No doubt the ease of Nev's movements had come with long practice. He crossed the security office, whirled a chair so that when he sat in it he was facing Kaz, and gave my ex a level look. "When you think about it, you've got to admit it's more odd than funny."

"It is." Kaz had loosened his black bow tie soon after two plainclothes detectives had plucked him out of the banquet and walked him into the office. Now, he played with the ends of it. It was a fidgety thing for a guy who is usually all about cool, calm, and collected, and just watching him, my stomach jumped.

It clenched into a painful ball when Nev asked the next logical question. "You want

104

to explain?"

"I do." Hearing those two particular words from Kaz did nothing to calm me. I'd been sitting at a desk flanked by monitors that showed the goings-on in the lobby, the hotel gift shop, and the loading dock behind the building, and I stood and paced to the other side of the room. When I turned around, Kaz's eyes were still on me. "It's kind of embarrassing," he said.

Believe me, it took every ounce of self-control I had not to throw my hands in the air and tell him it couldn't possibly be. Over the years, Kaz had done so many bone-headed and heartless things, adding another one to the list shouldn't have been a stretch.

Which made me wonder why this incident in particular was so different.

And that only made me more jumpy than ever.

I held my breath and watched Kaz twine his hands together on his lap. "I kind of need a place to stay," he said. "Just for a little while."

"That's why you went around to my apartment the other day!" OK, so raising an arm and pointing a finger at Kaz was a tad overdramatic. It's not like he didn't deserve it. "You were going to ask me if you could crash at my place. That's why you're being so nice to me here at the conference, too. Pretending to be my assistant and picking up Thad at the airport, and —"

"Did you? Pick up Mr. Wyant from the airport?"

This was one little detail Nev knew nothing about, and I had to give him credit. He stuck to his guns (no pun intended) and did his objective homicide detective best to ignore the current of emotion that shivered between me and Kaz like the electrical charge that builds before a thunderstorm. "Was that the first you ever met the victim?"

"Sure." Kaz nodded. "You don't think I hang around with this button crowd, do you? I mean, except for Jo. And Jo was there, too. At the airport, I mean. She'll tell you. It's not like I knew this Wyant guy or anything. It's not like I even cared. I was just trying to . . . you know, help Jo out."

"So I'd invite you to stay in my hotel room with me."

This came out sounding far more personal than I'd intended, but once I'd spoken, it was too late to call the words back. I couldn't do anything about the heat that shot into my cheeks, either.

Kaz's shoulders should have drooped. I mean, anybody else in this situation would have had the brains to look remorseful.

Instead, he pulled his shoulders back, and his eyes glinted.

"I knew you'd cave sooner or later," he said, proving once again that he'd never gotten to know me very well in the three years we'd been married or the year since we'd gotten divorced. "Last night I didn't know what else to do so I hung out in the bar and the lobby for as long as I could, and then . . . Well, I just sort of wandered around until I found my way down to that linen room."

"And what, got cleaned up in one of the washing machines?"

I don't do sarcasm well, which might explain why both Nev and Kaz looked at me like I had begun speaking in some foreign tongue. That is, right before Kaz shrugged. "You brought your briefcase down to the registration table this morning, and your room key was in it and —"

"You broke into my hotel room?"

"Well, technically, I had a key, and —"

The stress of the last hour exploded in me and I swung toward Nev. "You can arrest him, right? You heard what he said. He said —"

"I needed a place to clean up," Kaz admitted. "And I figured you wouldn't mind, Jo."

A memory clicked inside my brain. "You moved my comb!"

"Dang! Did I? I hate it when I'm careless. I used it, see, and I meant to put it back. I just . . ." Like one twitch of those broad shoulders was supposed to explain? "House-keeping knocked, and I figured I should get out of there as soon as I could. You know, before they noticed anything weird."

My hands curled into fists, I stepped toward Kaz.

Lucky thing, cooler heads prevailed. And that the cool head belonged to Nev. "We'll sort all that out later," he said. "For now —"

His cell phone rang.

Nev checked the caller ID, excused himself, and stepped out of the office.

"Sorry."

"Don't even try." I shot Kaz a look. "You've never been sorry in your life, and you're sure not sorry now. You've been playing Mr. Nice Guy just so I'd let you stay with me. And you broke into my hotel room."

"You gonna press charges?"

I crossed my arms over my chest. "It would serve you right if I did."

A smile shivered at the corners of his mouth. "But you won't."

"I should."

"But —"

Now, Kaz's cell rang. He answered, and that hopeful little shimmer in his eyes dissolved in an instant. "Amber! It's great to hear from you." Kaz turned his back and continued his conversation. "No, it's like I said; I'm in Paris, and I won't be home for at least a few more days. You understand, don't you?" He listened for the space of a heartbeat. "I knew you would. I'll call. Really. It's just that I have to catch the Metro now and —"

With that, he hung up.

"I can explain," he said.

I knew he was talking about the phone call, not about why his blazer was at the scene of a crime. I held up a hand to stop him. "I don't want to hear it."

"But —"

"And really, I don't care."

It was nice of Nev to walk back into the room so I didn't have to prove it.

"You're free to go," he told Kaz. "But not until you give these officers your clothes so we can test them for traces of blood. After that, you'll want to stay close."

"Sure." Kaz sidled out of the office.

"What next?" Nev knew I wasn't talking about Kaz. Or at least I hoped he did.

"We'll interview everyone tomorrow, starting with those people you mentioned earlier." He shook his head, and his hair fell in his eyes. "Who would have thought there could be this much drama at a button conference?"

CHAPTER SIX

"You really didn't have to —"

"I know." At the door of my hotel suite, Nev shifted from foot to foot, looking even more rumpled than he had when he first arrived at the crime scene down in the basement hours earlier. He rubbed a hand across eyes the color of a spring sky. Right about then, it was a sky streaked with every shade of sunset red. I imagined my eyes must have looked just as weary. They felt like they were filled with sand. "I know you could have gotten back to your room by yourself. But I didn't like the thought of you walking around on your own this late. There's already been one murder in this hotel tonight."

"There isn't going to be another."

He gave me a lopsided grin. "I know that and you know that. Let's hope the killer knows it, too."

It was an uncomfortable reminder of all

we'd seen in the linen room, and I shivered.

"You're tired." Nev stepped back. "And I need to go. I've got to wrap up downstairs and make sure the scene is secured, then get back to the station. There will be a mountain of extra paperwork to take care of, thanks to Thad Wyant. You are . . ." The elevator dinged to announce its presence on the floor, and he back-stepped toward it with more energy than he should have had considering how hard he'd already worked that night. "You're going to help me, right?"

"Investigate?" It was late, and my voice was loud. I repeated the question in a stage whisper but that did nothing to alter the uncertainty of it. Sure, I'd investigated before, and successfully, too, but I am a button dealer, not a detective. "I can introduce you around," I said, my voice just loud enough so Nev could hear it. "I can point you in the direction of the people we talked about earlier. But other than that —"

"You did a great job last time." The elevator doors slid open, and with one arm, Nev made sure they stayed that way.

"Last time, I helped because of a button."

"And this time, it's because of a button expert."

"But I can't —"

"Sure you can."

The elevator buzzed its displeasure at being held up, and I pictured people in the nearby rooms being awakened from a sound sleep and people on the floors below waiting impatiently for the elevator to arrive. Yeah, I know it was silly to be worried about things like that, but as I'd found out on that earlier investigation, when I'm faced with the overwhelming horror of murder, focusing on the little things helps keep me sane.

"I'll try," I said, mostly because I couldn't stand to hear that buzzing any longer. "See you tomorrow."

Nev checked his watch. "It's already tomorrow, so I'll see you later. And Josie . . ." He'd already stepped into the elevator and he poked his head out. This time, his smile was wide. "Looks like we've got something else to talk about, huh?"

We did, and though I couldn't say I was exactly happy about the circumstances, I realized I was glad I'd be seeing Nev again, and soon. Smiling, I slid my key card into the slot on the door, pushed it open, and stepped inside my room. But when I went to close the door again, a man stuck his foot in the way,

Startled, my adrenaline shot to the moon, and I gasped and pushed on the door harder.

"Ouch!"

I recognized the voice, and that adrenaline rush dissolved in a moment of pure annoyance. I wasn't the least bit surprised when I opened the door and saw Kaz jumping around the hallway on one foot. Yeah, like a little bump with the door hurt that much.

I crossed my arms over my chest. If it wasn't for that, I was sure he'd see my heart trying to batter its way out of my black-lace dress. I didn't need surprises. Not on a night I'd already been way too close to a murder. I looked down the hallway and realized there was a potted palm there. No wonder I hadn't seen Kaz when I walked up to the door. "So you were watching me from behind a potted palm? What are you doing here? And why are you dressed like that?"

He looked down at the blue top and drawstring-waist cotton pants, which reminded me of a doctor's scrubs. "They took my clothes. The cops," he said, answering my second question before he answered my first. "And you heard what your friend told me downstairs." He stopped hopping so he could tip his head toward the elevator. "He told me I had to stay close."

"He didn't mean this close."

Kaz reserved the really devastating smile

for occasions just like this. His sparked and lit up the hallway. "I can't stay down in the linen room again tonight. And the thing about me staying close . . . It is a police order."

"Why not just steal my room key again and make yourself right at home?"

Kaz doesn't recognize sarcasm when it hits him right over the head. That smile got even bigger. "I would if I had the chance. With the cops around and all . . ." His shrug was as casual as can be. "Hey, you don't want me to get in trouble with the cops, do you, Jo?"

My sigh was as much of an answer as he needed. I stepped aside, and he stepped inside.

"Suite, huh?" Kaz looked around at the living-room area and leaned forward for a peek into the bedroom and bathroom. "Pretty snazzy."

"It's not exactly the height of luxury, but we had to choose a reasonably priced hotel for the conference." I set my evening bag and room key on the coffee table in front of a chintz sofa in shades of blue and yellow and kicked off my shoes. "I needed the extra room." I waved toward the dining table, which was piled with extra conference booklets and the leftovers we had of the bags we handed out to each attendee, along with the giveaways we'd been sent by button manufacturers and vintage dealers. "But then, you've already been here. I'm sure you took a good look around then."

Kaz was immune to the steel in my voice. Always had been, and if I was smart, I would remember that he always would be. He strolled over to the minibar and had just put his hand on the door to open it when his cell rang.

"Hey, I've been meaning to call you!"

It wasn't like I had any intention of eavesdropping, but heck, it was my room, and I wasn't going to run and hide so he could talk in private. Instead, I listened to the hum of his conversation while I went into the bedroom and changed into my cotton pajamas and the terry bathrobe I'd brought from home. I washed up and brushed my teeth, and I'd just stepped out of the bathroom when Kaz said, "I'd better go. It's really late here."

He paused for a second, listening to the caller, then blurted out, "Early. Sure, that's what I meant. It's really early here in London. It's late in Chicago where you are, and I really should let you get to bed. I'll bet you're exhausted. I'll talk to you soon. Bye!"

"Paris," I said, as soon as he put down the phone. In answer to his *Huh?* look, I explained. "When you talked to Amber earlier, you told her you were in Paris. This time, you said London. Unless, of course, that wasn't Amber."

"It was." Kaz flopped down on the couch. "She's really terrific," he said.

"But . . ."

His sigh was monumental. The cops had taken his tuxedo jacket, pants, shirt, and bow tie so they could search for traces of blood on them (standard procedure, Nev had assured me) and had allowed Kaz to change into the one of the outfits the hotel staff members wore when they were at work in the basement laundry. He looked relaxed, at ease, and a little too comfortable on my couch. Well, except for the little shade of green that tinged his expression when he talked about Amber. "But . . . well . . . you know I'm not looking for anything permanent. I mean, not anymore."

I could have pointed out that I had come to the painful but inevitable conclusion that he never had been, but it was late, and I was tired, and rehashing our relationship wasn't going to get us anywhere. When it came to me and Kaz, there wasn't any place left to go.

Maybe Kaz realized it, too. He leaned back. "I met Amber down in Florida a month or so ago."

I cinched the tie belt on my robe and sank into the chair opposite the couch. "And let me guess, you're so darned charming, she just can't forget you. That's why she keeps calling."

"Worse than that. She's here. In Chicago."

The light dawned. "Which explains why you need a place to hide out."

"I'm not exactly hiding." He was, of course, and because he refused to face the truth, Kaz got up and did a turn around the room, moving aside the drapes so he could take a gander at the skyscrapers that surrounded us. "It's just that when we met . . . Well, Amber's pretty and blonde." He dropped the curtains back into place and turned to face me. "She's a school psychologist in Sarasota, and heck, I just work down at the Port of Chicago. I wanted to impress her, you know?"

"So you didn't tell her you were my assistant here at the button conference?"

"It's not funny, Jo."

"Neither is you pretending to be my assistant."

"Yeah, I know. But you've got to understand." He hurried back to the couch and sat down. Like looking me in the eye was somehow going to convince me of the righteousness of all he was saying. "I didn't know what else to do, and I had to help you out so you'd do me this favor in return and let me stay with you. See, when I met Amber, I told her some stuff that wasn't exactly . . . Well, I embellished a little bit, you know?"

I did. Whatever he'd told Amber, I was sure I'd heard some version of it somewhere along the line.

Too antsy to keep still, Kaz got to his feet again. This time, he went over to the minibar, took out a beer the hotel would charge me a bundle for, and offered it to me. When I declined with a tip of my head, he popped it open. "I guess you could say I made up a story. You know, about being a big-time developer and living on the Gold Coast. Stuff like that. I didn't think it would ever matter. I just thought Amber was . . . Well, you know. I just thought she was someone it was fun to be with for the weekend. I never thought she'd actually ever show up to visit. I figured once I left Florida, she'd forget all about me."

"Just like you forgot all about her."

At least he had the sense to look embarrassed.

I didn't feel the least bit sorry for him. That's why I didn't offer any advice. He wouldn't listen, anyway. "Trying to get by on your charm and your bullshit . . . It was bound to blow up in your face eventually."

"It sort of already has, because like I said, she's here. And she apparently went to my apartment to surprise me, and it's a lucky thing that I was at work. But now, of course, she's asking how can I possibly live in a walk-up apartment over in Bucktown when I said I had a killer view of the lake from my thirty-fourth-floor condo."

"So let me guess: you made up a second lie to explain the first."

He made a face. "Not a big lie. Just a little one about doing some renovations and helping out a friend and . . . You understand, don't you, Jo? You see why I needed your help for a couple days. After this week . . . Well, she's going to have to get back to Florida sooner or later, and if I can just keep out of sight and pretend I'm in Europe, then there's no way she'll ever find out I lied to her, because I mean, really, what cool woman would ever even think about a button convention or looking for me at one?"

"Not this cool woman, that's for sure." Another zinger that hit the wall of Kaz's incredible ego and dropped like a stone in

120

water. I got up and headed for the bedroom.

"Why not just tell the woman the truth? If she likes you — and she must or she wouldn't have come all the way to Chicago to see you — she won't care that you work at the Port. I never did."

"Yeah, but you . . ." I felt Kaz step up behind me. But then, it was impossible not to notice that the temperature shot up. I told myself to just keep walking, but some old habits die hard. I turned in time to see that his eyes were twinkling. "You're different."

"Dumber, you mean."

"Never!" He set down the beer and stepped even closer. "No way, Jo. You're the smartest woman I know. You run your own business, and you're doing a bang-up job with this conference, and I heard what that cop told you. He wants you to help him solve this murder. You know, like you solved the last one. You're plenty smart. After all, you —"

"Got talked into letting you stay with me?"

He rolled back on his heels. "Well, there's that."

"Your charm isn't always going to get you by, Kaz."

He turned up the wattage on that smile of his and looked beyond me and into the bedroom. "It got me where I am right now. You know, the two of us back together again."

" 'Back together' meaning together in the same building. Not together. Not like in a relationship way."

"No. Sure. Of course not. Only . . ." Another flick of those espresso-colored eyes toward the king-size bed in the room beyond. "Only it's kind of the perfect opportunity. You know . . ." He shuffled closer and put his hands on my arms. "To catch up on old times."

Yeah. Old times.

Like it or not, my brain played back over them at the same time my blood heated and my knees turned to mush. One place Kaz and I had never had any problems was the bedroom, and one thing he'd never been was unfaithful. In fact, Kaz knew more about the right way to romance a woman than any other guy I'd ever met.

He also knew more about offtrack betting, online poker, and lying to poor fools like Amber.

I thanked the gods of sensibility for reminding me at the same time I stepped back and pointed. "The couch pulls out."

"Yeah, I'm sure, but —"

He'd already made another move toward

me, which completely justified me stepping into the bedroom, grabbing hold of the doorknob, and swinging the door almost shut. "I've got to be downstairs tomorrow by seven. So you'll need to be in and out of the bathroom either earlier or later," I said.

The fire in his eyes was tamped back. "Got it," Kaz said.

And I chalked up one point for common sense and gave him a quick once-over. "The cops confiscated that blazer and the other clothes you left in the linen room. If you're helping me out at the conference tomorrow — and you are, by the way, as a way of paying me back for giving you a place to sleep — you may want to head home and pick up some other clothes."

"I can't go home. Amber might be lurking. But not to worry." His smile came and went. "I stopped at the gift shop and put a couple things on your conference account. I figured you wouldn't mind."

"Once again, Kaz, you figured wrong."

It wasn't exactly the stinging parting shot I would have liked, but the fact that I closed the door in his face said something to him.

The fact that I made sure I locked the door . . . Well, I guess that said something to me, too.

■ ■ ■ ■

Kaz's new clothes were delivered to the room early the next morning, and by ten minutes to seven, he was waiting at the elevator for me, decked out in black pants with a crisp pleat in them and a raspberry-colored sweater that fit as if a team of knitters had taken his measurements and worked their little fingers to the bone overnight.

I didn't bother to ask how much the sweater cost me. The bill wouldn't go to the conference but to my own personal account, and the way I figured it, seeing him look that good was worth it. Besides, now that he'd come right out and confessed what he was up to, I planned to make him work his butt off for the rest of the conference to earn both his couch to sleep on and his new clothes.

We rode down from the twenty-fourth floor in silence, and thank goodness, the elevator was empty of other conference-goers. I'd spent a good deal of the night tossing and turning and thinking about how I was going to break the news of Thad's death to conference attendees, and so far, I hadn't thought of anything that would satisfy everyone's curiosity about what happened to our guest of honor and didn't include the word *murder*.

"So, what are you going to tell them?"

Have I mentioned that Kaz has always been able to read my mind? I didn't question it, just went with the flow.

Which is to say, I shrugged.

"I suppose I could say Thad was called away for some emergency back home, but once Nev starts interviewing people, that's not going to hold up. I dunno." My sigh echoed back at me from the elevator's high ceiling. "I don't want people to panic. And I don't want them to worry. I don't want the conference to stop cold because all we can talk about is what happened to Thad. That's not what we're here for, and besides, like him or not, Thad deserves our respect. Especially because of the way he died." I hugged my arms around myself and the gray-and-black argyle sweater I was wearing with black pants and pumps that were sensible enough to get me through another day of panels and discussions, organizing, and overseeing.

"We'll just play it cool," I told Kaz as the elevator bumped to a stop in the lobby. "I'll talk to Nevin, and he'll know the best way to break the news. Maybe a gathering in the ballroom before the first session. Or an announcement at lunchtime. That would be good." The elevator doors slid open. "That will give me time to ease into things and —"

As if they'd been snipped with scissors, my words stopped. But then, I've found that it's pretty hard to talk when my jaw is hanging slack.

A hand-drawn poster that said "Mourning Buttons, Death Mementos, This Way" and pointed toward the dealer room will do that do a girl.

"Oh my gosh, Josie, you must be so frazzled!" A woman I didn't know raced up and pulled me into an embrace strong enough to squeeze all the air out of my lungs. "Imagine, finding a body like that!" She thrust me away as quickly as she grabbed me, so that she could press a flowered handkerchief to her nose. "It must have been awful."

I think that was right about when I realized we were surrounded by conference-goers and that none of them looked any less upset than the woman who'd waylaid me. One woman clutched a copy of Thad Wyant's latest book about Western buttons to her heaving chest. Another sniffed softly.

"He was such a great man." Sniffing Lady

sniffed even louder and shook her head sadly. "Such a loss to the button world, such a loss."

"It is." How's that for a noncommittal sort of statement? I think I stood there for another dozen heartbeats, looking around at the circle of miserable expressions and wondering what to say and how everyone already knew about Thad's death, when Kaz grabbed my hand and tugged me down the hallway.

"Got to go," I said, and since the ladies all nodded knowingly, I suppose they thought I had something important to accomplish rather than just that I was eager to escape.

"They know." I said this in a stunned monotone even as Kaz dragged me into the dealer room and I saw that there had been a transformation in there since I'd stopped in the day before. On Monday, the room was filled with eager dealers showing off their wares, everything from glass buttons to wooden buttons to the buttons we called realistics, those that are made to look like everything from dogs and cats to spaceships and pianos. Now, most of those buttons had been stowed away and replaced with mourning buttons.

Quick button lesson here . . .

Back in Victorian times, mourning was a

big business. The rules of how to grieve the loss of a loved one were specific, and the clothes people wore — and what they weren't allowed to wear — were part of those rules. Everyone's familiar with the black gowns, the crepe, the long weeping veils. But think about it — all those black clothes. That meant a lot of people needed a whole lot of black buttons.

The button producers of the nineteenth century stepped up to the task. These days, the buttons they made are a subspecialty of many a button collector.

And apparently, of button dealers, too.

Pikestaffed, I stepped through the dealer room surrounded by jet buttons (jet is a naturally occurring substance, a lot like coal, and it was used for expensive buttons), black glass buttons (for those who wanted to look like they were wearing jet but not pay the price), and buttons made from the twined hair of a deceased person. (OK, I love buttons, but those always creep me out.)

The dealers who didn't have enough mourning buttons to display capitalized on the news of Thad's death with Western buttons. Even as Kaz hauled me through the room and on toward the hospitality suite, where the morning's continental breakfast would be served, I noticed buttons shaped like horses, and cowboys, and cowboy boots, along with buttons fashioned from turquoise and silver, sweet little calico buttons, and even good old plain and reliable pearl buttons, the type that had once been on Geronimo's shirts.

"Amazing." Langston mouthed the word as we hurtled by. Others weren't quite so unobtrusive. They mumbled their condolences, though why I should be on the receiving end of them was a mystery to me.

Honestly, I was relieved when I stepped into the hospitality suite, where in addition to rolls and coffee and bagels, Grace Popovich, a nice lady from Baltimore, was scheduled to serve up a helping of button knowledge and a short talk on clear-glass buttons.

I hadn't expected a full room, but after just a couple minutes, we were packed in like sardines, and I figured it was time to introduce Grace. I did that and would have stepped aside and let her take the floor if a man at the back of the room hadn't raised his hand.

"Is it true?" he asked. "You're the one who found Thad Wyant's body?"

"And he was stabbed! Forty times!" A woman near the front of the room fanned her face with her conference booklet. "Should we be worried, Josie? Is someone out to get button collectors?"

Apparently, this was a new thought for most of the folks in the room, and not a good one. A murmur started and grew, like the sound of a bee swarm.

Since I'm not tall, I wasn't exactly a commanding presence. But I'd been a theater major, remember, and though I was a lousy actress, I knew a thing or two about projecting.

"There's nothing to be worried about," I bellowed; then, because I was embarrassed at bellowing, I cringed. The crowd quieted. "The police are confident Thad's death is an isolated incident."

"But it must have something to do with buttons. Good gravy!" A heavyset woman in the front row slapped a hand to her heart. "What if I'm next?"

Another steady buzzing started, and again, I was obliged to raise my voice. "The police are here in the hotel," I said. "And between them and the hotel's regular security staff, we're all perfectly safe." If they knew Ralph, they might know this was not necessarily true, but I wasn't about to spill the beans. "So just relax, and let's let Grace Popovich —"

"But what about the Geronimo button?" someone called out. "Does this mean we're not going to get to see it?"

"I came a long way to get a look at that button," another voice grumbled. "If a conference promises something, it should follow through."

"Hey, look at this!" This time, it was Kaz who did the yelling. He stepped back from the door and waved his arm in that direction just as a member of the waitstaff carried in a spectacular arrangement of fresh fruit. Two waiters followed behind: one with a supply of orange juice, the other with champagne. "The least we can do is toast Thad Wyant," Kaz said, and gave me a wink. "Line up right here," he waved people into a neat line. "And once we all have our mimosas, we'll drink to his memory."

I leaned in close to him. "I suppose I'm paying for this."

"Call it the price of a little peace of mind," he mumbled back.

And I suppose I would have if Daryl Tucker hadn't come shuffling up at that very moment.

"Josie," he said. His eye twitched. "I need to talk to you."

I was standing near the front of the mimosa line, debating between greeting each attendee with a warm smile and words of assurance and grabbing one of the bottles of champagne and downing it. "Talk," I told Daryl.

His cheeks turned the color of Kaz's sweater. "I mean . . ." He lowered his voice and leaned closer. "I mean in private."

This was hardly the time for one of Daryl's half-baked come-ons. I hoped the smile I gave him didn't say that as much as it did that I was busy and maybe later . . .

"Maybe later," I said out loud, just in case he didn't get it. "I'm kind of busy and —"

"But Josie . . ." Daryl bounced up on the balls of his feet, as nervous as a Chihuahua. "But Josie . . ." He moved close, and since I had nowhere to go, it was really close. Daryl was a half a head taller than me and he bent to whisper in my ear. "I need to talk to you, Josie," he hissed. "Because . . . because I think I know who killed Thad Wyant."

CHAPTER SEVEN

Yes, I said I was going to make sure Kaz earned his room and board. That didn't mean I trusted him to keep things running smoothly there in my breakfast meeting turned feeding frenzy. Luckily, I spotted Helen in the crowd of mimosa drinkers, and even before I could beg for her help, she volunteered to do whatever I needed. To show her how much I appreciated it, I officially put Kaz at her beck and call.

That taken care of, I invited Daryl to join me for coffee at the Starbucks across the street.

Oh yeah, I was dying to talk to him right there in the hospitality suite and ask what he meant when he said he knew who killed Thad. But I am smarter than that, even on mornings when I haven't had enough sleep the night before, thanks to murder and the fact that, all night, I could hear my ex gently snoring in my living room. I'd already seen the news of Thad's death spread through the community of usually levelheaded button collectors like kudzu on steroids, and I wasn't taking any chances. If Daryl and I were going to have a heart-to-heart (in a murder-investigation sort of way only, of course), and if Daryl was going to name a suspect, I couldn't let word of our conversation get out. Especially not if the suspect happened to be someone at the conference. Or if just talking to me might somehow put Daryl in danger.

Discretion was the best course of action.

Honest, the fact that Starbucks served my favorite, Caffè Misto, and the hotel didn't have a coffee that came even close, had nothing to do with it.

So even though I was itching to grill Daryl, I kept my mouth shut as we walked through the lobby side by side, and outside while we waited for the light to turn so we could head across the street.

I wanted to make sure no one was watching.

And that no one overheard whatever he was going to tell me.

"So . . ." I'd waited long enough, and once I had my coffee and sat down opposite Daryl at a table far from the window, I couldn't wait a moment longer. "What did you mean, Daryl, about knowing who killed Thad? How do you —"

"Well, I guess I can't say for sure."

My heart sank, and yes, I admit, I was a little cranky. Lack of sleep, remember, and Kaz on my couch. "If this was some kind of goofy way for you to get me alone —"

Daryl's eyes glimmered behind those Coke-bottle glasses of his. "Is that what you think?" He smiled. And twitched. "Are button collectors always so narcissistic?"

"Am I? Narcissistic?" Call me crazy, but as dorky as Daryl was, I was more than a bit surprised he not only knew the word, but could use it properly in a sentence. "You said you had to talk to me alone. Naturally, I thought —"

"That I was coming on to you."

"No." I popped the top on my cup of coffee, the better to keep my hands busy so I didn't reach across the table and punch ol' Daryl in the nose. "You're the one who said you needed to talk to me, Daryl. You said it was because you knew who killed Thad."

"And you don't believe me. You don't think it's possible for a guy like me to know important things. You think I'm just another button collector."

My shoulders shot back. "And what's wrong with being a button collector?" I demanded. "Some of my best friends are button collectors. I'm a button collector. As a whole, button collectors are educated, interesting, well read, and a heck of a lot better company than a lot of the non-button collectors I've met. If you think being a button collector means being boring —"

"Doesn't it?" Daryl's eyes were so big and so sincere that I wanted to give him a shake.

Instead, I pulled in a breath. "Look . . ." I gripped my coffee cup and let the warmth seep into my fingers, through my hands, up my arms. Once it had soothed and calmed me, I knew it was safe to speak again. "I think we got this conversation off on the wrong foot. So let's start again. Back at the hotel, you told me you thought you knew who killed Thad Wyant."

"Yes. I did." Daryl had ordered a cup of green tea and he dip, dip, dipped the bag into the steaming water. "Maybe . . . Maybe I just got carried away. You know, with all the excitement and all those people at the meeting asking about Mr. Wyant and what you knew about the investigation. That's why I thought I should talk to you. You seem . . ." He carefully removed the bag from his cup, set it on his saucer, and stirred sugar into his tea. "You seem to know an awful lot," he said when he was done. "About the investigation, I mean. Like you're some kind of . . . oh, I don't know . . . like you're somehow connected with the police."

"Only because I was the one the security guard came to when he found the body." It seemed a simpler explanation than telling Daryl about the murder I'd already solved and how I sometimes dated the lead detective on the case. "I was the one who called 911."

He thought this over and nodded. "So if the police . . . If they knew anything about what really happened, they would tell you."

"No way." As if it would actually put some distance between me and what Daryl inferred, I scraped my chair back from the table. "They don't talk about cases. Not with civilians. And I'm definitely a civilian."

"Then maybe I shouldn't have mentioned it to you at all. You know, about what I saw."

Another deep breath as I thought over how I was going to handle this. I'd just come right out and told Daryl that when it came to investigating, I was as far from being professional as it was possible to get. But he had turned to me in confidence. And besides, I was dying to find out what he knew.

"I've helped the police," I admitted. "Once before. A little. And since I'm chair of the conference —"

"They want you to help again. Of course. So you were the right one to come to."

"Maybe." How's that for wishy-washy? "Why don't you tell me what you think you know. Then we can take it from there and see if it's something you should talk to Nev — I mean, Detective Riley about."

It was clear that Daryl wasn't the type who jumped into decisions. He thought over this one while he sipped his tea. "I was at the banquet last night. You remember, Josie, because we were sitting near each other."

He was right. My chair and Daryl's were back to back.

I nodded and waited for him to go on.

"And we talked. And then my phone rang, and I went out to the lobby to take the call. It was the least I could do. I mean, don't you think people talking on their cell phones in public . . . Don't you think it's the rudest thing ever?"

We weren't there to pass judgment on other people's manners. Eager for him to continue, I leaned forward.

He got the message. "I was standing in the lobby talking on my phone and . . . well, that's when I saw him."

"Thad Wyant?"

"Yes." The artwork on the wall nearest to where we were sitting was pretty nondescript, but Daryl studied it for a long moment. "He was outside," Daryl said. "In front of the hotel."

"And . . . ?"

"And he was with another man. They were arguing."

"You were inside, and they were outside? How do you know they were arguing?"

Daryl scrunched up his face, and his glasses rode up the bridge of his nose. He adjusted them before he said, "Well, you can tell, can't you? I mean, just by looking at people. Mr. Wyant's face . . . Well, I didn't know the man at all, but I remember seeing him on the cruise the other night, and he seemed . . ."

Something told me Daryl was thinking exactly what I was thinking, and what I was thinking was that when we saw Thad together on the cruise, Thad was arguing with Beth Howell.

"Well, I guess the cruise doesn't count," he said, confirming my suspicion. "That was an awkward moment for Mr. Wyant and that woman, whoever she was." He looked at me to supply that information, and since I didn't want to get off track, I didn't say a word.

Daryl sighed. "A man as well respected as Mr. Wyant, he must be studious and careful and knowledgeable, right?" He didn't wait for my answer, but gazed over my head with a faraway look in his eyes. "That's not how he looked when he was talking to that man outside the hotel. Mr. Wyant's face, it was red and his hands were . . . you know . . ." Demonstrating, Daryl curled both his hands into fists. "A couple times, Mr. Wyant even pointed his finger in the other man's face."

"And how did that man react?"

"He was even madder than Mr. Wyant. His eyes were all squinched up. You know . . ." Daryl gave me what was supposed to be a sinister glare. Coming from Daryl, it was more of a puppy-dog look, but I didn't let on. There was no use spoiling things for him. "He got up real close in Mr. Wyant's face, and . . . Well, I don't know what he said. I couldn't hear. But I can tell you this; whatever it was, it wasn't pretty and it wasn't friendly."

"Was the man anyone you recognized from the conference?"

I didn't even realize I'd slipped right into investigation mode until I saw the way Daryl smiled knowingly. I hadn't meant to be that obvious, and I started to make an excuse, but he didn't give me a chance to finish it.

"You are working with the police," he said. "That's good. Because I'll tell you what, Josie. I can tell you're smart. And they're going to need somebody smart to help them figure this out." Daryl tipped his head back. "Was the man someone I recognized from the conference?" He paused, thought about it, shook his head. "No. And I don't think he was from the conference. Because he was wearing a raincoat. You know, like he'd come into the hotel from the outside. Or like he was outside waiting for Thad. If he was part of our conference, he would have been down at the banquet, and he wouldn't have needed a coat."

It was a good point, and I reminded myself to mention it to Nev when I recounted what Daryl told me.

"The police will want to hear about this from you," I said out loud.

Daryl's shoulders shot back. "Do you think they will?" Just as quickly, he folded in on himself and glanced from side to side, as if he was afraid someone might be watching. "Do you think . . . Do you think I saw the killer?"

"I can't say, and you can't, either, so there's no use worrying about it." It was the truth, so I didn't feel guilty for trying to soothe his fears. "But I'll make sure I mention it to Detective Riley, and I'm sure he'll want to talk to you. He'll probably have you work with a police sketch artist. You know, to come up with a drawing of the man in the raincoat."

The muscles of Daryl's jaw tightened. His eye twitched. "I can do that," he said. "I mean, if it will help the police, I will do it. But only . . ." He glanced at me quickly, then glanced away. "Will you come with me when I talk to them?" he asked. "I mean . . . as a friend?"

Was Daryl a friend?

I wouldn't go so far as to say that, but I wasn't stupid. If it took having someone along for Daryl to feel comfortable enough to tell Nev what he knew, I wasn't about to question it.

I promised I'd be right there at his side.

I was saved from any further uncomfortable revelations about friendship when the beeping alarm on my cell phone went off.

The sound hit me like that bell in Pavlov's dog experiment, and I shoved the paper top on my coffee cup and rose from the table, scrambling to get organized. "Oh my gosh. We've got judging this morning! I completely forgot about the button competition.

Helen's supposed to be supervising the judging, and I left her at the breakfast. She's going to need plenty of help, and I can't leave her high and dry."

Daryl clutched his teacup with both hands. "I'm not nearly good enough to enter competitions yet," he said.

I was just reaching for my purse, and Daryl touched his hand to mine. Normally, I would have been on my toes enough to see it coming. Or at least cool enough to extricate my hand slowly.

The way it was, my head was spinning with all Daryl had told me about the man Thad Wyant had argued with, and my heart was doing the sort of tap dance it always did when judging was about to start and I was involved in seeing that everything was in order, working smoothly, and as impartial to our contestants as it was possible to be.

I guess that explained why I stood there and stared.

"Thank you," Daryl said, increasing the pressure on my hand just enough to make the encounter shoot right past friendly to uncomfortable. "I won't forget this, Josie. In my book, we didn't really need Thad Wyant here. You're the real star of this button conference."

■ ■ ■ ■

I wasn't feeling much like a star.

Then again, I wasn't exactly liking the attention I was getting from Daryl, either.

I reminded myself to keep my distance, and next time Daryl mentioned the police, it might not hurt to say something about the fact that Nev and I were an almost-couple. Stretching the truth? Yeah, a little. But all in the name of getting Daryl to back off.

The thought firmly in mind, I headed back to the hotel and right into the conference room where the button judging would begin in just another hour. Sounds like a lot of time, doesn't it? Believe me, it's not. Not when there's so much to do before the judging can even begin.

See, when a person enters a tray of buttons in a contest, that tray needs to be cataloged and put into the box with the other trays in that category. And the categories . . . Well, in a show as big as this one, there were dozens of categories and hundreds of button collectors vying for first, second, and third place in each one. Our teams of judges would be looking at pewter buttons and glass buttons and buttons with birds on them and buttons that featured pictures of women and flowers and . . .

Suffice it to say that it was a huge job, and it took teams of dedicated volunteers to make it all happen.

Helen, of course, was the most dedicated of them all, and she had plenty of help from the most dedicated of our members, including Gloria Winston. I was glad. Gloria might be a tad bluff, but she was thorough and well respected. She was also always level-headed and objective. Those were two of the most important assets for any judge.

Just as the thought occurred, I watched as the door to the conference room swung open, and Helen marched in along with Gloria and the volunteers, who would do a final count of the trays and make sure all the paperwork that went with them was checked and rechecked.

"I'm so sorry." The words were out of my mouth before she was even close. "I forgot."

"About the button competition?" I couldn't blame Helen for sounding so incredulous. Or for giving her fellow volunteers a look that pretty much came right out and said she was hearing it, but she wasn't believing it. There was a time Josie Giancola never would have let anything get between her and a button competition. Of course, that was the time before murder entered her life.

"I know. I know." Because Helen hadn't moved, I stepped forward and took the pile of scoring sheets she was carrying out of her hands. Talk about symbolism! I guess I was doing what I could to lighten her load. "It's just that —"

"You were busy with other things. Of course."

Leave it to Helen to be understanding. Even when I didn't deserve it.

"I got sidetracked." Because I was too embarrassed to admit my shortcomings to Helen, my mentor and my friend, I glanced around at the other volunteers, all women and all of whom looked just as disappointed as Helen did. In fact, Gloria was so puckered, she looked as if she'd just sucked on a lemon. "I'm here now. And everything is organized, and —"

"That's because I was here at six this morning." Helen didn't say this like it was any big deal; she was just reporting the facts. Her chin came up a fraction of an inch, and her cheeks had two bright spots of color in them the same shade as the pink sweater she was wearing with neat khakis and cute little loafers that had buttons slipped into the slot on the front where some people put pennies. "I knew you'd be distracted, Josie. You were bound to be, with all that happened last night. I mean, really, how can something like that not affect your performance here at the conference? Even the chair of an event as important as this can't keep that many balls in the air."

"But she should be able to. I should be able to." Another glance around by way of apology. "I'm here now and —"

My cell phone rang.

I held up one finger as a way of excusing myself and saying I'd be right back, turned my back on the woefully wronged committee, and crossed to a quiet corner of the room.

"Hey."

"Hi, Nevin."

"I'm up in Thad Wyant's room. I thought maybe you'd want to come up and have a look around."

I glanced over my shoulder at the waiting committee. "I would. I can. But —"

"There's a bunch of button stuff up here." I could tell by the way his voice faded that Nev was taking a look around the room. "I could use your help. You know, to explain what all this stuff is and what it's for."

"Are there . . ." I could barely get the words out from behind the sudden ball of emotion that blocked my throat. "Have you found the Geronimo button?"

"Got me!" Nev didn't chuckle often, which made the sound all the more startling. "That's why I need your help up here, Josie. You're the expert."

I was.

And I was also the chair of a conference that was quickly spinning out of control.

I clicked off the call and crossed the room. Helen met me halfway.

"Don't even say it." She patted my arm. "I can tell by that look in your eyes. You're on a mission."

I grimaced. "The police need my help, and —"

"Of course they do, dear. You're smart and you're knowledgeable and —"

"And the judging is going to start soon."

"We've got everything under control." Helen's cadre of volunteers had followed at a discreet distance. When she looked over her shoulder, they nodded in unison. "See? No problemo." Helen gave me a nudge toward the door. "Go do what you need to do; I've got everything under control."

She did. And I was grateful.

Which explains why in the elevator on the way up to Thad Wyant's suite, I called down

to the gift shop and had a dozen roses sent
to Helen's room.

CHAPTER EIGHT

"Don't touch anything."

They were the first words out of Nev's mouth when I walked into Thad's suite, and I understood the wisdom of keeping my hands to myself, but really, it was too bad. He hadn't been kidding the night before when he said he had to get back to the station and work on the case. He was wearing the same khaki suit and that same god-awful tie. The good news was that he apparently kept a clean shirt at the station; the blue Oxford cloth shirt had been replaced by one in a shade of beige just this side of oatmeal. With his fair skin, light eyes, and monochromatic outfit, Nev looked worn out, and my fingers itched to smooth away his wrinkles. It would have done nothing to relieve the bags under his eyes, but it would have played into my irresistible impulse for neatness.

A tendency apparently not shared by Thad

Wyant. Unless . . .

"The room was ransacked?" I asked, and at the same time, I glanced around in horror at the clothing tossed over chairs and the couch, the empty beer bottles on the credenza against the far wall, and what had been the contents of the welcome bag we gave conference attendees spilled half on the dining table, half on the floor.

"Hard to say." Nev had been talking to a crime-scene tech just as I walked in, and he finished up with the woman, and she went off to check out the bedroom. That taken care of, he stepped toward me. "It was like this when we got here last night to seal the room and get started on the investigation, but I don't know . . ." He looked around, too, and I guess Nev and I had one more thing in common than just murder, because he shivered at the sight of the chaos. "Maybe somebody was in here looking for something, or maybe our Mr. Wyant was just a plain old garden-variety slob."

"It actually wouldn't surprise me." I carefully stepped between the couple days' worth of newspapers scattered across the carpet and a chair where a piece of Thad's luggage was opened and half unpacked. "It's hard to believe that a man who was so precise in his work could be so . . ." Words

151

failed me, and I guess Nev understood because he shook his head in sympathy.

I had no doubt he was going to get right down to business. After all, that's why Nev had asked me to meet him up in the suite the conference was providing for Thad. That thought hit me like a ton of bricks, and I realized there was one more thing Nev and I had in common. I was thinking business, too.

"Will we have to keep paying?" The question popped out before I could edit it, and I didn't want to sound cheap, but . . . "We were covering his expenses," I explained. "And if Thad is checked out . . ."

"Yeah, permanently." Dark humor. No doubt, it was one of the things that kept cops sane in the face of the evil and stupidity they encountered every day. "I think you're off the hook. Unless you'd like to move Kaz in here."

Impossible, since Thad's room was considered important to the investigation, and no way they'd let someone else stay there and mess up whatever evidence might exist there, so I knew Nev was joking.

Unless he wasn't.

I gave Nev a careful once-over, wondering as I did what was going on behind that calm, oatmeal exterior, and I guess I had at least a bit of the answer when he broke off eye contact.

"You knew Kaz was waiting in the hallway for me last night," I said.

Nev gave me a lopsided grin. "It's kind of hard to miss a guy trying to look inconspicuous behind a potted palm."

"I did."

"You had other things on your mind."

"So did you."

He shrugged. "I told you I wanted to walk you back to your room because I didn't like the thought of you wandering around the hotel by yourself at that hour. So really . . ." The tips of Nev's ears turned a shade of red that looked particularly vivid with his pallid outfit. "Really, I had you on my mind," he said. "I knew Kaz wasn't any threat to you."

"You could have warned me he was lurking."

"You let him stay in your room?"

Was that a personal question? From Nev? Or was he just doing his job and keeping tabs on the guy who'd already admitted he'd been squatting in the basement laundry room where the murder had been committed?

Before I could decide, the tech called Nev into the bedroom, and I was left on my own.

153

"Don't touch anything," I reminded my-self while I strolled through the room and took as close a look as I dared at the mess. The carry-on Thad had with him at the airport was tossed in one corner, open, and I nudged it with the toe of my shoe (that doesn't count as touching) just enough so that I could peek inside and see that it was empty.

Hands on my hips, I looked around, wondering where Thad might have put the Geronimo button and, more important, if it was still there.

"So what do you think?"

When Nev stepped back into the living room, his question snapped me out of my thoughts, and I spun to face him.

"About this disaster? Or about you asking where Kaz spent the night?"

Something told me Nev wasn't caught off guard very often, so I had every right to smile when he flinched.

"Natural curiosity," he admitted.

I wasn't about to let him off the hook so easily. "Not really," I pointed out.

Nev's cell rang, and I cursed my luck. At this point in my life, I wasn't looking to jump into a serious relationship with Nev or anyone else. But I did think he owed me an explanation. If there was more to our friendship than the occasional dinner and a movie — or if there could be — I had every right to know.

And an obligation to do my part and not play games.

I waited until Nev finished his call.

"I didn't know what else to do with him, and the hotel is full so I couldn't get him a room of his own. Kaz did stay in my suite," I said. "In the living room. On the couch."

Nev did his best to control a smile. "It's none of my business."

"It isn't, but I don't mind telling you. Kaz and I are . . ." It was difficult to explain. "*Friends* is the wrong word."

"But you do have a history."

"Undeniable."

"And you do still have feelings for him."

"Not those kinds of feelings." I walked over to the window and looked out. Thad's room was on the opposite side of the hotel from mine. Where all I could see from my room was buildings and more buildings, Thad's view included a wide swathe of Lake Michigan, glittering in the morning sun. "There are times I want to shake Kaz until his teeth rattle," I told Nev. "There are times I'd like to punch him in the nose. But there are times I want to help him out, too, and I've convinced myself that's the worst

155

thing I can do, so I do my best to back off and back away. Like I said, we aren't friends, but there are times I think we can still be friendly. But just so you know, there is never, ever a time I think we could still be married."

Was that a sigh of relief I heard from Nev?

Unfortunately, I didn't turn around fast enough to confirm it. I did see that, with our personal issues settled (at least for now), he was all set to get back to the investigation. He pulled a small leather notebook from his back pocket and reached for a pen. "What can you tell me about Thad Wyant?" he asked.

"Not much more than I told you last night. Oh, and something I found out this morning." I recounted what Daryl had told me, and Nev took copious notes. "Do you think Daryl saw Thad's killer?"

"Do you?"

Leave it to Nev to remember what I'd told him the night before about not wanting to get involved in another investigation, and to respect my wishes. Leave it to Nev to ask my opinion without asking my opinion. Thinking about his question, I strolled over to the minibar, which was just like the one in my suite. "You want to know if I think Daryl's telling the truth. I can't say." I left out the part about how Daryl wanted to get to know me better in a way I didn't want to know him, and settled for "I never met him before the cruise on Sunday night, and I've only chatted with him a couple times since."

"But he confided in you."

"He did." There was no question about it. "Daryl is a little . . . Well, you'll see when you talk to him. I guess *dorky* is the right word, even if it does sound mean. He doesn't seem to have any friends here at the conference, and he's not Mr. Personality. I think because I'm the only person he knows here, he turned to me."

"Fair enough." With his leather notebook, Nev waved me closer. "Look at these things, will you, and tell me what they are."

He pointed behind the couch, where Thad — or whoever had trashed his room — had tossed a pile of stuff, and when I got over there, he handed me a pair of latex gloves like the kind I'd seen crime-scene investigators wear on TV. I slipped them on and bent closer to the pile for a better look, picking my way through it carefully so I could put it right back the way it was when I was done.

"Plastic sleeves for keeping button trays protected, card stock for mounting the buttons —"

I glanced over my shoulder at Nev. "These

are the things Langston Whitman said Thad stole from his booth down in the dealer room. And that awl with the cherry handle . . ." I remembered the scene down in the linen room, and the awl that had been thrust into Thad's neck, and I sat back on my heels. "Langston was right. Thad did steal all this stuff, and one of the things he stole ended up being the murder weapon." I yanked off the latex gloves, stuffing them in my pocket, and hugged my arms around myself. "How creepy is that?"

This interested Nev, and he made a note about it, then offered me a hand up.

It wasn't until we were toe to toe that we realized we were still holding hands and scrambled to untangled our fingers.

I was glad. Not that I didn't enjoy the sensation, but the last thing we needed was a skin-to-skin moment with a crime-scene tech in the room just beyond and murder on our minds.

I told myself not to forget it. "Why would a man like Thad need to steal button supplies?" I spoke even as I glanced around the room again and didn't see a sign of what I was looking for. "And where are the buttons? If he needed card stock and sleeves, he must have had buttons to mount. More important, Nev, where's the Geronimo button?"

"As far as we can tell . . ." He lifted his arms, taking in the entire suite. "There isn't one button in this room, and believe me, we've looked everywhere."

My stomach turned to ice. "Then whoever killed Thad . . ." My mouth was suddenly dry, and I ran my tongue over my lips. "They killed him to steal the Geronimo button?"

"Too early to know."

Of course Nev would say that. He didn't understand button collecting — or button collectors. Not really. If he did, he'd know that collectors took buttons very seriously. "It's an important button," I said by way of explanation. "I hate to think that any collector would value a button over a life, but if somebody wanted the Geronimo button bad enough . . ."

He scribbled a few more notes. "How valuable?"

It wasn't often I was put on the spot. Not when it came to buttons. I am, after all, one of the country's leading experts. Still . . .

"It's hard to say," I admitted. "The button itself . . . Well, according to the articles I've read that Thad wrote about the button, it's made of mother of pearl. What we in the business call MOP." I remembered this would not mean to Nev what it would to a collector and explained. "Don't think of the pearls that are found in oysters out in the ocean. Mother of pearl was harvested from mussel shells found in the Mississippi River. Hundreds of thousands of MOP buttons were made during the nineteenth and early twentieth centuries. Button production was a huge industry in places along the river."

"Hundreds of thousands translates into not so valuable."

"Except that we know Geronimo owned the button and sold it to a man who came to visit him. That takes it from just another vintage button into a whole new realm."

Nev understood and he nodded. "Impossible to pawn and hard to resell."

"But so satisfying to keep in a personal collection and call your own!" I was afraid I sounded a little too wistful, so I shook away my pleasant button daydream. "I can't believe anyone here at the conference —"

"Would kill for a button? Come on, Josie, you said it yourself. It would be something of a coup to own that button."

"But if you can't ever tell anyone . . ."

"I've seen people kill for weirder things: a pair of sneakers, a jacket, some skewed notion of how they'd been done wrong. Of course, killing for a button —" He realized what he'd almost come right out and said, and he bit off his words.

"Don't apologize." I held up a hand to stop him before he could start. "I get it. Most people don't understand about button collecting, and there's no reason they should. Buttons are small; they're common. From the outside looking in, this whole button-collecting thing looks as crazy as crazy can be."

"Maybe. To some people." Nev tucked his notebook back in his pocket. "I was actually going to say that killing for a button . . . Well, that makes this whole investigation trickier because buttons are small and easy to hide, and for those of us who aren't experts, they're easy to overlook, too. I was going to ask if you'd have a look around. You know, just to make sure that button isn't here and we missed it completely."

He didn't have to ask twice. When it came to the Geronimo button, I wasn't just anxious; I was dying to look.

Poor choice of words considering the circumstances.

I put the latex gloves back on and started a methodical search of the room, poking through drawers, Thad's luggage, and even inside the minbar. The only interesting thing

I found . . .

I was at the table in the dining area of the suite, and I bent at the waist for a better look.

"Nev." I waved him over. "Two things. Take a look."

He did, first checking out the upholstered chair. There was a tiny, rusty colored spot on it that looked as if it had been smeared.

"Blood?" I asked.

He looked closer. "Certainly a possibility."

"And this," I said, pointing again.

Nev looked down at the table, then glanced at me with more than a little skepticism. "Dust. So the housekeeping staff isn't all it's cracked up to me."

"Only it's not dust. It's little bits of card stock. You know, like the kind collectors use to display their buttons."

"You think so?" He took another look.

"I'm sure of it." I was, but I leaned in nice and close, holding my breath so I didn't disturb one little scrap. "I've mounted a ton of buttons in my lifetime, and that means I've cleaned up a whole bunch of flecks just like this."

Nev stood up. "And that means . . ."

"Well, it's weird, don't you think?" I stood, too, and since I'd been bent over so long, I pressed a hand to the small of my back. "Thad stole card stock for mounting buttons. And he stole an awl. And he obviously used both, because when he poked the awl through the card stock, it left these little scraps on the table. So he was mounting buttons, but . . ." I don't know what I expected to see, but I did another quick scan of the suite. "The Geronimo button isn't here. There aren't any buttons here."

"And you think that means somebody stole the buttons Thad was working with."

It wasn't a question. Nev and I looked at each other, and his expression fell.

"So you're telling me . . ." He pulled in a breath, and believe me, I knew just how he felt. My stomach was doing flip-flops, too. But then, I had every right to feel queasy; I think I understood the enormity of our task even better than he did.

Nev's already wan complexion paled. "You're telling me we need to find buttons," he said. "At a button convention."

Helen had everything under control in the judging room — as usual — so I didn't feel guilty about cutting out of the conference for a couple hours.

At least not too guilty, anyway.

Then again, I had a perfectly good excuse. All my button research materials were at my shop, and if I was going to be any help to Nev, I would need them. In the interest of saving time and getting back to the conference as soon as I could to relieve Helen, I hopped a cab and headed to Old Town. Just a short while later, I was in front of the converted brownstone that was my dream come true, the Button Box.

I pushed open the robin's-egg-blue front door, breathed in the scent of lemony furniture polish, and sighed. There was something about every single one of the twelve hundred square feet of this real estate — from the hardwood floors to the old tin ceiling — that soothed me and made my soul sing. Maybe it was the thousands and thousands of buttons in my inventory, buttons that were stored in antique library catalog files and displayed in glass-front cases and in frames on the walls. And buttons always made me smile. Or maybe it was because the Button Box was my badge of independence. My shop. My buttons. My responsibility. Yes, the shop had been open for about six months, but there were times when I still woke up in the middle of the night in a cold sweat, worried about if I'd be able to make a go of it, if my dream would, indeed, last a lifetime. But hey, worry comes with the small-business territory, and besides, the worry wasn't nearly as important to me as the exhilaration, and the exhilaration of being a business owner and indulging my passion for buttons . . . There were times that still took my breath away.

"Hey, kiddo!" Stan Marzcak, my friend, neighbor, and shop sitter for the duration of the conference, came out of the back room carrying my steaming "I ♡ Buttons" coffee mug. "Good to see you! And here I thought I finally had a customer."

"None, huh?" Well, what did I expect? All the customers I usually dealt with were at the conference. "That's OK," I said so Stan wouldn't feel as if he'd somehow let me down. "I've got plenty to do without new orders, and once the conference is over, I know they'll come pouring in. That's how it always works. Collectors hear lectures and their interest is captured, and they decide to venture into a new specialty. Or they see other people's trays in the competition, and they're convinced they can't live without buttons just like that. Not to worry. I've got plenty to keep me busy."

"Yeah, so I saw in this morning's paper. Murder, huh? Who woulda thought a button conference could be that interesting." Stan tapped one finger against the newspaper open on my rosewood desk. "You need help investigating?"

This might have seemed like a funny question coming from anyone else, but Stan is a retired Chicago Police Department detective, so it was only natural he'd ask. He's also a bit — how should I say this? — not comfortable with his life of leisure. Stan might be in his seventies, but his mind is as sharp as a tack. No doubt, when it came to Thad Wyant's murder, he'd have all sorts of advice to offer. Just as certain, I'd take every bit of what he had to say to heart.

I set my purse down on the chair behind my desk, took a folded tote bag from it, and went into the back room, where I kept not only that coffeepot Stan had used to fill his mug, but a worktable, packing supplies for the buttons I sold and shipped, and a library's worth of reference materials. "I don't think Nev actually needs help with the investigating part," I told Stan, and I'd bet anything he agreed; in spite of the fact that Nev had taken over what was once Stan's job on the force, Stan respected Nev, both as a person and as a police officer.

"What he can use some help with is research." Along one wall of the back room, there were bookcases filled with button reference books, button magazines, and various and sundry publications that came from button clubs around the country, and I stood in front of it, scanning titles and doing my best to remember what information I'd seen where.

"It's all about the Geronimo button," I told Stan, skimming my finger over the books until I found the one I was looking for, *Nineteenth-Century Buttons of the Old West,* by Thad Wyant. I flipped open the chapter on the Geronimo button and saw that my memory served me well. Just like I'd told Nev, the button was a MOP. Along with Thad's narrative of how he'd come to own it, there was a full-page color picture of the button.

"Doesn't look like much," Stan commented from over my shoulder. "You don't think that guy really got killed for that little button, do you?"

"I'm afraid so. At least that's what I think."

"Riley doesn't." Stan didn't sound disappointed at this news. In fact, a smile lit his face. "The kid's got a good head on his shoulders. He knows not to make a decision about motive until he's got more of the facts."

"Maybe. But why else would someone kill Thad Wyant?" I flipped to the back of the book. There was no picture of Thad there,

and I wasn't surprised. Up until this conference, he'd always kept a low profile. His bio
was there, though, and I glanced over it and
grumbled.

"Something interesting?" Stan asked, leaning closer.

"It says he's a devoted vegan." I remembered the Italian beef sandwich Thad had
requested, and the scene he'd made on the
cruise when the roast beef didn't meet his
red and mooing standards. "Guess he wasn't
all that devoted."

"But nobody killed him because he started
eating meat."

"You think?" I glanced at Stan. OK, I
wasn't expecting him to say it actually might
be a motive, but I was hoping he would.
Somehow, a crazy vegan getting revenge on
the fallen sat better with me than a greedy
button collector.

I tucked the book into the tote bag, then
grabbed a few of the magazines that I knew
contained articles Thad had written over
the years. "At least Nev can see what the
button looks like," I told Stan. I headed
back to the door, grabbing my purse on the
way by. "You can close up early if it's not
busy."

He waved away my offer. "Getting ready
for that cocktail reception you've got sched-

uled here Friday night. You know, dusting and polishing and all. It's keeping me out of trouble."

As I got to the door, I turned to find Stan leaning against one of the display cases, his arms crossed over his chest, his legs crossed at the ankles, and a spark in those rheumy blue eyes of his.

"It ought to be way more interesting now that Wyant's dead, don't you think? Not that I don't think those button friends of yours will be fascinated with this place," he added when he thought I might be offended. "But it seems to me, talk of murder always adds a little zing to any festivity."

CHAPTER NINE

Tote bag in hand, I made it back to the hotel in record time.

Good thing, too.

Otherwise, when I stepped into the lobby, I wouldn't have seen Gloria Winston race into the nearby ladies' room. If I didn't know better, I could have sworn she was sobbing.

Of course, that wasn't possible. I knew this deep down inside because deep down inside, I knew Gloria was the most well-adjusted and composed person in the world. That didn't stop me from automatically following her.

Which meant I was doubly surprised when I found Gloria standing in front of the mirror, both her hands clutching the faux-granite countertop and her shoulders heaving.

"Oh my gosh. Gloria, what's wrong?" I set my tote bag on the floor so that I could put an arm around her. No easy thing considering that Gloria towers over me and is just as wide as she is tall. "Something terrible happened. Don't tell me. Not another murder?"

"N . . . n . . . no." The word was barely audible, what with her sniffing and sobbing. "Oh, Josie, no one was supposed to see me like this. I'm so . . . so embarrassed."

"Well, don't be." Warm and fuzzy Gloria is not. That didn't mean she didn't deserve a little consolation. I pulled her into a hug.

Gloria's whole body shook like a grass skirt on a hula dancer, and I kept my arms around her until I felt her breathing slow and her sobs quiet. "Now . . ." I plucked a couple tissues from the box on the nearby counter and handed them to her. "Tell me what happened."

The tip of Gloria's nose was an unattractive shade of red. "It's s . . . stupid."

"Not if it's got you this upset."

She sniffled, wiped her nose, and reached for another tissue. "It's the judging, I'm afraid."

I groaned. "What went wrong? No, don't tell me. Not yet. Just know that whatever it was, I'll take full responsibility. The committee shouldn't take the rap. This is my conference, and I have to step up and face the music, especially when things go wrong. Please, please don't think any of it is your fault."

Gloria sniffed a little more, and when two ladies came into the room, laughing and chatting, she turned her back so they wouldn't see her swollen eyes. It was obvious she didn't want to talk when she knew they might hear, so I grabbed my tote and led the way out of the ladies' room and into the coffee shop on the other side of the lobby. It was late afternoon, and the place was nearly empty. I slipped into a seat at the table farthest from the door and facing that way so Gloria would have her back to whoever might come into the coffee shop, and when the waiter arrived, I told him we needed two glasses of water and two pots of tea. Settled, I patted the table as a signal to Gloria to sit down.

She did. Even as she mumbled, "I'm so embarrassed."

"Yeah, you said that." I tried to keep things light, figuring it would help her regain her composure. "But you haven't told me why."

Our water came, and Gloria finished off her glass in three long guzzles. Chin down, she glanced up at me through the coating of mascara on her sparse eyelashes. "Measles," she said, and the tears started all over again. "And now you know what a fool I am."

The light dawned.

Measles, see, are what we button collectors call the little red circle stickers that are put on the plastic sleeves that hold competition trays when one of the buttons on the tray is not appropriate to the category. One measle disqualifies the entire tray from competition.

"You mean you —" I wasn't sure how to say it without insulting Gloria, but really, it was hard to fathom. Gloria was an expert and meticulous about her competition trays. "One of your trays was disqualified?"

Tears streaming over her cheeks, Gloria nodded. She slipped the paper napkin off the table and touched it to her eyes. "Can you believe it? The category was ivory buttons, and I could have sworn every single button on that tray of mine met the criteria." Her glass was empty so she reached for my water and took a gulp. "Well, I guess that's what I get for being so sure of myself and entering a category I've never attempted before. You know me, Josie, when it comes to moonglows and realistics —"

"There's nobody who knows more."

"Well." Gloria hung her head. "Maybe there's nobody who used to know more.

These days . . . Well, maybe I'm losing it."

I sat back and laughed. "Not a chance. You're the sharpest —"

"What?" Gloria's head came up, and her eyes narrowed. "Old lady? Is that what you were going to say?"

I had seen her be cold, and even rude, but I'd never seen Gloria angry, and I chalked it up to how upset she was. "I was going to say you're one of the sharpest button collectors I've ever met," I said. "Gloria, no one thinks you're old."

"Not now. Not yet. But once word of this gets out . . ." With one hand, she mashed the paper napkin into a ball. "I'll be the laughingstock of the conference. Of every conference."

I doubted it. Though button collectors can be precise, exacting, and focused on details, I had never known them to be cruel. Except, of course, if it was a button collector who had killed Thad. Murder, it seemed to me, went even beyond cruel.

"Why don't you just tell me what happened. Something tells me once you put it into words —"

"It will make me feel better?" There was no amusement at all in Gloria's rough laugh. "OK. Yes. You're right. Of course you're right." She grumbled. "I'm acting

174

like a prima donna, and you know that's not like me. I suppose I was just caught a little off guard by that measle. Damn!" She pressed her lips together. "I was so sure I'd win first place; I swear when I looked through the judged trays and saw that little red mark on mine, you could have knocked me over with a feather. I suppose that's the price of pride, right? Or maybe it's just what I get for falling in love with a button. You see, the button that disqualified me . . ." She traced an invisible pattern over the table with one finger.

"It was a button I saw at a show in Philadelphia a couple months ago, and I was so taken with it, I did what I've told every button collector north, south, east, and west never to do. I scooped it right up. The dealer assured me it was ivory, and I never questioned him. I should have. I should have double-and triple-checked it before I put it on that tray. But I was busy with other things, and the time just sort of got away from me. The judges' remarks — you know, the ones they write on the slip of paper attached to my tray — the remarks said the tray was disqualified because that button was bone. Bone!" An unbecoming flush raced up her neck and into her cheeks. "Even a first-time button collector should be able to tell bone from ivory. And I missed it completely. There's a lesson to be learned. I'm so embarrassed; I could just die!"

With all that had already happened at the conference, I didn't like to hear her talk like that. "Not to worry," I said. I resisted the urge to pat Gloria's hand because I didn't want to seem condescending. "Your name isn't on the tray. No one knows that measle belongs to you."

"You're right." She gave me a begrudging smile. "But if someone asks how my tray did —"

"You can tell them the truth. Not every tray can be a winner."

"Yours always are."

Was that jealousy I heard edging Gloria's voice? I decided instantly that my ears were playing tricks on me. Gloria was too matter-of-fact to be the jealous type.

"Oh, come on." Again, I went for upbeat and hoped I succeeded. Our pots of tea had arrived, and I toyed with the string on my teabag. "Everybody makes mistakes on their competition trays now and again."

"Not you."

I scrambled through my memory banks, back to all the competitions I'd entered over the years, and found comfort telling her, "There was that time in Kansas City —"

"Kansas City. Hah!" Gloria's jaw was tight. "That was years ago, Josie. You were just a kid. These days, you'd never make the kind of mistake I made on that tray of ivory buttons."

"Maybe not, but —"

"But you have royally screwed up this conference." Apparently cheered by the thought, Gloria sat up and her shoulders shot back. She softened the blow of her remark with a smile so genuine, I couldn't take it personally. At least not too personally.

"See?" I harnessed my irritation behind a smile of my own. "We all make mistakes. I messed up on the scrimshaw buttons —"

"And the salads at lunch, remember," she reminded me. "And some of the nametags for the cruise, and —"

"The point is . . ." There's only so much self-reflection any woman can take, and I'd had enough. "We all make mistakes, Gloria. It's not the end of the world."

"But if anyone found out . . . about that bone button, I mean . . . my reputation . . ." She paled and lowered her voice to a whisper. "I'm a judge at competitions all over the country. And I'm asked to speak at club meetings and conferences. If word gets out that I'm careless, that I don't know my stuff . . . Promise me, Josie. Promise me you won't tell anyone about the . . ." Langston Whitman walked into the coffee shop and called out a hello, and Gloria mouthed the last word. "Measle."

I crossed a finger over my heart. "Your secret is safe with me."

"Secret?" Langston stopped at our table and put one hand on Gloria's shoulder and one on mine. "What are you two talking about behind my back?"

"Oh, just girl talk." Gloria was back to her old self. Which pretty much sent the message that Langston should back off and mind his own business. She pushed back from the table and stood, making sure she kept her head down and her tearstained face turned away from Langston. "It's getting late," she said, "and I'm having dinner with the Colorado club this evening. I think I'll just head back to my room for a little catnap before it's time to go."

And before either one of us could stop her, Gloria marched away.

"Well, that's not like her." Langston took the seat Gloria had just vacated. "She's usually eager to talk buttons, any time of the day or night."

I hoped my shrug said it all. "You heard her. She's got a busy evening ahead.

Now . . ." I could tell by the way Langston sat with his hands clutched together on the table that this wasn't a social call. "What can I do for you?"

He drew in a breath and let it out slowly. "I know I shouldn't ask," Langston said.

"But you're going to, anyway." I made sure I punctuated my statement with a laugh. Langston's shoulders were rigid; his back was ramrod straight. He was telegraphing his tension and stressing me out in the process, and I had to do what I could to lighten the atmosphere. "Get it over with, Langston. We've been friends forever; whatever you're going to say, it's not going to surprise me."

His jaw was rigid. His lips were set. "I think I might be a suspect in Thad Wyant's murder," he said.

I was right; this didn't surprise me. Then again, as far as I knew, Nev hadn't narrowed down the field. Everyone at the conference, and that mysterious man Daryl had seen arguing with Thad outside the hotel's front entrance — we were all suspects.

I poured my tea, added milk, and took a sip. "Do the police have reason to suspect you?" I asked.

Langston rolled his eyes. In an elegant way, of course. "I couldn't stand the man."

"From what I saw, not many people could."

"Then maybe they should be suspects."

"Maybe they are."

Thinking this over, he cocked his head. "That detective came and talked to me. I know you know who I'm talking about because he's cute, and I'm sure you noticed him. He showed me some things that were found in Wyant's room: plastic sleeves, card stock, and such. He asked me if I could identify any of it, and of course, I could. It was exactly what Wyant had looked at Sunday evening. Exactly what was missing after he visited the booth on Monday."

"So it's official. Wyant did steal from you. That doesn't automatically make you a suspect."

"I should hope not."

"But you're worried, anyway."

Langston tugged on his left earlobe. "I just felt . . . I don't know . . . uneasy, I guess. I didn't like the questions that detective was asking."

"That's his job."

"Yes, of course. But I thought if you knew anything . . ."

"About the case?" First Daryl and now Langston. I wondered what kind of reputation I was getting in the button community.

"If they know anything —"

"They wouldn't tell you. That's what you were going to say, right? But they must have questioned you, too. After all, I heard you were the one who called the police. Did you see anything, Josie? Did the police tell you they found anything?"

"You mean like clues?"

Langston leaned over our table for two. "Like the Geronimo button."

"What makes you think it's missing?"

He sat back. "I didn't say it was. I just thought if they were going to come poking around asking questions, I should get an idea of what they're after. So they didn't say anything?"

"About clues? And the Geronimo button? Not a thing. Not to me."

"That's good. Maybe." Again, he leaned closer. "Maybe it's bad."

"It isn't good or bad. It isn't anything. It's just the police doing their jobs and not telling me anything because whatever they find, it's none of my business."

"But you are helping them."

Again, I wondered about the button grapevine. "Who says?"

"Nobody. Everybody." Langston lifted his hands in a gesture that said it was the truth and that's just how it was. "Everybody's talking about that actress who was killed in your shop last summer and how you helped the police find out who did it. They know you've got connections with the police. And they're worried."

"About me?"

"About you finding out things that maybe you shouldn't know."

"And are you worried about something like that?"

"Me?" I would have been convinced by Langston's laugh if he didn't refuse to meet my eyes. "My life is an open book. You know that, Josie. I don't have a thing to hide."

"But you were carrying an awl when I saw you march across the lobby yesterday." I threw out this comment casually, like it really didn't matter to me, but it might to the cops.

He tsked. "That was early in the day. Believe me, I put down the awl long before Thad Wyant met his maker. Although the cops . . ." Langston bit his lower lip. "They showed me the murder weapon. It was one of Elliot's awls. Of course, I recognized it. The workmanship is superb. There was . . ." He ran his tongue over his lips. "There was dried blood all over it."

"So you can see why they had to talk to you. And there is one other thing . . ." Not that I was accusing Langston or anything. But I was curious. "You arrived at the banquet late, and from what Detective Riley tells me, Thad died not too long before Ralph the security guard found him. Which means you weren't in the ballroom at the time Thad was killed."

"Yes. Well . . ." Langston shifted in his seat. "If you must know, Elliot and I had a bit of a tiff yesterday afternoon. Not to worry. We've smoothed things over." His smile was brief. "At the time the banquet was scheduled to start, we were in our booth, kissing and making up. Elliot will be happy to share the story with you and with the police if they ask. He's an artist, and you know how they are, never shy about baring their souls. Or the details of their personal lives."

"You know I believe you."

"And you know the police might not."

"They will if you're straight with them."

"Straight." For the first time since he walked into the coffee shop, Langston's smile was wide and sincere. "One thing I am definitely not."

I smiled, too. "You know what I mean."

"I do, and I thank you for listening to my rant. You're a good friend, Josie." He stood and the smile faded from his face. "This whole thing has upset me terribly. Word is out that it was one of our awls that killed Wyant, and I've seen the way people look at me when they walk past the booth now. You know, like they think it automatically means I'm guilty. Our business is down from yesterday, too, and I'm sure it's because people are uneasy about dealing with us. Maybe Elliot and I should just pack up and go home."

"I can't say for sure, but something tells me the cops wouldn't be happy about that."

"No. Of course not. I suppose it would only make me look even more guilty." He smoothed a hand over his impeccable Italian silk tie. "You know I'd never hurt anyone, Josie. Not in the way Wyant was hurt. I couldn't. I mean, for moral reasons. But aside from that, I'd never risk my reputation or my freedom, not because a two-bit cowboy like Thad Wyant swiped some things from my booth. That would be . . . well . . ." He backed away from the table and headed to the door. "That would just be crazy."

"Yes, it would." Since Langston was gone, I was talking to myself. "But I've seen crazier things happen around here so far this week."

Apparently, the universe was looking to

confirm my statement because at that moment, an elevator opened onto the lobby and Nev raced out, caught sight of me through the glass walls of the coffee shop, and stopped so fast that he skidded across the granite floor.

I got money from my wallet and left it on the table before I hurried out to the lobby to see what he was up to.

And didn't it figure, that was just when his phone rang.

"Nothing, huh?" Nev spoke into the phone at the same time he held up one finger, signaling that he'd be right with me. "You're going to try again in the morning? I sure would appreciate it. And if you'd give him my number —" He listened to what the person on the other end said, expressed his thanks, and hung up.

"Santa Fe police," Nev said. "They've been talking to his neighbors and found out Thad Wyant has a brother out in California. The guy is apparently a small-time actor. They've been trying to get ahold of him, but —"

"No luck?"

Nev's sigh was all the answer he needed to give, but he put aside his disappointment in a heartbeat and latched on to my arm. "Hey, I'm glad I found you," he said. "I was up in Wyant's room, and I got a call from the security office, and I was on my way over there. You know, to watch the tapes from yesterday. You want to come along?"

He knew I did.

"Got the tapes you wanted all set." A security guard, who thankfully was not Ralph, waved Nev over to the desk with the three monitors in front of it. "I didn't bother with the gift-shop tapes or the ones from the loading dock," he explained. "If you're looking for the person who vandalized those posters, those cameras aren't going to help you at all. There weren't any posters hung in those areas. But the lobby camera . . ."

He pointed to the live feed running on the monitor in front of us. "There's the registration desk and the concierge, and see, if you look right here . . ." The guard pointed to the far left of the screen, where a smidgen of the area outside the lobby-level elevators showed. "If I remember correctly, there were posters hanging there."

"Yes, there were." I confirmed his theory. "When I came downstairs yesterday morning, they were fine. But later, that's when I saw that Thad's eyes had been gouged out."

The security guard nodded, went to a console behind us, and popped in a tape, and both Nev and I turned that way. "That's what I was thinking," he said. "So I tried every tape from yesterday after eight in the morning." He fast-forwarded through what must have been hours of tape, then put the video on pause. "It's pretty quick," he said. "So you're going to have to pay real close attention. Remember," he tapped the upper-left-hand corner of the screen. "Look right there, near the elevators."

He started the tape again, and as one, Nev and I got up and stepped closer to the monitor, watching the comings and goings as hotel guests got on and off the elevator. At one point, there was no one in the little alcove outside the elevators, and something told me that would have been the perfect moment for our culprit to strike. I held my breath.

"Here it comes," the guard said. "There." He stopped the video.

And I gasped. Sure, the image was small and hard to see, but there was no mistaking the woman who strolled up to the poster on the wall opposite the bank of elevators, no mistaking that she lifted her right hand toward the poster at the level of Thad's eyes and that something metallic flashed from her hand.

187

There was no mistaking who she was, either.

Small and gray. A little mouse on a mission.

I put a hand on Nev's shoulder and said, "That's Beth Howell."

CHAPTER TEN

"Ms. Howell, it's the police. Open the door."

Nev rapped on Beth Howell's hotel-room door, and when no one answered, he looked at the manager, a man named Mike, who'd come up to the sixth floor with us. "Will you unlock it, please?" At the same time Nev asked, he put out an arm as a way of telling me to stay back while he entered the room.

It wasn't a suite like mine or Thad's, so it didn't take Nev long to look around and signal the all-clear.

"So . . ." I stepped into the room and looked around, too, relieved to see that Beth Howell — though she might have had felonious tendencies of the destroying-the-posters sort — did not share Thad's penchant for extreme sloppiness. "The place is immaculate."

"Sure is." Nev didn't say this like it was a simple matter of fact but more like he thought it was plenty curious. He went into the bathroom, and I saw him run one finger carefully over the shower wall. He looked toward Mike. "You must have the world's best cleaning crew. Or . . ." Nev swung his gaze in my direction. "This room hasn't been slept in for a while."

Since there were no clothes hanging in the closet, no sign of a toothbrush or toothpaste, and those tiny hotel samples of shampoo and soap had obviously never been touched, I was going with Nev's last theory.

This was confirmed when Mike called down to the housekeeping office, and the woman who cleaned this end of the sixth-floor hallway showed up.

"Never seen no one." The housekeeper's nametag said she was Darla, and she glanced around, too, just like we'd been do-ing, and shook her head. "I come in every morning, but I never seen the bed rumpled or the towels used. Asked Bernice." This was apparently Darla's supervisor. "Asked her this morning if the person in this room was gone, and Bernice, she checked with the folks down at registration. Said the room's reserved, all right. Has been since Sunday night."

"For Beth Howell, the woman who paid

for a room but has never used it." Weird. Which was why I mumbled to myself — to try to make some sense of it, even as Nev called the crime-scene techs so they could come in and dust for prints. "We'll wait here for them," he told Mike and Darla, and when they were gone, he closed the door and leaned against the far wall, his arms crossed over his chest.

"A little strange, don't you think?" he asked.

I did. "Why pay for a hotel room you're not going to use? And come to a button conference if you're not going to attend any of the functions? After that night on the cruise . . ." I thought back over the last two days. "I only saw Beth once, and I tried to catch up with her so I could ask about that fight she had with Thad and if she was OK, but I never had the chance. And believe me, I've tried. I check for her at every panel. Well . . ." I am nothing if not responsible, and the fact that I hadn't exactly been a shining example of what a conference chair should be weighed on me like a ton of bricks. "I've checked at every panel and every meal I've actually been able to attend."

"My fault." Nev pushed away from the

wall. "If I hadn't talked you into helping
—"

"Really. Don't feel bad." I was standing
near the entertainment center that held the
TV, and I waved away Nev's apology with
one hand. "Buttons mean the world to me.
I guess you know that by now. But nothing's
more important than a human life. Even a
human as disagreeable as Thad Wyant. If
there's anything I can do to help —"

"You said you didn't want to." Nev's smile
was kinder than *Gotcha!* but it sent the same
message.

I gave in with a smile of my own. "But
I'm helping anyway. I guess that tells you
something else about me."

"You like to solve puzzles." He took
another step nearer.

And like there was some sort of magnetic
pull tingling in the air between us, I couldn't
help myself. I took a step closer to him, too.
"And I guess I like to help when I can."

"Kind of like me."

By this time, Nev was just a couple feet
from me. I closed the distance between us.
"Looks like we have two more things in
common."

When he reached out to put his hands on
my arms, his eyes sparkled sapphire. "Before
you know it, we'll practically be best

friends."

It was the worst time for his phone to ring.

Or maybe it was the best.

Either way, he knew he had to answer it, and his eyes reflected his disappointment. Apparently, the crime-scene techs had been close by, because they were already down in the lobby, and he told them what room we were in and said they should come up. By that time, that magnetic sizzle in the room had pretty much evaporated, and I suppose it was just as well. It was time to get back to business.

Nev realized it as surely as I did. He stepped back and rubbed a hand over his chin. "So that fight Beth Howell had with our victim the other night . . . Tell me about it again. What were they fighting about?"

I moved to the window, the better to make sure all that tingly energy had a chance to scatter, and did my best to report as much as I remembered as accurately as I could. "Beth accused Thad of not caring. Not caring about what . . ." I shrugged.

"And Wyant?"

"Whatever Beth was upset about, he couldn't have cared less. He was his usual, annoying self. He told Beth he didn't know what she was talking about, and it was almost as if . . ." I pictured the look on

Beth's face when she turned and fled the scene. "It was like just hearing those words shattered her into millions of pieces. Once she was gone and I apologized to Thad about the commotion, he said he didn't know why she was angry, because he had no idea who Beth was."

"And that seems a little strange, too, don't you think?"

"It does. Because she obviously knew who he was. Otherwise, she wouldn't have been so devastated by the way he treated her. And I don't think she would have gone through the effort of defacing those posters. Unless she thought he was someone else. But I don't know . . ." Again, I let my thoughts wander to the events of the last couple days. "Seems to me you don't pick a fight with a man unless you're sure of who he is. And you don't destroy posters with his pictures on them. Not unless you're carrying one heck of a grudge."

"Agreed. And I sure would like to talk to her and find out what that grudge was all about."

I could only imagine. But then, Nev was obviously a man with a mission. His chin was set. His shoulders were steady. When he finally caught up with Beth Howell — and I knew he eventually would — I had a feeling he wouldn't waste much time with niceties. Then again, a man was dead. There was nothing nice about murder.

I wanted to help as much as I was able, and I thought back to the cruise and the two days of conference that followed. "After Sunday night, the only other time I saw Beth was before the banquet."

"Which would have been just about the same time our victim was killed."

I knew where Nev was headed, and in the great scheme of things, I knew it was a good thing. After all, the whole point of this investigation was to get to the bottom of the mystery and find out who had taken that glorious hand-carved awl and plunged it into Thad's throat. That didn't stop my stomach from flipping when I said, "You think Beth is our killer?"

"Can't say for sure." We heard voices and footsteps from out in the hall, and Nev went to the door and held it open so the three techs who arrived with their cases of dusting powders and brushes could come right in. He told them he needed a thorough sweep of the room, and they got to work, starting in the bathroom.

That left Nev and me alone again. "It sure makes Beth Howell look suspicious," I said.

"Especially since she's apparently disappeared into thin air. We've got the tapes, but they're not exactly great. I'd like you to work with a sketch artist when you have the time. You've got a good eye for detail. I'm sure you can give us a better idea of what Beth Howell looks like."

"Of course. Sure. Only . . ." That chill in my stomach turned to a solid block of ice. "You don't think the reason she hasn't been around is that she's another victim, do you?"

Something told me Nev had already thought of this. Of course, cops are trained not to wear their emotions on their sleeves like we ordinary mortals do. "I'm not ruling anything out," he said. "Not until we can figure out what the heck is going on. But don't worry. If Beth was somehow involved in Thad's murder and if she was a victim, too, I think we would have found the body by now. And you know we haven't. We haven't found anything."

I'd been careful not to touch anything since I came into the room, but believe me, I'd done my share of hands-off snooping. My sigh reflected my opinion of what I'd found. Or hadn't found. "Not even a button," I said. "That's two people — Thad and Beth — who've shown up at a button conference and haven't brought one button with them that we've been able to find. And that's just weird."

Nev's cell rang again. When he answered and his eyes flew open and he said, "Really?" I decided I had to revise my previous thought about cops not wearing their emotions on their sleeves. Apparently, there were things that could surprise even a cop, and eager to know what this one was, I waited impatiently for him to get off the call.

"That was Ralph, down in the security office," he said. He told the techs he'd be back and headed for the door. When he held it for me, I figured I was invited along. "They just found something."

My stomach soured and I gulped. "Not . . ." I prayed I was wrong at the same time I gasped, "Not Beth's body?"

"Nope." Nev pushed the button to call the elevator. "The Geronimo button."

We caught up with Ralph on the first floor outside the vendor room. He was standing next to a trash can, and when a woman walked by and tried to toss her empty water bottle in it, he held up one hand like a no-nonsense traffic cop.

"Crime scene, ma'am," Ralph said, his chin on his chest. "No gawkers. Move on."

"Crime scene?" I am usually more trusting than skeptical, but after all, this was

Ralph. The looks Nev and I exchanged said as much. Together, we peered into the trash can expecting to see nothing but . . . well . . . trash, and again, we exchanged looks. This time, they weren't as skeptical as they were thunderstruck. Not sure I could trust my eyes, I turned back to the trash can for another look at the piece of mat board lying at the top of the heap as if it had been gently and deliberately placed there and — much more important — the MOP button attached to it. My breath caught, and I grabbed Nev's sleeve and tugged like there was no tomorrow. "It's the Geronimo button!"

Nev was two steps ahead of me. But then, the sight of a historic button was not enough to make his non-button-collecting heart beat double-time like it had mine. He untangled himself from my grasp, slipped on latex gloves, and took an evidence bag out of his pocket. He opened it, gently lifted the card holding the button, and slipped it into the bag.

"And the papers." I pointed to the folded papers that were under the button. It was hard to tell, what with them being in a trash can and all, but they looked official to me. "Provenance papers," I said, after Nev had rescued those, too, and I had a chance to take a better, albeit quick, look. "The papers that prove the button is the real thing. But why —"

I didn't need Nev to remind me that this wasn't the time or the place for speculation. Sensing that something was up, conference attendees had already gathered around us, their voices buzzing with curiosity.

"Is that it? The Geronimo button?" One woman dared to dart forward, but a well-placed look from Nev drove her back.

He instructed Ralph to wait there until a tech arrived to collect the garbage can, and the evidence bag and its precious contents safely in one hand, he walked right past the gawkers without a word.

"I need to get this back to the station," he said, once we were past them and their buzzing had risen to a din. "You want to come along?"

I glanced down at the legendary button inside the bag and my blood raced. He didn't need to ask me twice.

"So why would somebody go to all the trouble of killing Thad so they could steal the Geronimo button and then throw the button away?" I wasn't going to get an answer from the button, but I was staring at it through the plastic evidence bag, anyway, so enthralled to be this close to it, and so confused by all that had happened back at the hotel, I couldn't help myself.

"You think it's real?" Across his desk, Nev was staring, too. In fact, if I shifted my gaze just a smidgen, I could see his face, distorted by the plastic so that it looked as if I was glimpsing him through an aquarium full of water. His nose looked smooshed; his blue eyes seemed even more pensive than usual. Thanks to the way the plastic made him look as if he'd been cut apart, then glued back together with overlapping pieces, his hair looked messier than ever.

I looked up from the bag and the button inside and saw that when it came to Nev's hair, it really wasn't an optical illusion. He must have been tugging at his sandy, shaggy hair; it *was* messier than ever. I resisted the urge to smooth down the lock of it that stood straight up at the top of his head. It was too personal a gesture, and personal was the last thing I wanted to be in the bullpen-like office, where dozens of gray metal desks were lined up like soldiers in formation and plainclothes detectives and uniformed cops worked side by side, answering phones, talking to witnesses, and writing reports. I kept my hands in my lap, curling my fingers into my palms to remind myself to stay on task — and off anything that even smacked of intimacy — and dared to speak the words that had been eating away at me in the hour we'd been at the police station. "If we could take the button out of the bag so I could have a closer look at it . . ."

It says a lot about Nev that he humored me. He opened a desk drawer, got out a pair of latex gloves, and handed them to me. He put a pair on, too. "Ready?" he asked, and honestly, he shouldn't have had to. Now that the big moment had arrived, I was vibrating like a car with the idle set too high. I guess maybe he noticed, because he finally took pity on me and opened the bag.

"The techs tell me there are no fingerprints," he said, slipping the poster board and button out of the bag and setting it on his desk. "So we don't have to worry about messing anything up."

Awed, I didn't dare grab the poster board. Instead, I ran my tongue over my lips, pulled in a breath, and looked to Nev for the go-ahead, and when he gave it with a nod and a smile, I lifted the board.

"Geronimo." I whispered the name and stared at the button. "It's the right size for a shirt button of the late nineteenth century." I confirmed this by glancing from the buttons on Nev's shirt to the one on the card. "Men's shirt buttons haven't changed much. And it's a sew-through, see?" With my finger poised just above the center of the button, I pointed.

"Because you can sew through the holes to keep the button on the shirt." Three cheers for Nev — he was falling into discussing buttons like he'd been born to it. "That makes sense in terms of that story you told me, that when Geronimo sold one button from his shirt, he sewed another one on, then he sold that one, and so on and so on."

"And the button feels . . ." Since Nev told me I didn't have to worry about messing up any fingerprints, I touched the button to my cheek. "Mother of pearl is cool against the skin," I said, and to prove it, I held the button to Nev's cheek, and yes, I guess it looked a little weird, the two of us sitting there and me holding this eight-by-ten piece of poster board to his face. That would explain why another detective walked by and chuckled and why Nev mumbled, "Working here, Lewis, if you don't mind."

I pulled my hand back, but Nev pointed to his cheek, and I put the button against it again. He nodded, feeling the coolness, too.

"You wouldn't get that feel with a plastic

button," I told him. "Plastic buttons are great for a whole lot of things, but they are not a product of Mother Nature. They feel manufactured. Dead. And if we look at the back of this button . . ." Again, I waited for permission, and when Nev gave it, I turned over the card, unwound the piece of coated wire that Thad had used to fasten the button to it, and took the button off the poster board.

That's when I had to stop to catch my breath.

"I'm holding a piece of history," I said. Hearing my voice waver, I realized I must have sounded like an idiot, and I glanced up at Nev. "You must think I'm crazy."

"I think it's . . ." He paused for a heartbeat before he added, "Nice. I think it's nice that a woman as sophisticated as you can be impressed with such a little piece of history."

Sophisticated? I liked the sound of that, and before I could decide I liked it a little too much and forget where we were and what we were supposed to be doing, I turned back to the button.

I flipped it over and looked on its underside. "See here." I pointed so Nev wouldn't miss what I was talking about. "These little ridges and lines are what we call striations.

That's a sure sign that it's a MOP. And if you turn the button toward the light . . ." I did. "You can see the coloring of the mussel shell. The mussels . . ." I set down the button and cupped one hand to demonstrate. "Say my left hand is a mussel shell . . . The buttons were punched out of them." With my right hand, I made a stamping motion. "They came out as little blank circles; then the sew-through holes were drilled in them." I let go a reverent breath. "This button looks to be the right age. And it's made of the right material. The papers . . ?" The provenance papers were in a nearby evidence bag.

"The techs will be taking them for testing in a couple minutes, but I looked them over quickly." Nev lifted the bag that contained the papers we'd found in the trash under the button, then set it down again. "Everything looks to be in order. This is the Geronimo button, all right."

"The Geronimo button." I put it in my palm and stared in awe. "Imagine Thad being killed for a little thing like this."

"Except we don't know that was why he was killed."

"But we can assume it."

"We can't assume anything. Not in a murder investigation. Take Beth Howell, for instance. You said she was upset after talking to Thad on Sunday night. To me, upset and buttons don't go together. Don't get me wrong." Like he expected me to jump all over him for insulting button collectors everywhere, he sat back, and when I didn't go on the attack, some of the starch went out of his shoulders. "I know you and other button collectors take your buttons very seriously, and like I said, I think that's pretty cool. But from what you said, Beth Howell's reaction to the way Thad treated her on the boat, that was personal."

"But Thad said he didn't know her."

"That's why they call it a mystery." Nev shrugged. "And we won't get answers until we question Beth Howell. That's why —"

This time, it was my phone that interrupted us. I was tempted not to answer until I saw that it was Helen's number that popped up. I groaned. "What is it?" I asked her before I even said hello. "There isn't something wrong, is there?"

"Oh no, dear. Everything's just fine. In fact, we're just setting up for the evening function."

"The sock hop." I said this to prove to Helen that I had not completely forgotten about my duties as conference chair, even if I wasn't at the hotel to carry them out. "I'll be there," I promised, looking at Nev as a way of sending the message that I had to go. "I'm sure there's a lot to do and —"

"Not to worry." Helen's voice was breezy. "I've got everything under control, and people are really excited and looking forward to it. I just saw a woman out in the lobby wearing one of those old-fashioned poodle skirts. Only hers was decorated all over with buttons. How cute is that! No, no . . . Don't hurry back, Josie. People won't mind. About the milkshakes, I mean."

Sure, my head was filled with thoughts of murder, buttons, and clues that were leading us nowhere. But through it all, I managed to dredge up the details for the night's sock hop. "We're showing episodes of old TV series on the screen in the big conference room. We're serving popcorn and cookies and milkshakes and —"

"Afraid not." I could picture Helen shaking her head in sympathy. "You see, dear, you forgot." Like there were people nearby and she didn't want them to hear, she whispered. "There were supposed to be two spots set up in the conference room where folks could go up and order milk-shakes, right? Well, I was just in there a couple minutes ago, and when I didn't see any sign of anything that looked like it could be used for making milkshakes, I checked with catering. Josie, honey, you completely forgot about the milk-shake stations. Catering didn't know a thing about it."

"Forgot?" I held out my phone and gave it a look Helen obviously couldn't see, my mind racing back to the day the past spring when I'd gone over to the hotel to make final arrangements with the catering manager. "But I'm sure I did. We even mentioned it in the conference booklet."

"Oh yes. We surely did. I've already had people tell me they can't wait for a good old-fashioned chocolate shake. I hated to tell them, but sooner is better than later when it comes to something like this. A few of them were mighty disappointed."

I pictured button collectors, thirsty from a day of judging and buying, anxious to slurp a nice, frosty shake and —

And cursing me for dropping the ball.

My shoulders flagged when Helen said, "I told them it wasn't your fault, dear. I didn't come right out and tell them what you're up to, but I did explain how the mind can play little tricks like that on us when we're preoccupied. They'll get over it."

I swallowed my disappointment. It wasn't so easy to get rid of my embarrassment. "And everything else?"

"Like I said, not to worry." Helen's voice was breezy. "I've got everything under control."

I hung up and groaned, only since Nev was giving the button to an evidence tech, he didn't hear me.

"What?" Finished, he took one look at my face and knew something was up. "Something happened at the conference?"

"Something *didn't* happen at the conference." I collected my purse and stood. "I need to get back there as soon as I can. People are expecting milkshakes, and I completely forgot and —"

"Hey, don't be so hard on yourself." Nev stood, too, and he'd already put a hand on my arm when he remembered where we were. He backed off instantly, glancing around to make sure none of the other cops noticed. I could tell by the way they looked away that of course they had.

"You're doing a great job," Nev said.

"Maybe with murder, but not with buttons. I've got to go see what I can do to make it up to everyone."

CHAPTER ELEVEN

What I did to make it up to everyone was order ice-cream sundaes for the crowd (since there was no special equipment involved, it was more doable than milkshakes at late notice), and honestly, everyone was having such a good time watching the old TV shows and dancing to the music of Elvis and Ricky Nelson, I don't think they minded. Thank goodness! I'd seen the way a couple attendees looked at me when I walked into the hotel late that afternoon — like I had a lot of nerve showing up at my own conference — and I didn't like it at all. I vowed right then and there to pay more attention to the details and make sure the rest of the week went as smoothly as possible.

With that in mind, I had just finished a sweep of the ice-cream stations to make sure there was plenty of hot fudge, whipped cream, and sprinkles and was heading back across the room to check on the sale of raffle tickets when a voice from behind me brought me spinning around. "You want to dance?"

I turned to find Daryl Tucker in skinny jeans, a white T-shirt, and black-and-white sneakers. He looked like he belonged in one of those old TV shows, like the stereotypical class nerd — well, a nerd with a bushy beard — and I almost complimented him on his costume. Until I realized it was probably what he would have worn no matter what the party theme happened to be.

He looked over my black-and-red-checked skirt, my crisp white blouse, and the light-weight red cardigan, which matched the chiffon scarf that tied back my ponytail.

"You look nice, Josie," Daryl said. "That's why I thought you might want to —"

"Would love to. Really. But . . ." I poked a thumb over my shoulder toward the doors, where Helen was selling raffle tickets, and it was a good thing I acted fast; the music switched from something with an upbeat, rocking rhythm to a slow song. My heart jumped into my throat, and I poked faster. "I can't leave Helen high and dry."

"You mean high and dry again."

This was an especially perceptive comment from Daryl, and I narrowed my eyes and looked him over. "What you're saying is —"

"Nothing. Really." With a twitch, he retreated back into his shell in a nanosecond, head down, voice stammering over the words. "There's just been some talk. That's all. You know. About how you haven't been around because you're investigating Mr. Wyant's murder and —"

"I'm right here, right now." I tapped one saddle shoe against the floor to prove it.

"Does that mean you found out who the murderer is?"

"I haven't found out anything." We were standing at the edge of the dance floor, and a couple sashayed by and practically ran into me. I figured that was my cue to escape. "If you'll just excuse me, Daryl, I'll . . ." And before he could say anything else, I scampered away.

"Is that any way for the class good girl to treat the nerd who's nuts about her?"

Kaz.

Of course.

He intercepted me before I had a chance to cross the room, grinning as he looked me up and down. "Figures you'd be dressed like a 1950s Goody Two-shoes."

"Figures you'd be dressed like a bad boy." He was, too, in butt-hugging jeans, a black

T-shirt that was molded to his chest, and a black leather jacket. He even had his hair slicked back and greased. Rather than ask where he got the costume, worry about my next month's credit-card statement, and spoil my mood, I enjoyed the view. That is, right before I asked, "What's wrong with being a Goody Two-shoes, anyway?"

"Nothing. If you want to be boring." Before I saw it coming and had a chance to counter, he looped an arm around my waist and sailed me onto the dance floor, and once we got there, he locked his arms tight around me and whispered in my ear. "But I know your secret." He braced a hand behind my back and dipped me until I was practically on the floor, then lifted me and swung me around, tightening his hold. "You, Jo, are anything but boring," he growled.

"I'm anything but feeling well after all this twirling and whirling. Besides . . ." I did my best to extricate myself from his hold long enough to peek over Kaz's shoulder. Just as I suspected, Daryl was watching us, and I cringed. "You're making me look bad. I told Daryl I didn't have time to dance."

"What you meant, of course, is you didn't have time to dance with Daryl. You wouldn't say no to me."

"Or maybe I would if you'd just give me a

chance."

"You owe me."

His smile was tight, and I knew what that meant. That's why I laughed. "Let me guess, Helen ran you ragged today."

"Understatement." He grabbed one of my hands and, as if I were a yo-yo, pushed me away, then pulled me in again. That is, right before he curled his arm around my waist again and pulled me close. "The woman is like some evil incarnation of the Energizer Bunny. She never stops moving."

"There's a lot to do to keep a conference going."

"So she tells me." He made a face. "I didn't mind when I thought I was going to be your assistant."

"You are." Thank goodness the song ended. My head was spinning, and the scent of Kaz's aftershave — the one I always bought him for Christmas because it made me crazy — was destroying what was left of my equilibrium. "By helping out Helen, you're helping me out, too."

"Not what I had in mind." He pulled a pack of cigarettes out of his jacket pocket, and when my jaw dropped, he rolled his eyes. "Not to worry. I haven't picked up any bad habits. Any new bad habits, anyway. The cigarettes just add to the image. You know, rough and tough."

"If only Amber could see you now!"

He winced and looked over his shoulder at the doorway. "Thank goodness she can't. She's called like a dozen times today."

"And where are you now? Still in Paris?"

His shoulders shot back. "As a matter of fact, I'm in Scotland. And the weather is terrible. I was supposed to leave for home tomorrow, but it looks like that's not going to happen. Fog, you know."

When I shook my head, my ponytail twitched. "Poor Amber."

"Yeah." Kaz is a nice guy. Honest. I knew he felt bad about leaving Amber in the lurch. But not bad enough to risk any sort of personal contact that might be construed as commitment in any way, shape, or form. "She came all the way here just to see me and now she's in town, all alone."

"Not what I was talking about." I leaned in close. "I meant that poor Amber is a sucker to believe a word you say."

And with that, I spun around — and realized I was facing the wrong way. So much for all that twirling and whirling. I turned again and marched to the door.

"He's a sweetheart." Helen was waiting for me, raffle tickets in hand. She was dressed in pink, of course, a tailored dress with a matching hat. She was wearing little wrist-length white gloves, too, and I noticed they were adorned at the wrist with tiny MOP buttons. Authentic vintage gloves. Leave it to Helen. "He was a great help to me today."

"I appreciate you keeping him busy. That way, he stays out of trouble."

"Oh, you can't be serious. He's such a sweet boy."

Kaz was a lot of things. A sweet boy wasn't one of them.

Rather than get involved in a debate I knew I wouldn't win, I asked about raffle-ticket sales. I was one of the retailers who'd donated buttons for prizes, and it was nice to hear sales were brisk.

My good mood was dashed when a lady walked by holding a bowl overflowing with ice cream and hot fudge. "Not exactly the same as a milkshake," she mumbled, loud enough for me to hear and quiet enough that if I'd confronted her about it, I was sure she would have said I heard wrong.

I never had a chance to find out. That was because my cell phone rang.

This time, Nev didn't even bother with an opening "Hey." He launched right in with "I'm up in Wyant's room, and I think there's something here you should see."

"Now?" Truth be told, I couldn't decide what would be worse, ducking out of another button conference function or letting Nev see me in my 1950s throwback outfit.

"Now or later, it doesn't really make much difference." Nobody could be as matter-of-fact as a cop. "But it is pretty interesting. I think you're going to want to come now."

I guess he knew me better than I thought he did. There was no way I was going to miss out on a suggestion that tantalizing.

As casually as I could — maybe my fellow sock hoppers would just think I was headed to the ladies' room and not abandoning ship again — I sidled toward the door, and once I was out in the hallway, I hurried to the elevator. A couple minutes later, I was up in Thad's suite.

A smile sparkled across Nev's face when he looked me over. "You look like Olivia Newton-John. You know, in *Grease.*"

Now that he mentioned it, I guess I did. Except she is a blonde, and my hair is chestnut brown. "Maybe at the beginning of the movie, but remember, John Travolta liked her better at the end, when she put on that bad-girl outfit. You know, black leather, tight pants."

As if he was picturing me dressed like that, he cocked his head and pursed his lips.

216

"Yeah, that would be all right. But really . . ." His cheeks got rosy. And I knew he would have come out with a compliment if we hadn't heard a bump from the bathroom.

Nev cleared his throat and explained. "Crime-scene team. Here to do one final sweep."

I suppose that made sense. Nev being here? Not so much. "What about you? Last I saw you —"

"The station. Yeah." He scraped a hand through his hair. "Didn't think I'd get back here today, but the techs called me a little while ago. They were being a little more thorough this time. And they found something very interesting."

Nev led the way over to the far end of the room and pointed toward the heating-and-cooling vent up where the ceiling met the wall. "The stuff was in there," he said, pointing to the opening and the slatted vent cover, which had been removed and put into an evidence bag and propped against the wall. "I guess I shouldn't be surprised at where people hide things." He waved me over to the dining area.

There were five plastic evidence bags on the table. Four of them contained white, business-size envelopes. "You can look them

217

over," Nev said.

I did, picking up the first bag. "There's something in the envelope," I said, running my fingers along the length of it. "Paper, maybe. At least that's what it feels like. And on the front . . ." I took a close look. The envelope I was holding had words scrawled across the front of it. "Number one," I read out loud. "Sunday after the cruise."

When my inquiring look at Nev got me no answer, I picked up the second bag. It felt as soft and as squishy as the first. "Number two," it said in a loose, scrawling hand. "Tuesday morning. Hotel workout room." I set this bag down, too, and reached for the next ones. "Number three. Hotel bar, after banquet. Number four. Laundry room. Before the banquet."

My head came up. "The laundry room before the banquet. That's where —"

"Yeah, apparently Wyant had a date to meet his killer."

"And that last envelope?"

Nev picked up the bag and handed it to me. "Take a look."

I did, and saw that it contained a ticket to Fresno with Thad Wyant's name on it. The plane was scheduled to leave Tuesday afternoon.

"He was leaving? The conference?" I

didn't believe my eyes, so I took another look. "But Thad was supposed to show off the Geronimo button all week. He was going to be on a Western button panel on Wednesday and . . ." One more look, and I finally admitted to myself that the ticket was real. "I bought him a ticket to leave Chicago late Sunday. But he wasn't going to use it. He was all set to leave on Tuesday."

"What's in there might help explain why he was so anxious to get out of town." Nev stepped nearer and picked up one of the evidence bags with an envelope in it. "Ten thousand in each one," he said. "Cash."

"Wow." There was a chair nearby, and I dropped into it. "So he met four different people and was giving each one of them ten thousand dollars?"

"Or he got ten thousand from each of them. And he marked each of the envelopes with a note about when he was supposed to see them again."

I wrinkled my nose, thinking this over. "But how do we know that? Maybe he just met them and got the money and — oh." I felt my cheeks get hot. "If he was meeting with them once and getting the money then, the money from Monday night wouldn't be here."

Nev nodded. "Because that was the night he was killed, and he would have had the money with him when we found his body. Or the killer would have snatched it back after Wyant was dead. That seems more likely."

"So he got money from four different people." I dangled the idea like a worm on a hook, and when Nev didn't tell me I was wrong, I ran with it. "And then he met with each of these people and, apparently, sold them something. I mean, why else would he have received ten thousand dollars from each one of them? And he did this on Sunday night. And he did this on Monday morning. And he was supposed to do it Monday evening, too, but —" The full meaning of what I was saying sunk in and my heart thumped. "Number four is our killer," I said, breathless.

Nev sat in the chair across the table from mine. "Looks that way."

"And the Geronimo button?" I did my best to think through the scenario to its logical conclusion, but rather than making more sense, it only made less. "Do you think Thad sold the Geronimo button to one of these people? Is that what the ten thousand was for? But if you paid ten thousand dollars for a button —"

"Why turn around and throw it away?" Nev didn't sound any more sure of any of this than I felt, and I have to admit, that discouraged me. If he knew where we were headed with these questions, it would have made me feel like we were on more solid footing. He crossed his arms over his chest and the cream-colored shirt, which looked as droopy as the curl of hair that fell over his forehead.

"And if Wyant sold the Geronimo button to one of these people, what was he selling to the others?" Nev asked, thinking out loud. "You're the expert. What kind of button could possibly be worth that kind of money?"

It was my turn to be completely baffled, and I admitted as much. "The Geronimo button has historic value, and I can see that certain collectors might be attracted to it for that reason alone."

"But ten thousand bucks? For a button?"

Nev didn't mean this to be patronizing, and I knew it. Which is why I didn't take offense. "It is hard for a noncollector to understand. As for a collector . . ." I was talking about myself now, and I took a few seconds to think through the problem. "I've been reading Thad Wyant's articles about Western buttons ever since I started collecting," I said. "He loved that button. He loved the lore. He loved the history. He loved talking about it and writing about it. If he was willing to sell it, he must have been awfully hard up."

"Would you?"

"Sell a button with that sort of historical significance?" Nev nodded, and again, I paused to think over the question. "If the Button Box was about to go under and that money was the only thing that could save it. Or if some friend or relative was in need of an operation or something. Yeah, maybe. Who knows?" I lifted my shoulders. "Maybe something like that was going on. Maybe Thad was desperate. I just can't imagine it though . . ." Not that they would tell me anything, but I lifted the evidence bags, one after the other, feeling the heft of the ten thousand dollars inside each.

"I can't imagine he'd have anything else of this kind of value to sell. I mean, other than big chunks of his button collection, and if that was the case, we would have found buttons here in his room. I can't imagine there is much of anything else worth that much. Certainly not cavalry buttons, and that was one of Thad's specialties. Unless he had a button personally worn by Custer at the Little Big Horn or something."

I dismissed the very idea with a shake of my head. "There would be no way to prove it, no way to authenticate a button like that." I dropped the bag I was holding back on the table. "Maybe we've got this all wrong. Maybe Wyant was a drug dealer. Or a money launderer. Or —"

"We're checking into every possibility," Nev assured me. "But buttons make the most sense."

Thinking, I tapped my fingers on the table. "It would explain why he suddenly showed up at a button conference when he's never come to one before. If Thad had something to sell —"

"And he knew button collectors were the only ones who'd be interested enough to buy —"

"He might make an exception and come to a conference. It would be worth coming out of his hermit shell if there was enough money to be made."

"And forty thousand bucks isn't exactly chump change."

"But why . . ." We'd been going along pretty well, and I hated to interrupt the flow, but really, we had to consider all the possibilities and all the pitfalls. This was a pretty big pitfall.

"But if the killer bought something from

Thad and already gave Thad his money, why kill him?" I asked.

"Buyer's remorse?" Nev was guessing and he knew it, but he threw out possibilities. "The buyer found out Thad had something even more valuable and was going to sell it to someone else? The Geronimo button was a fake?"

"It didn't look like one."

"I know. I know." I guess my jumpiness was contagious, because Nev rapped the table with his knuckles. "I'm grasping at straws, but hey, brainstorming is a tried-and-true method for thinking through a problem. Maybe we'll hit on something that actually makes sense."

"OK, so let's walk through it again." I pulled in a breath. "Thad Wyant has something to sell. He contacts collectors he knows might be interested, gets ten thousand bucks from each of them, then arranges a meet. I think we can safely say that at the meet, that's where the buyer is supposed to get the product."

Nev didn't say I was right. He didn't say I was wrong, either, so I went on.

"Apparently, the meet on Sunday night goes well. So does the one on Monday morning. So whatever Thad was selling, the buyers must have been pleased. Unless, of course, one of those buyers bought the Geronimo button and then, for some weird reason, decided he — or she — didn't want it anymore. Then it's time for the meet on Monday evening, right before the banquet."

"And something goes terribly wrong." Nev took over the conjecture. "Langston Whitman says that the murder weapon is the awl Thad took from his booth in the vendor room, so we can assume that Thad had it with him. Maybe in his pocket or something. Or maybe he took it along for protection because he wasn't sure about this particular buyer and he didn't feel comfortable. They make the exchange —"

"And we know that, because we know there weren't any buttons found with Thad's body. Whatever he was selling, the killer took it with him. Or her."

"Exactly." Nev pursed his lips, thinking through the rest of the puzzle. "They make the exchange and something goes wrong. The buyer questions Thad. They argue."

"Thad pulls out the awl."

"And somehow, our killer gets ahold of it."

"The rest . . ." The rest made my stomach queasy, so I didn't want to spell it out. "It makes sense," I said.

"It does."

"But it still doesn't explain who killed Thad Wyant."

Understatement, but before Nev could point it out, his cell rang. From what he said by way of greeting, I figured out he was talking to the police in Santa Fe, and I figured they'd tell him what they'd been telling him for the last twenty-four hours: that they hadn't had any luck locating Thad's brother.

Which was why my heart bumped to a stop when Nev's eyes popped open. "What?" he asked into the phone.

I couldn't hear a word the person on the other end of it said, but that wasn't from lack of trying. I leaned nearer.

"Of course," Nev told the caller. "I understand this changes everything. We've got a lot to discuss, Detective Martinez. Yes." Nev listened for a moment. "Yeah, let's say tomorrow morning, eleven my time. That will give you time to get the scene secured and looked over. Yeah. Right. Until then."

Like a guy who'd just been whacked over the head with a baseball bat, Nev's eyes were fixed, and his expression was dumbfounded. He set his phone on the table, shook himself out of the stupor, and looked at me.

"Well, that settles that," he said. Only not

in a way that said anything was settled. "We don't have to worry if someone killed Thad Wyant because of buttons."

This sounded like good news to me. "We don't? Does that mean —"

Nev's face was pale. His sandy brows were low over his eyes. "The Santa Fe police just found Thad Wyant's body," he said. "It was in the basement of his home, stuffed in the freezer."

CHAPTER TWELVE

Like anyone could blame me for not being able to get a wink of sleep that night?

Thad Wyant was dead.

Only Thad Wyant wasn't Thad Wyant.

Because Thad Wyant was dead.

See what I'm getting at here? It was enough to make anyone's head spin!

And the next morning, it was enough to make me station myself at the door to the room where the panel on molded-glass buttons was taking place, just so I could keep an eye on the hotel lobby. The second I saw Nev walk in, I ducked out of what was an interesting conversation about the differences between the glass buttons made in Czechoslovakia in the 1940s and those made today and intercepted Nev outside the dealer room.

"So?"

He gave me a quick look out of the corner of his eye. "So what?"

"So who is he? Or I should say, who was he? If Thad Wyant wasn't Thad Wyant —"

"We really shouldn't talk here." With a quick look around to make sure we hadn't been overheard, he took my arm and steered me away from the lobby and into a quiet corridor. "The longer we can keep this under wraps, the better."

He was right. And I was embarrassed. By now, I should have known enough about murder investigations to keep my mouth shut. What I was not, however, was sorry when Nev kept his hand on my arm — even after we were tucked between a vending machine that featured plastic bottles of Coke and Mountain Dew for two dollars each and an ice maker.

When Nev realized he still had ahold of my arm, he stepped back, but he didn't let go.

"It was Brad," he said.

"Brad?" I didn't think something as small as the touch of Nev's hand could throw my equilibrium completely off balance, but it must have because I wasn't exactly following. I raised my voice over the chunky, clunky sound of the ice machine doing its thing. "Brad who?"

"Brad Wyant."

"No, Thad. Thad Wyant. He's the button expert."

"He is." Nev nodded. "But he's not our dead guy. Well . . ." He scrubbed a hand over his face. "He is our dead guy. Only he's our dead guy out in Santa Fe. Our dead guy here is —"

"Brad Wyant." It was starting to make sense. A little. The ice machine finished replenishing its supply, and we were suddenly hemmed in by a silence punctuated by the hum of the vending machine and the thump of my heart. "And Brad is —"

"Thad's brother. You know, the actor."

"Which explains . . ." I shuffled through what I remembered, which wasn't as easy as it sounds. If there was one thing I'd found out in the course of the murder investigation I'd been part of earlier that summer, it was that the information just keeps on comin'. There are times it's hard to tell the good guys from the bad guys without a scorecard, and times when the info piles up and my brain feels like it's in overdrive.

"That explains why you couldn't get in touch with Brad to tell him Thad was dead," I said to Nev. "Because Brad was dead here in Chicago, and Thad was —"

"According to the Santa Fe police, the real

Thad Wyant's been dead at least a couple of months. It's kind of hard to tell because of —"

"The freezer. Yeah." Guilt by association. I stepped away from the ice machine. It was horrible to think of Thad Wyant — the real Thad Wyant — stuffed in there and . . . I gulped. "Please tell me he was dead before he was put in that freezer."

The pressure of Nev's hand on my arm increased just enough to reassure me. "It looks that way."

"And you think he was murdered, and that the killer —"

"Well, we don't know for sure yet, but my gut says it must have been Brad." Rolling his shoulders, Nev leaned back against the wall. "Thad's neighbors say Brad went to visit his brother last summer. They remembered because Brad didn't come around very often. After he left, they don't remember seeing Thad. I guess that didn't cause them to be too suspicious because, as you know, Thad was something of a hermit, but hey, he did leave his house once in a while. But nobody saw him come or go after Brad left, not that they can remember, anyway. That was a couple months ago; the timeline is right. And Thad's credit cards have been used steadily since then. It doesn't take a leap of logic to figure out that Brad scooped them up and has been living high off the hog. The stuff he's been charging went way beyond Thad's credit limit."

"Which is why Thad's charge was declined when Brad tried to use it at Langston's booth in the dealer room." This made a whole bunch of sense. "And no doubt, Brad wasn't paying the charges —"

"Because he knew there was nothing anyone could do to him. If they were going to come after anyone for the payments, it would be Thad. And Thad was —" The ice machine made another clunky sound and even Nev — seasoned cop that he was — caught the symbolism and made a face. "Obviously, Thad wasn't able to make the payments. Brad's plan was probably to float by as long as possible."

"And Thad really being Brad . . . I mean, the Thad who was here really being Brad . . . That explains it!" Honestly, I would have slapped my forehead if I wasn't afraid I'd leave an ugly mark. "When I was reading through Thad's articles about the Geronimo button, his bio said he was a vegan. And yet on the dinner cruise . . ." I remembered the scene about the meat that had been too overcooked for Thad's . . . er, Brad's . . . liking. "It explains why he didn't seem to know very much about buttons. I mean, on the dinner cruise, when Langston said he specialized in supplies, Thad . . . er, Brad . . . thought that was some kind of button. It also explains why he didn't act the way I thought a Western button expert would act, either. I expected a man who was academic and quiet. And I got —"

"Brad Wyant, pretending to be his brother and acting the way he thought a Western button expert would act. According to the neighbors, Brad didn't come around unless he needed something. And their phone records don't show any calls between the brothers. Brad was playing a role, and since he didn't know Thad all that well, he didn't realize he was playing it all wrong. Anyone heartless enough to kill his brother and stuff the body in a freezer wouldn't realize that a man can be an expert at something and not have to wear his ego on his sleeve."

Something told me Nev knew a lot about this. He was an expert, too. An expert at crime and investigation and getting people to talk, even when they didn't always want to. He was an expert at handling the bad guys, and that meant the good people of Chicago could live their lives securely. Nev wasn't flashy or loud. He wasn't showy or pushy. Like Thad Wyant — the real Thad

Wyant — he didn't wear his ego on his sleeve.

There were usually too many wrinkles on Nev's sleeves to accommodate it, anyway.

In spite of the fact that we were discussing murder, I found myself smiling. But then, it was hard not to when a sudden thread of warmth tangled around my heart.

Nev, of course, was completely unaware of what I was thinking. Thank goodness!

"I got an e-mail this morning," he said. "Pictures from the state coroner's office in New Mexico, and I have to say, Thad and Brad, they looked enough alike to be twins even though they were born a year apart. Thad was so reclusive, Brad just naturally thought he could get away with impersonating his brother. He was an actor, remember. Even if he wasn't a very good one."

"Good enough to fool all of us." I hated to admit it. "He would have gone right on fooling us, too, if he hadn't been murdered. I guess that was something he never figured on when he came up with his scheme. Whatever it was. It's crazy, isn't it? I mean the whole identity thing and . . ." I gave Nev a look. "You're sure?"

"That our Thad is really Brad and that the real Thad is . . ." Even Nev was having trouble keeping it straight. He wrinkled his nose. "Between us and the police in Santa Fe, we've checked fingerprints, and everything matches up. Of course, the people from the medical examiner's office have taken DNA samples from our victim, but I'm willing to bet —"

I didn't know Nev well enough to go into details when it came to discussing what my life had been like with Kaz, but — duh! — he was good at picking up on clues. At that last word, his cheeks got dusky. At least he didn't patronize me by apologizing. Instead, he went right on.

"After seeing those pictures from Santa Fe," he said, "I'm sure of it, and I bet that speck of blood we found in his suite will confirm it. It was Brad Wyant, all right, and he killed his brother and assumed his identity. Whatever he was up to, whatever he was doing with all that cash we found in his room, he figured he could come here to Chicago where nobody knew him and get away with it."

I groaned, and because even that wasn't enough to convey my frustration, I threw up my hands. "It was staring us in the face this whole time, and we never saw it. The way he was acting, it should have sent up a huge red flag. All that hokey talk about varmints and heck; he even called me little lady. Nobody talks like that. Not for real. Nobody but somebody who's read too many bad scripts for B Westerns."

"Don't beat yourself up about it, Josie. Nobody suspected."

"But we should have." I was so sure of this that a muscle jumped at the base of my jaw. "He was a cartoon. The dusty cowboy boots and the hat and those embroidered shirts. He was an actor portraying a button collector. The only question is, why?"

Nev looked at me hard and that made the pieces click.

I nodded. "The money. Sure. Of course. The forty thousand dollars you found. Brad Wyant killed his brother and took his place so he could come to the conference and sell whatever it was he was selling. Then Thad Wyant . . ." A new thought struck, and my shoulders slumped. "I really have made a mess of this conference. Here I thought getting Thad Wyant to come and give our keynote address was a coup. But Thad never agreed to it at all. It must have been Brad who answered my letters. Which explains . . ." Just thinking about it made me cringe. "I wrote to Thad Wyant more than a year ago," I explained. "I invited him to the conference. And when I didn't hear in a couple months, I wrote again. Just in case he hadn't gotten the first letter. And again, I didn't hear. Not for months and months, anyway. Then a few months ago, just when I'd pretty much lost all hope, that's when he responded. And the fact that I invited Thad . . ." I pressed a hand to my stomach. "It's my fault Thad is dead. If I'd never invited him —"

"Oh, no!" Before I could say another word, Nev pulled me into his arms. "I'm not going to let you talk like that," he said, his mouth close to my ear. "It's not your fault, understand?" His hands on my shoulders, he pushed me just far enough away to look into my eyes. "You're not responsible. Not for what Brad Wyant did. He's the only one who has to answer for that. And he did. Somehow, this crazy charade of his resulted in his murder. It has everything to do with him and nothing to do with you. You get that, don't you?"

I did. At least I think I did. It would have been easier to figure out if I wasn't feeling a little dazed and confused by that hug. I reminded myself this wasn't the time or the place and got back on track. But then, that wasn't so hard. A new thought struck, and I sucked in a breath.

"Then on the cruise, when Beth Howell

confronted the man she thought was Thad
—"

"She was really talking to his brother. And he actually might have been telling the truth when he said he didn't know who she was or what she was angry about."

"Which means if she's our killer . . ." I hated when the universe thumbed its nose at us mere mortals. Especially when a big dose of irony was involved. "She was angry at Thad, and she may have killed the wrong man."

"But not an innocent man," Nev reminded me. "Don't start feeling sorry for Brad Wyant. There's Thad's body in the freezer, remember."

Like I could ever forget?

"So . . ." This close to Nev, it was impossible to not think about that hug and lose my train of thought, so I stepped back closer to the ice maker, and realizing it, I sidestepped to stand in front of the vending machine. "Maybe, somehow, Beth really did know Thad. I mean, the real Thad. Maybe she knew him years ago, and maybe Brad fooled even her."

"Just like he fooled everyone else."

"I wonder." I flipped through my mental Rolodex, remembering the last few days and the button collectors who'd had run-ins with Brad Wyant. "Langston had never met Thad Wyant before," I said. "If he had, he would have noticed the differences between Thad and Brad for sure. Langston is a details kind of guy. And Helen . . . She's been around for years, but she's never been interested in Western buttons. Even if she had crossed paths with Thad, it would have been years ago, and as you said, the brothers looked an awful lot alike."

"That leaves Beth Howell." Nev pushed away from the wall, and I knew what that meant. Although the cops had been looking for Beth all this time, he was about to initiate a full-court press.

"And Chase Cadell," I added. "Let's not forget him. He and Thad have been rivals for years." Again, I felt like giving myself a good swift kick in the pants for missing out on the clues. "The man we thought was Thad didn't blink an eye when he cut in line in front of Chase on Navy Pier before the cruise. They hated each other. You think he would have reacted somehow. And Chase . . . He and Thad must have met each other in person somewhere along the line. He had plenty of opportunities to see Thad . . . er, Brad . . . at this conference. If he noticed anything was off —"

"Then he might have figured out that the

Thad who showed up for the conference wasn't the person he was supposed to be."

"And he might have confronted him and —"

I was getting way ahead of myself. I knew it, and of course, Nev did, too. Again, he put a hand on my arm, this time to stop my imagination from running away with me. "That still doesn't explain all that money," he reminded me.

"I know. I know." I marched out toward the lobby and the conference rooms beyond, already scanning the groups of people leaving this hour's scheduled panels, looking for Chase Cadell. "But it might give us a lead, right? Thad and Chase weren't what anybody would call old friends. In fact, they were more like old enemies. And something tells me one old enemy might know a whole lot about the other one. A whole lot he might not want to talk about."

I had no luck finding Chase at any of the panels scheduled in the next hour, or at lunch, either, and by the time our luncheon crowd was breaking up to head into the afternoon sessions and I'd already called Chase's room three times and gotten no answer, I was desperate. I was about to pick up the house phone and try his room one more time when Kaz breezed by. He was dressed in those black pants with the crisp crease in them and a killer black-and-gray houndstooth jacket. White shirt. Black tie. Heck, he looked more like the chair of the conference than I did. But then, he didn't have black smudges of sleeplessness under his eyes, and I did.

Kaz was pushing the wheelchair of Betty Cartwright, a lovely woman and longtime button collector from Colorado, and he excused himself, asked a nearby conference attendee to take over the Betty duties, and zipped over.

"What's up?"

I hated to think that he knew something was wrong just by looking at me, so I answered noncommittally. "Nothing. Why would you think something is up?"

"That little crease. Right there." He tapped his index finger to the spot squarely between my eyes. "I always know when you're worried about something because that crease shows up. It's cute."

"Being worried is not cute." He should have known this, since three years of living with Kaz had left me plenty worried plenty of times. I would bet not one of those times was cute by anybody's definition.

"Then there's that little crease. Right

there." This time, he touched his finger to my bottom lip and left it there just long enough for me to taste a hint of the sugar-coated shortbread cookies that had been served after lunch. "Another telltale sign that you're thinking about something and that whatever it is, you're not happy about it."

I shoved away from the alcove where the house phones were located. "It's Chase Cadell," I admitted. "I need to talk to him, and I've looked all over the place and he's not answering his phone and —"

"That's because he's at Cowboy Bob's."

This sort of out-of-left-field comment might have thrown me for a loop coming from anyone else. From Kaz, I knew better than to dismiss it out of hand. "Explain," I said.

"Chase and I talked. Last night. He said he was looking for a place he could hang out and relax. You know, a place with a sort of Western atmosphere. I remembered Cowboy Bob's, north of the city. It's a great little country-and-western place, and when I saw Chase this morning, I mentioned it, and he said that's where he was going. You know, to get away from the conference for a while and chill."

"And this Cowboy Bob's is where?"

Kaz's face lit with a grin. "No need to ask, little lady," he said, bowing and sounding a little too much like the fake Thad Wyant for my liking. "I'll just mosey on over there with you."

Apparently, Cowboy Bob's had risen from the same imagination that spawned Brad Wyant's skewed stereotypical view of the West. Lots of cowboy paraphernalia (like chaps and spurs and hats) hanging on the walls and from the ceiling fans that spun in slow motion overhead. Hardwood floors coated with a sprinkle of sawdust. Dance floor. Bar along the far wall, complete with bartenders wearing cowboy hats, waitresses in dance-hall-girl getups, and country music wailing from the sound system.

Oh yeah, it was a little slice of the Old West in Illinois, all right. Or at least a slice of the Old West as people like to imagine it.

As it happened, though, there was more to Cowboy Bob's than met the eye. Turns out Kaz was more than willing to mosey on over there with me because in addition to being the mother of all corny honky-tonks, the place featured off-track betting on horse races, greyhound racing, and jai alai from around the country.

Let's be kind and just say I was less than

pleased when Kaz went right into the betting room the moment we were in the front door.

I bit my tongue.

It was one way to get my mind off the way my stomach suddenly soured.

And a not-so-gentle reminder that what Kaz did was none of my business. And definitely not my problem.

Not anymore.

Chase Cadell, on the other hand, and what he might — or might not — know about the real Thad Wyant, was.

Steeling myself against the hair-raising high notes of the woman howling a song about her lost love and the rent money he'd taken with him, I squared my shoulders and did my own moseying — right up to the far end of the bar, where Chase was seated on a stool, one hand wrapped around a glass of amber liquid.

He looked up when I slid onto the stool next to him. "Fancy seeing you here. You come to apologize?"

When the bartender approached, I signaled that I wasn't interested in anything at the moment. "Apologize?" I asked Chase.

"For invitin' Wyant to be your guest of honor instead of me." Chase laughed, the sound like sandpaper on gravel. "At least I woulda lived long enough to give your banquet speech."

"You're not upset that Thad's dead." Understatement. Yeah, I got that. But sometimes people need to hear the obvious, just to nudge them toward telling the truth.

Chase was dressed in jeans and a yellow golf shirt with blue embroidery over the heart that said "Pike's Peak Mini-Golf." So much for the cowboy motif. "Come on, Josie. You know I couldn't stand the guy." He sipped his drink, glancing at me over the rim of his glass. "Now you gonna ask me if I killed him?"

"Did you?"

"I wish." He chuckled and coughed and pounded a hand against his chest, and when he was done gagging, he took another drink. "Can't imagine the whole, entire button world wouldn't erect a monument in my honor. You know what I mean? Wyant was lower than a snake's belly and as nasty as a coyote with a migraine. I won't miss him, that's for sure."

It was early in the afternoon, and the bar was less than crowded. The bartender came by again and, feeling guilty for taking up space and contributing nothing to his wages, I ordered an iced tea. "When was the last time you saw Thad Wyant?" I asked Chase.

He sucked on his bottom lip for a while; then, done thinking, he propped his elbows on the bar. "You mean before this conference? Dang if I can remember. Twenty, thirty years ago, maybe. It was the first time we met. The last time, too. We was at a button conference in Boise and me, being the charming sort I am . . ." He gave me a sparkling smile that hinted at the fact that this might actually be true if the subject wasn't Thad Wyant. "I went up and introduced myself. Wyant was a legend, after all. I figured it wouldn't hurt to cultivate his friendship and maybe learn a thing or two from him."

"And Thad . . . ?"

"Blew me off." Chase harrumphed. "Told me there was no use me even getting into Western collecting because he had a corner on all the good buttons and there was nothing left for an amateur like me to buy. Told me he had a Geronimo button, and you can just imagine the way he said it. I . . ." Chase sat up and raised his chin, putting on a pretty good fake Thad Wyant accent. "I am the owner of the one, the only, the original Geeronimo button, my friend. Ain't another one like it in all the world. Not one anybody

246

can authenticate, anyway. You're just wastin' your time trying to come up with anything half as interestin'." Finished with his Thad impersonation, Chase grumbled and took another drink.

"And is that what he sounded like?" I asked.

"Thad, you mean? Sounded? You heard him yourself, Josie."

"I did. I know. But thirty years ago when you met him, was he as —"

"Rude and obnoxious?" Chase finished the sentence for me. "He was certainly no prize. But . . ." Thinking, he squeezed his eyes shut. "Bah!" His eyes popped open, and he brushed away my concerns. "The man was some kind of nutcase. Seems obvious, don't it, the way he got himself killed?" Chase leaned near enough for me to catch the whiff of whiskey on his breath. "You know anything about that?"

I did. But it wasn't like I was going to spill the beans, so I guess it was just as well that Kaz came racing out of the betting room, zoomed over, grabbed my hand, and yanked me off the bar stool.

"We gotta go," he said, and when I hesitated, he gave me a tug. "Now, Josie. Come on."

"I'm not done talking to Chase," I said,

my teeth clenched in a way that should have told Kaz I wasn't happy.

"Doesn't matter." He gave Chase a quick smile by way of apology, and I managed to drag out a couple dollars to pay for the iced tea I'd never been served and wouldn't have a chance to drink and slap them on the bar before Kaz said, "We're leaving. Now."

I may have been caught off guard, but honestly, as we zipped past the betting room, I realized I wasn't surprised. Outside, I untangled myself from Kaz's grasp. "Let me guess, you met somebody you owe money to."

"Worse than that." Before I had time to get settled, he propelled me along the sidewalk and toward the parking lot. "Apparently, there's a few things about Amber I never knew."

"Like — ?"

We were already standing next to his Jeep and he was fumbling with the keys when a woman popped out of Cowboy Bob's and looked our way. She was blonde, voluptuous, and a whole head taller than Kaz, and she was wearing a red, low-cut top that showed off her curves to their best advantage, along with jeans so tight that I wondered how she was able to sit in them, much less breathe.

I now officially knew what Kaz saw in Amber.

"Kaz! Kaz, honey, is that you?" The woman called out and waved one perfectly manicured hand, and even then, Kaz never missed a beat. But then, he was an expert at ignoring things he didn't want to hear. He pulled open the car door, hopped in, and with a gesture, urged me to do the same, and as fast as I could.

A second later, we were on our way out of the parking lot. It goes without saying that Kaz used the exit farthest from Cowboy Bob's front door.

"Amber has plenty of time to kill since you're not around, and apparently, she likes country music," I said, as casual as can be. "And Kaz, honey . . ." I had picked up on the lilt of a Southern accent in Amber's voice and I wasn't above echoing it, just to get Kaz's goat. "She's gonna be real disappointed to hear that the handsome guy in Cowboy Bob's wasn't really you."

He wiped a bead of sweat from his forehead. "I don't care if she's disappointed," he said. "As long as she believes it."

CHAPTER THIRTEEN

Kaz wasn't the only one with problems.

The second I got back to the hotel, Helen was on me like white on rice, and it didn't take more than a heartbeat for me to realize something was very, very wrong.

Helen's usually perfectly styled hair stuck up at the top of her head, and she was wringing her hands. Her cheeks were a shade darker than the flamingo-pink sweater she wore with tailored gray pants.

"I can't explain it, Josie," she said, her voice bumping along with her emotions. "No one can. But I'm telling you right now, we've got to do something, and we've got to do it fast." Just as she said this, a group of conference attendees walked past, and I don't think I was imagining it: they were grumbling. Let me go on the record here and say that button collectors are — usually — the most unruffled folks in the world. That is, until something goes wrong that involves buttons. Grumbling collectors mean button trouble. And button trouble late Wednesday afternoon —

I swallowed hard. "The contest winners are supposed to be announced tonight," I said, even though Helen, of course, already knew that. I was hoping she'd jump right in and tell me I was on the wrong track, and when she didn't, I sucked in a breath. "Something's happened with regard to the contest."

"I'll say." A single tear slipped down Helen's cheek, and she wiped it away with a trembling hand. "I don't know how, Josie. I swear I don't. But some of the trays . . ." She leaned in close and whispered. "They're missing."

"What?" I staggered back. The entries had been kept in a conference room that was locked when the judges weren't in there, and they'd been monitored every day. There was no way!

A look at the ashen hue of Helen's face told me otherwise.

I groaned, and I don't know whether I was trying to console her, or myself, when I said, "It's OK. It's all right. Hotel security will help us find out what happened to them, and if this is a worst-case scenario and those trays really are missing, the conference has an insurance rider, and most of our collectors carry their own policies on their inventory. They're protected. We're protected."

"Our assets, yes." Helen sniffed. "But what about our reputation? What about yours, dear? You've worked so hard on this conference, and you've had nothing but bad luck from the start. First a guest of honor who was less than cordial, then all those mix-ups with salads and microphones, and now this. Not to mention the murder, of course."

A not-so-gentle reminder I didn't need. "We'll take care of it." I patted Helen's arm. "I'll go over to the conference room now and check things out. Any idea of how much is missing?"

She shook her head. "I didn't do a complete count. What I mean is, I just couldn't. I started to, and when I saw that something was wrong . . . Oh honey, I was so taken aback, I came right out to look for you. But of course, you weren't here. You were out doing other things. Not that I'm blaming you or anything," she added quickly, when I opened my mouth to defend myself. "I know you have places to go and people to talk to. Kaz tells me you're helping the police solve Thad's murder."

So far, my *helping* hadn't gotten us very

far, and I told her as much, even if I didn't bother to point out that the Thad we knew wasn't who we thought he was.

"That's a shame, dear." It was her turn to pat my arm. "No success on the investigation and all this trouble here at the conference . . ." Helen sighed. "You're having a tough time of it."

I didn't need to hear that as much as I needed to know what I was in for as far as the missing trays, and when I urged Helen, she got right back to her story.

She clutched her hands at her waist. "Like I said, I went into the conference room to prepare the final list of winners to be read at this evening's dinner," she said, "and when I realized something was wrong, I was so taken by surprise . . . Well, I suppose I should have just kept my mouth shut." She bit her lower lip. "But I was upset. I'm sure you understand. And when I walked out of the conference room . . . like I said, to find you . . . and some of the girls from the judging committee were there . . . I just couldn't help myself. I suppose I might have said something. You know, about what a horrible mess we had on our hands."

"And word travels fast, which explains why people are grumbling." My stomach flipped.

Helen nodded. "A couple people have stopped me. To talk, you know, and —"

"Never had problems like this in other years." Before Helen could finish what she was saying, Gloria Winston broke into our conversation. Gloria was nobody's version of a shrinking violet, and there was fire in her eyes. "You owe us an explanation."

I do not need to point out that she looked square at me when she said this.

"I do." There was no use saying anything else or trying to dodge the undodgeable. "And as soon as I have a chance to look into things —"

"The sooner the better." Gloria impaled me with a look, and I knew exactly what it meant: she had no intention of keeping her mouth shut about how unhappy she was. "People are talking, and I for one can't blame them. We never had these sorts of problems when Helen was in charge."

"Now, Gloria . . ." Helen began, but I didn't give her a chance to finish. As much as I appreciated Helen's support, I didn't deserve it. Not if I couldn't keep things running as smoothly as our attendees expected.

"On my way over there now," I said, and I scampered toward the conference room.

Less than a half hour later, I knew for certain that Helen and Gloria were right.

Our inventory list showed three hundred and forty-seven trays had been entered in the various competition categories. My count — I did it three times just to be sure — only turned up three hundred and thirty-three trays. Fourteen had simply disappeared.

Maybe I'm just a glutton for punishment. I looked over the entries again, rechecking categories against what I knew about each of the people who'd entered.

A couple of the entries were from some of the better-known collectors, and I had no doubt the buttons on those trays were worth a pretty penny. But a few others were relatively common buttons with little monetary value. Whoever stole the buttons — if, indeed, they'd been stolen — wasn't very discriminating.

Of course, that didn't matter to collectors. True collectors loved more about their buttons than just the fact that some were worth a pretty penny. There was the history of each button to consider, and the effort that went into assembling a collection of them that could satisfy the exacting standards of each judging category.

And as it turned out, one of the trays that was missing was Gloria's collection of ivory buttons, the one that had included the bone button that caused her tray to receive a measle. When I realized it, I dropped my head into my hands. If she was mad before, she would be doubly mad when she found out her tray was among the missing.

Just thinking about the scene Gloria would cause made me feel worse than ever, and I slumped against the nearest table, working through what I had to do and what I'd tell our conference attendees. Unfortunately, no matter how many times I went over it, I always came back to the same thing: there was only one thing I could do and that was talk to the entire group. And there was only one thing I could tell them.

The truth.

At dinner that night, I stepped to the podium before the salads were served and did exactly that — I told the truth about the missing trays and faced the collective wrath of the button community. There were plenty of questions, and I was woefully short on answers. All I could do was promise to do my best to find the missing buttons and get to the bottom of the mystery of how they got that way. That, and delay announcing the contest winners until all the trays were returned and could be judged all over again.

Fortunately, that was good enough for most folks.

Unfortunately, *most folks* doesn't mean *all*.

By the time I finished up at the podium, I'd been accused of fixing the contest for my own gain (though my accuser couldn't say what that gain could possibly be), stealing the buttons so I could sell them at the Button Box, and even making off with the buttons because (and follow closely here because this gets a little complicated) Thad Wyant was a government spy, I was in on his secret mission, and the buttons on those missing trays were clues linked to a mystery that was vital to national security.

Conspiracy theories are us.

I handled all this as best I could, and honestly, I think I was cool and calm enough on the outside to fool every person in that room. My insides, though, weren't cooperating. When I sat down at the dinner table reserved for the conference committee, my knees were weak, my stomach was in knots, and I couldn't eat a bite. I excused myself on the pretext of having to use the ladies' room, but I had no intention of going back into the ballroom. One look at the baked chicken, mashed potatoes, and green beans on the plate that was set in front of me, and

I knew I had to get up to my room, put on my jammies, and hide under the blankets.

All that might actually have been possible if Kaz wasn't waiting just inside the door of my suite when I got there. He had a bottle of wine in one hand and two glasses in the other.

It wouldn't have been a surprise (well, except for the wine) if his wasn't one of the faces I'd just seen looking up at me from the audience in the ballroom. "You were just —"

"Watching you do your public mea culpa, yeah. I ducked out before you did. Figured you'd need a breather after going through that. Button people can be brutal."

I tried to shrug, but my shoulders felt as if they were weighted with lead. "They're disappointed. They have every right to be. They come to a conference with expectations, and I'm pretty sure murder and larceny aren't among them."

The wine bottle was already open, and Kaz set down the glasses on the coffee table in front of the couch, poured, and handed one to me. "Drink," he said. "You're as wired as a cat with its tail in an electrical socket."

He was right.

I tossed my purse down on the floor next

to the couch and accepted the glass of wine. I didn't so much drink as I did sip, and when the fruity nip of the Riesling hit the back of my throat, I sighed.

"Better?" Kaz asked.

He was sweet to think of me, and I hated to disappoint him, but that night was all about laying the facts on the line. There was no dodging the truth, so I didn't even try to mince any words. "No."

"There's talk . . . you've probably heard . . . about replacing you as conference chair." Apparently, Kaz knew to lay it on the line, too, but he softened the blow by quickly adding, "Not from many people, of course. But some of them —"

"Maybe they're right." I dropped onto the couch. "Maybe getting the Button Box off the ground and running the conference at the same time gave me too much on my plate. Maybe I'm just not as capable and together as I like to think I am."

He sat down next to me. "You know that's not true. It's just —"

"What? Bad luck?" I took another sip of wine to get rid of the acid taste in my mouth. "The murder, sure, that was bad luck. But everything else that's happened . . . Gloria Winston was right. We didn't have these kinds of problems when

Helen was in charge. Her conference ran like clockwork. Mine, not so much."

"You've been distracted."

"Yeah, but I shouldn't be."

"You've been showing up at every event you can and helping the cops at the same time, and that's not easy. I'd like to see anybody else do it."

"Yeah, but —"

"No buts." Kaz slipped his arm around my shoulders. "You're terrific. You know that, don't you? You're terrific and you're more than capable, and it's not your fault if some numbskull stole a bunch of buttons."

"But how —"

"It doesn't matter. You'll figure it out. Just like you'll figure out who killed Thad Wyant. And when you're all done, you'll get all those buttons judged again, and you'll announce the winners, and everyone will leave for home happy."

"Except for the people who don't win."

"Hey, I'm not responsible for that. And neither are you." Kaz clinked his wineglass against mine. "We can only worry about what we can control. Everything else is out of our hands."

It was a philosophical take on things from a man who is usually anything but, and thinking it over, I took another drink of wine and felt some of the tension inside me ease. I didn't even realize just how much talking to Kaz had helped me unwind until I realized my head was on his shoulder.

"Don't," he said when I made a move to sit up. "It's OK. You need to relax."

"I'm not sure this qualifies."

"Sure it does." He leaned forward and set his wineglass on the coffee table so that he could crook a finger under my chin and tip my face up to his. "You know I'm always here for you, Jo."

In an evening that was supposed to be all about telling the truth, this was one big whopper of a lie, but I didn't point it out. I couldn't. Not when those espresso-hot eyes were locked with mine, and the scent of Kaz's aftershave was clouding my brain. He bent his head a little closer and waited for me to make the first move. If I allowed it, I knew he would kiss me, and if I allowed Kaz to kiss me —

Maybe button dealers/collectors/ conference chairs have a special fairy godmother looking over their shoulders to help prevent them from doing incredibly stupid things.

That would explain why, just at that moment, there was a knock on my hotel room door.

Kaz sat back. I jumped up and made it to the door in record time. Was I trying to be polite to whoever was knocking? Or running away from my own baser instincts? I had no idea, but when I realized I was being a little too jumpy and feeling guilty about something that almost — but didn't — happen, I sucked in a breath and threw open the door.

Nev was waiting in the hallway.

"Glad you're here." He sailed into the room, took one look at Kaz and those two glasses of wine, and stopped cold. "I'm interrupting something," he said.

"Yeah, me trying to talk my ex down from chucking the button business and this conference-chair thing and running away to join the circus." As casually as can be, Kaz got up. "I was just leaving. Maybe you can convince her she's the best at what she does and she shouldn't let other people make her crazy." Instead of adding that he was one of those people, he headed for the door, stopped over at the countertop that held the mini-fridge and microwave, and got another wineglass. He handed it to Nev and walked out the door.

Nev watched Kaz go. "Really? He was trying to help?"

"In a Kaz sort of way."

"Which means . . ?"

I shrugged. It was impossible to explain, and besides, I was too exhausted to even try. "He has a good heart. It's his self-control and his bad habits he just can't restrain." I rolled my glass in my hands. "You want a glass of wine?"

"On duty." Nev set down his glass. "If it can keep until we've got this case wrapped up . . ."

The way things were going, I was afraid the wine would be long past its expiration date by then.

Rather than let my pessimism show, I set down my glass, too. "What can I do for you?" I asked Nev.

"I heard what happened. About the buttons." He didn't say he was sorry. He didn't have to. Nev's mouth was pulled into a thin line of regret. "More trouble than you need, huh?"

"That's putting it mildly." I sat back down, instinctively avoiding the spot that was still warm from the heat of Kaz's body. "You don't suppose the missing trays of buttons have anything to do with Brad's murder, do you? And the Geronimo button we found in the trash?" Just trying to make sense of it made my head ache, and I pressed my fingers to my temples. "It's crazy."

"It is." Nev dropped into the seat next to me. "But hey, don't give up. I've just been talking to the guys down in the security office, and they found something that might help us out. Well, actually, they found nothing, and that might help us out."

I hadn't had enough wine to make me foggy, but I still didn't follow. "And this is good news, why?" I asked.

Nev sat forward. "I was thinking about what Daryl Tucker told you, about the man Brad Wyant argued with the evening he was killed. We went over the security tapes again."

"And found nothing."

"Exactly." Why this was a good thing, I didn't know, but Nev seemed pleased enough. "The tapes don't show the outside of the building. Not clearly," he explained. "But if you watch the tapes from the lobby camera really carefully, you can see a sliver of the front entryway. On the night of the murder, they show Brad Wyant going through the lobby, and a little while after, Daryl Tucker walking by, his phone in his hands. He turned down the hallway over by where your vendors are set up, so after a while, I couldn't see him, but I did see

Wyant come through again. He headed in the direction of the elevator that would take him down to the laundry room."

I wasn't sure what he was getting at, but I sensed it was important. I sat up, too. "But . . ."

"But Wyant never went outside."

"Which means —"

"He couldn't have argued with a man outside."

"Which tells us —"

"Daryl Tucker is lying."

"But Daryl was at the banquet, and his phone did ring, and he did go out into the lobby."

"I'm sure of it. I saw it with my own eyes. But what happened out in the lobby —"

"Didn't happen the way he reported it." I thought of how Daryl had been coming on to me since the conference started, and goose bumps prickled over my arms. "You think he's our killer?"

"I don't know. The tapes don't show him going toward that service elevator, but he might have used the stairs. But even if he's not our guy, it's pretty obvious he's hiding something."

"And you're going to take him down to the station to question him, right?"

Nev stood up and scraped a hand through

his hair. "Come on, Josie, you've seen the guy. If I approach him and tell him I'm taking him in to be interrogated, he won't just clam up; he'll fold like an origami stork. He'll never talk."

"But you cops, you have ways of making him."

"Not as good a way as you have."

It wasn't my imagination. My stomach was back to flip-flopping around, just like it had been down in the ballroom when I had to confess that button trays had been filched from under our noses and our contest was in jeopardy. "You're kidding me," I said and hoped against hope Nev was.

"It's not like I'm asking you to run off to Vegas and marry the guy or anything."

I hopped to my feet. "Good thing."

Nev grinned. "Yeah."

Have I mentioned that Nev is cute?

And that if there's one thing I hate, it's being played for a fool?

So far, Brad Wyant had done a plenty good job of that. He'd killed his brother and assumed Thad's identity, and none of us had been the wiser.

Then there was Brad's killer. He'd done a pretty good job of playing us for patsies, too.

"I want to find out what happened," I told Nev.

"That means you'll talk to Tucker?"

I hesitated. I supposed if I talked to Daryl someplace public, like in the hotel coffee shop or right outside the ballroom . . . I supposed it wouldn't look like I'd succumbed to his not-so-obvious charms.

"He was down at dinner. I saw him there." I stepped toward the door. "I'll just wait for people to leave the ballroom and have a talk with him."

Nev grabbed my hand to stop me. "I was thinking Tucker might be more likely to talk in a more casual setting."

I'd had those couple sips of wine; my throat shouldn't have been dry. But suddenly, it felt as if it was coated with sand. "Are you asking me to ask Daryl Tucker out on a date?"

Instead of answering, Nev reached over and retrieved my glass of wine so he could hand it to me. "Maybe you better finish this," he said and grinned. "You know, for courage."

CHAPTER FOURTEEN

All right, I admit it — I was a mess the next day. And not just because things had gotten so out of hand at the conference and the murder investigation was going nowhere. Too much of a weenie to do it in person, I had called Daryl Turner's room the morning after Nev talked me into this little fishing expedition and left a message, asking if Daryl would like to join me for dinner that evening. Within minutes, he phoned back. Excited? From the way Daryl's voice quavered, I could picture him hopping around his room, eager for six o'clock to roll around, the time we set for our date.

Daryl.

Our date.

Words that, just a few days earlier, I would have sworn I would never use in the same sentence. Not in a million years.

"You remember what you're going to say, right?" Nev didn't look all that calm himself.

I was trying to brush my hair and he hovered behind me like a nervous mom on her daughter's wedding day. I ignored his fidgety reflection in the mirror, slapped on some lipstick, turned to leave the bathroom —

And ran right into Nev, who was planted in the doorway.

"You remember, right?"

I controlled a screech. Barely. But since I cut him that much slack, I decided it was perfectly acceptable to throw my hands in the air. "You're the one acting like I'm running off to Vegas with Daryl," I said, sidestepping around Nev and into the living room of my suite. "It's just dinner, remember? That's what you said to convince me to go along with this goofy plan of yours."

"It is just dinner. Yes." Nev had flattened himself against the wall when I sailed past him, and now, he pushed away and closer to me. "But there are some serious questions you need to ask Tucker."

"I know. I get it." I grabbed my purse. "What did he really see the night of the murder? More important, why did he lie about it? And what is he covering up?"

"You don't want to ask that last one. Not outright, anyway." Nev shifted from foot to foot.

"What?" Another toss of my hands, which might have been easier (or at least a little more graceful) if I wasn't holding my summer straw clutch. "What on earth do you have to be so nervous about?"

Nev shoved his hands in his pockets. Took them out again. He scraped a hand over his chin. "I'm not nervous," he said. "It's just that —"

"Oh, I get it." I'm not usually the type who teases. At least not the type who teases a guy I think is cute when we are still trying to get our relationship on some sort of even footing. But let's face it: Nev deserved a little figurative kick in the butt for acting like such a mother hen.

I clasped both my hands and my summer straw clutch to my heart. "You're afraid I'll discover Daryl is the man of my dreams. My soul mate. The love of my life! And that I can't live without him." I'm not the type who bats her eyelashes, but I batted for all I was worth. "Maybe we really will run off to Vegas together."

Nev frowned. "That's not funny."

"It's also not possible, and you know it." I was back to being my real self, matter-of-fact, not a batting eyelash in sight. "Come on." I leaned forward and pinned Nev with a look. "What's really bugging you?"

Nev doesn't beat around the bush, either. In his job, he doesn't have the luxury. He stepped back. "There's a chance he's our murderer. You know that."

I wrinkled my nose. "I do. But . . . Daryl? Really? You think?"

Nev shrugged. "Not really, but —"

"But that would be perfect, wouldn't it?" The realization sparkled through me like the bubbles climbing up the side of a champagne glass. "I mean, it would be great if he was our murderer and if I could actually find out something from him tonight that would prove it."

"And put yourself in danger? There's not a chance I'm going to allow that."

Aha! We were getting to the meat of the problem. And the reason for Nev's sudden case of the jitters. It was sweet. And I was touched.

Right before I realized I was also insulted.

I pulled back my shoulders. "I can take care of myself, especially in a public restaurant where —"

"I know. Believe me, I do. But a man who's capable of murder —"

"Which we don't know Daryl is."

"But if he is, he might also —"

"Yes, of course he could, but you know I'm not going to take any stupid chances."

"Even if you don't, he might —"

"He won't. This is Daryl, remember. Nerd with a capital *N.*"

"Yeah, nerd who lied to us about what he witnessed the night of the murder."

"He did, but —"

"Nerd, who's obviously trying to cover something up."

"He is, but —"

"Nerd, yes. But like it or not, there's a chance he's a dangerous nerd."

Have I mentioned that we were getting nowhere fast? I guess that's why, this time, my screech was fully justified. "This was your idea," I told Nev, and I poked a finger in his direction just to emphasize it.

"I know. I know. And it's a good idea. But . . ."

"But?"

If his sigh didn't say it all, the fact that he moved to the door and opened it for me did. "Be careful," he said.

I didn't bother to tell him I would be. Instead, as determined as I'd ever be and likely to talk myself out of this cockamamie tryst if I didn't get moving and do it fast, I marched toward the hallway. I stopped only once. That was so I could stand on tiptoe and give Nev a quick kiss on the cheek.

His face flushed with color. "What was

that for?"

He's a smart guy, so I figured he knew. I also figured it never hurts to spell things out.

"It's the least you deserve," I told him. "For caring."

When it comes to an investigation, I might be willing to swallow my pride, but I am not a complete moron. I deliberately avoided any restaurant that even hinted at candlelight and romance and went for sleek, casual, and well lit instead. One within walking distance of the hotel so we didn't have to ride in the backseat of a cab together. Murderer or garden-variety nerd, it didn't matter; I was determined to spend as little time alone with Daryl as it was possible to get on any date.

I ordered the shrimp and red-pepper pasta. And a dirty martini for courage.

Daryl asked for chicken tenders, extra fries, and a beer.

Had I been with anyone else (Nev, for instance), this is the part where the conversation would have lagged, and what started out as a promising evening crashed and burned. As hard as it was to believe, that meant there was an actual plus to dating Daryl. (I mean other than trying to find out something that would lead us to Brad Wyant's murderer.) Two button collectors at dinner together? No way we could ever run out of things to talk about.

"So . . ." I scooted forward in my seat, my hands clutched around the stem of my martini glass. "It's been so busy at the conference, we haven't had much of a chance to get to know each other, Daryl. What kind of buttons do you specialize in?"

"Specialize?" He had just lifted his beer mug, and he looked at me through the golden liquid in it. It wasn't until after he'd taken a drink and set down his glass that he replied. "I'm too new to collecting to specialize in any one kind of button."

"I remember those days." I did. Just barely. Still, it seemed like a first-date (and there-will-never-be-another-one) thing to say. "When you first get into collecting, they all have a special appeal, don't they?"

I could have sworn Daryl was listening intently, but then, there was a light hanging from the ceiling right above our table, and its glow reflected in his glasses. Maybe his gaze wasn't glued to me the way I thought it was. "What's that you said?" he asked, adjusting the lapel of that hideous plaid sport coat and leaning forward. "About every button being —"

"Special. Sure. I'll bet you feel the same way. At first, they're all so interesting."

"They. Meaning the buttons."

"Of course. But there must be one certain kind that really attracts your attention."

A slow smile spread over Daryl's face. "One certain kind of button? I thought for sure you were talking about one certain kind of woman." He slipped his hand across the table toward mine.

I tucked mine in my lap.

The way Daryl's cheeks darkened above his bush of a beard, I was pretty sure he got the message. He took another sip of beer. "I like colorful glass buttons, and Western-themed ones, of course. But then, that's the whole reason I came to this conference in the first place, so I could hear Thad Wyant speak."

It was an uncomfortable reminder of why I was really there, but trust me, I was grateful for it. Better to think about murder then to get carried away with my ruse and even begin to consider Daryl as potential boyfriend material.

He scratched a hand through his beard. "Have you heard anything?" he asked. "From the police?"

"You mean about the murder. Funny you should ask . . ." The waitress delivered my pasta, and I sat back and bided my time. Maybe it was a good thing I did; it was the first I realized Nev was seated at a table across the aisle and two down, facing my way. He looked as casual as can be, sitting there drinking a cup of coffee, but I could feel his eyes on me. Not sure if that was reassuring or annoying, I ignored him, twirling my fettuccine onto my pasta spoon and keeping up the conversation.

"The police mentioned something to me that sounds a little odd," I said, and because I didn't want to seem too anxious, I ate that forkful of pasta, and since it was incredibly delicious, another one, too. "They were questioning me. You know, about the night of the murder."

"That first night of the conference. Sure." Daryl took a bite of chicken fingers and left behind bread crumbs in his beard. "I remember. We were just getting seated for the banquet, and I went out to the lobby to take a phone call."

"And you told the cops that's when you saw Thad Wyant outside the hotel arguing with another man."

Daryl was in the middle of chewing, so he didn't so much answer as he did grunt.

That gave me the opportunity to go in for the kill.

"Only you didn't, did you, Daryl?"

He was still chewing, and he excused himself by pointing to his mouth, swallowing, then washing down the chicken with a sip of beer. "What are you getting at, Josie?"

"I'm not getting at anything. I'm saying it plain and clear. There are security cameras all over the hotel." The aroma of shrimp and red peppers tickled my nose. I took another bite before I continued. "They've got video," I pointed out. "Video of you in the lobby, talking on your phone."

Daryl nodded.

"And video of Thad Wyant," I added, even though, technically, the video wasn't of Thad Wyant, but of Brad. "He never left the building, Daryl."

Daryl adjusted the glasses on the bridge of his nose. "You mean —"

"That you couldn't have seen Thad outside arguing with a man in a raincoat, because he never went outside."

"Oh."

"That's it?" My fork clattered against my plate, and when the noise brought Nev up and out of his seat, I warned him off with a little shake of my head. Before we attracted any more attention, I schooled my voice. "You lied to me, Daryl, and you lied to the cops, too. I was hoping for a little more of an explanation than *oh.*"

A fidgety smile came and went from somewhere inside of that dark, shaggy beard. His left eye twitched. "Can this get me in trouble?" he asked.

"That all depends . . ." I picked up my fork again, the better to make it look like we were having a dinner conversation, not a showdown. "What did you see that night, Daryl?"

He was about to grab a french fry, and he stopped and sat back. "I wasn't lying when I said I saw Thad Wyant in the lobby."

"I didn't think you were." Not technically correct because ever since Nev had told me about the security tapes and what wasn't on them, I wasn't sure what to think of Daryl. "But like I said, you didn't see him go outside. You couldn't have."

"No." He picked up a french fry, dipped it in ketchup, then set it down again. "That's true."

"So if you didn't see him go outside, you didn't see him argue with a man out there."

Daryl hung his head. "That's true, too."

"Then why . . ." Honestly, I didn't get it. Too antsy to just sit there and wait for answers I wasn't sure were anywhere near coming, I picked up my glass and sipped my martini. A minute later, I felt steadier, and ready to start again. "Why lie?" I asked Daryl. "It doesn't make sense."

His white shirt suddenly matched the color of his skin. Except for the two bright spots of color peeking out at the place where beard met bare skin. "I thought . . ." Daryl's voice caught, and he coughed, twitched, and took a swallow of beer. When he was done, he gave me a level look. "I thought it would make me look more important," he said. "To you."

"To . . . me?" Big points for me, I didn't groan when the truth hit like a ton of bricks. Then again, Daryl didn't exactly give me the chance.

My hand was on the table and he grabbed it and clutched it in his sweaty palm. "I had to do something to get you to notice me," he said, the words rushing out of him. "I mean, I knew, ever since that first evening when we went on that cruise . . . I knew you were special, Josie. And I knew there was no way a woman who's as smart and as beautiful and as accomplished as you are, I knew there was no way you were ever going to notice me."

Were my eyes as big as saucers? I'd like to think I'm a little more subtle than that, but at that moment, I wasn't so sure. I had been expecting the truth from Daryl. Heck, I'd been hoping for it.

But not this truth.

Talk about subtle — I raised my free hand in a sort of *help!* gesture I hoped Nev could interpret.

He drank his coffee.

"You understand, don't you, Josie?" Daryl's hand closed tighter over mine. "You can see how a guy like me . . . Well, I know you might find this hard to believe, but I don't have that much experience when it comes to romancing a woman. I thought —"

"That lying to the cops would get me to notice you?" Since Nev ignored my first signal for assistance, I tried again. My left hand shot up; then, to try to make it look like the most casual thing in the world, I ran it through my hair.

Bad move.

Number one, because Nev still didn't get it. In fact, when I sent a desperate, pleading look his way, I found him studying the dessert menu.

Number two, because Daryl's gaze moved to my hair, and his eyes lit up.

Oh no — he thought my little gesture was sexy, and I was coming on to him!

What little I'd eaten of my dinner soured in my stomach. My hands were suddenly as sweaty as Daryl's.

I can't even begin to explain how grateful I was when my cell rang.

I shot Daryl an apologetic smile, snatched my hand out of his reach, and grabbed for my phone.

"Looks like you need saving."

"Kaz?" Automatically, I scanned the restaurant and found him sitting on a stool at the bar, where he had a clear line of vision to our table. "How did you —"

"Bad time to ask questions, don't you think?"

Since I couldn't sit there staring at him, I looked away, but I knew he was smiling.

"Ask me what's happening at the conference," he said.

"The conference?" That sourness in my stomach ratcheted up a notch, and I squeezed my eyes shut. "Please, don't tell me something else has gone wrong."

"It's a great excuse, don't you think?"

I realized what Kaz was getting at and tried not to breathe a sigh of relief. At least not so Daryl could see it.

"I need to get back?" I said into the phone. "Right now?"

"I always said you were smart." Kaz hung up.

I did my best to look and sound disappointed. "I've got to get back to the hotel,"

I said, pushing back my chair and grabbing my purse. "There's a problem. At the conference. And —"

"Sure. I understand. Only . . ." From behind his thick glasses, Daryl's eyes were fixed on mine.

I prayed that wasn't supposed to be some come-hither look, gulped, and parroted. "Only . . . ?"

"You invited me," Daryl explained. "I think it's only right that you pay before you leave."

I did. As quickly as I could. I left Daryl sitting there munching his chicken fingers and bolted for the door.

I was out on the sidewalk before I realized Kaz was already out there waiting for me. And Nev wasn't far behind.

When I started for the hotel and he stepped up beside me, I shot Nev a look. "Thanks for nothing," I said.

"Thanks? For nothing?" Some detective! He didn't have a clue what I was talking about. Nev stopped in his tracks. And me? I never looked back. But that didn't mean I didn't hear Kaz when he walked up to Nev.

"Riley," Kaz said, his voice tinged with barely controlled patience, "we need to have a serious talk."

CHAPTER FIFTEEN

The conference would officially wrap up after lunch on Sunday. That gave me two and one-half days to accomplish two things:

1. Figure out who killed Brad.
2. Redeem myself in the eyes of conference-goers.

Notice I didn't say they were two easy things.

Which, believe me, didn't mean I wasn't going to try my darndest.

The thought firmly in mind, I vowed to devote all of Friday to conference activities and nothing but conference activities and think about the investigation later. First thing in the morning, I met with the security staff and found out they didn't have any leads on our missing trays of buttons. After that, I called a meeting of the judging committee and left them with the charge of figuring out the most equitable way to handle the contest. Before I attended one panel on calico buttons and another that focused on Oriental-themed buttons, I talked to Stan half a dozen times; he was at the Button Box, and at seven that evening, I was hosting a cocktail party there for any attendees who wanted to stop by. Stan and I went over last-minute details, checked and rechecked the catering menu, and even though I never mentioned it because I was sure he had everything under control, he told me — twice — how he'd vacuumed and dusted and made sure everything in the shop was shipshape.

So far, so good.

I was just on my way into another panel — this one was on military buttons, and I was anxious to hear it — when I saw Nev get off the elevator and walk into the hotel lobby. As soon as he scanned the groups of people walking out of one conference room and into another, I knew he was on the lookout for me.

I'd bet any money it wasn't to apologize for abandoning me to Daryl's amorous advances the night before, either.

"Hey." He closed in on me before I had time to duck and run into the military-button panel. "I've been looking for you."

"Like you were last night?"

His lips puckered. "I wasn't looking for you last night. I knew exactly where you were."

"Yeah, at dinner with a nerd . . ." I glanced around to make sure no one — especially the nerd in question — was listening, and just to make sure, I lowered my voice. "At dinner with a nerd who declared his undying love."

Nev grinned, then wiped away the expression in an instant. Or maybe it just melted beneath the heat of my glare. "He said he loved you, huh?"

"Not in so many words."

"But he didn't say anything about the murder."

So much for trying to shake the resolve of a determined detective. Nev wasn't about to get personal. Not when we had business to discuss. "Daryl admitted he lied about what he saw in the lobby that night," I said, and with a look, I dared him to grin again when I added, "He said he did it to try to sound important. So he could impress me."

OK, so I shouldn't have gotten all defensive. I couldn't help myself. Not when one corner of Nev's mouth twitched.

I crossed my arms over my burnt-orange suit jacket. "You think it's impossible for a guy to want to try to impress me?"

He bit his lower lip.

"You do. Of course you do." I was a big girl, so the sting shouldn't have been as sharp. I told myself not to forget it and turned to go into the conference room before the doors closed.

Even though I already had my back to him, Nev put a hand on my arm to stop me. "I think," he said, his voice warm and close to my ear, "it's impossible for any guy to meet you and not want to impress you."

If Nev's goal all along was to make me feel all warm and fuzzy, he got his way. I turned to find him looking into my eyes, and rather than get carried away by the blueness and the soft expression in them, I glanced down to where his fingers caressed that oh-so-sensitive spot where forearm and elbow meet. "Why . . ." My breath caught on what would have come out as a sigh of epic proportions if I let it. "Why were you looking for me?" I asked.

Nev grinned and tightened his hold. "Was I? I don't remember."

Don't think I was going to let him off the hook so easily. "Is that what Kaz told you to say?"

To Nev's credit, he didn't try to hedge. "Kaz tried to give me some advice last night, yeah. But believe me, this wasn't part of it. He talked about wining and dining and candles . . ." Nev winced. "Something tells me he's much more of a romantic than I am. Which makes me wonder why —"

"I dumped him?" The sound that escaped me was more snort than laugh. "There's more to being a perfect man than just romance."

"But romance is important. At least that's what Kaz said."

I couldn't deny it. "So is dependability," I pointed out. "And responsibility. Trustworthiness. A good sense of humor. Always telling the truth. Those things are just as important."

"He didn't mention any of that."

"He wouldn't. He doesn't know the meaning."

"But maybe that means some other guy . . ." Nev adjusted his hand just a smidgen, just enough to make tingles dance up and down my arm. "Maybe some guy who's reliable and dependable and who always tells the truth —"

"And doesn't pay attention when a woman is sending him come-and-rescue-me signals?"

Nev groaned and backed off. "You can't hold that against me. If I thought you were in real trouble, I would have come running. You know that. I knew you could take care of yourself, and besides, I was concentrating. You know, thinking about the case. Oh yeah, the case." He put a hand to the small of my back and urged me toward the elevator. "That's why I was looking for you. We need to get up to Brad's room."

A few minutes later, the conference was once again a distant memory, and we were back in the same messy suite we'd visited just a few days before. For a couple of moments, I couldn't understand why. That morning, it looked pretty much just like it had the last time we were there.

Pretty much being the operative words.

When the realization hit, I took another look around, and I felt Nev's gaze on me, watching expectantly.

"You see it, too, don't you?" he asked.

"I see . . ." I took a couple steps further into the room. "That suitcase was on that chair." I pointed to the now-empty spot. "Not on the floor. And those papers on the dining-room table . . ." Keeping my hands to myself, I checked them out. "They've been shuffled around. I can tell because Thad . . . er, Brad . . . had them all jumbled up, and look, somebody's tried to straighten them. Like they didn't remember how they found them and they figured they must have been piled neatly."

Nev nodded.

"Someone's been here."

He confirmed my guess with a second nod.

"And it wasn't your people, because if it was, you wouldn't think it was weird."

This time, he didn't need to confirm or deny. We both knew the crime-scene techs would have done their work without displacing any of the items in Brad's room.

That left me with only one question. "Who?"

Nev puffed out a breath. "I wish I knew."

"And what —"

"Don't know that, either. If I knew what they were looking for, it might help explain everything that's gone on around here this week."

"And how —"

He shrugged. "Just came to have a final look around. Before we release the room back to the hotel for them to use. The techs will be here this afternoon to gather up Brad's things and put them into storage. Until then . . ." His grunt spoke volumes about his frustration. "I guess I just needed you to confirm what I suspected. It never hurts to have another pair of eyes look things over."

"And nothing's missing?"

"It's hard to tell." Nev strolled over to the table and took a look at the brochures and booklets that Brad had dumped out of his welcome bag. "We'll check for fingerprints."

"You don't sound encouraged."

"There's not much about this case that's encouraging. With any luck, by the time the techs are done in here, we'll know more."

His words were all about hope. The way his shoulders sagged told me he wished he could believe them.

Done there, we walked out into the hallway just as the door to the room next to Brad's snapped open.

"Oh." A woman wearing a terry bathrobe and yellow rollers in her hair frowned when she saw us. She had a green avocado mask spread over her face, and it cracked just under her lower lip, revealing a narrow strip of pale skin. "I thought maybe you were that housekeeping woman finally coming back. When I saw her this morning, I told her I spilled coffee on the rug in my bedroom, and I figured she'd want to clean it up right away. Before it left a stain. By now, it's probably too late to get the stain out. That was hours ago."

"Hours?" I checked the time on my cell

phone. It was late morning, and I knew that at least on the floor where I was staying, the housekeeping staff didn't come around until after noon. "They clean this floor that early?"

"Well, now that I think about it, I guess not." The woman wrinkled her nose, and this time, the mask cracked along the lines of her apple-round cheeks. "I've been here three days, and every one of those days, they've come around later, right around lunchtime. But when I heard the commotion out here this morning —"

"Commotion?"

Nev and I were thinking the same thing, so it was no surprise that we both spoke at the same time.

The woman in the terry robe nodded. "Rattling at that door." She glanced toward the room I'd reserved back in those blissful days when I thought the real Thad Wyant would be staying in it — and staying alive. "You know, sometimes it's hard to tell if those key cards go in one way or the other. Happens to me all the time in hotels. But you'd think a cleaning woman would know. She couldn't get it right. Not at first, anyway. And I figured that was a good thing, because it gave me time to come out here and tell her about the coffee on the rug.

And she said she'd be back."

"And she went into that room?" Nev asked.

The woman nodded, and as if the cleaning woman in question was still there, she glared at the room next door before taking a step back in her own room. "I've got half a mind to call down to the desk and tell them their housekeeping staff is slacking off."

"And you can certainly do that." Nev put a hand on her door to stop her from closing it. "Only before you do, can you describe the woman?"

She narrowed her eyes and looked us both up and down. "You're from the hotel?"

Nev pulled out his badge, and the woman's eyes opened so wide that the dry green goo on her forehead chipped.

"Now that I think about it," she said, "that woman wasn't wearing the blue pants and tops I've seen the other housekeeping people wear." Her jaw went slack. "I guess I should have noticed that right away. But when I asked if she was from housekeeping, she said she was, and really, who was I to doubt her? Does that mean —"

"We can't say for sure. Not yet." Nev headed off any questions before she could voice them. "Do you remember anything else about her?"

The woman concentrated again. "She was small," she said. "Tiny, and kind of quiet. Or at least she was trying to be quiet. But she moved really fast, like she couldn't wait to get in and out of that room as quickly as possible. She reminded me of a little mouse."

I managed to keep my mouth shut at the same time I tossed Nev a look. He thanked the woman, and we headed for the elevator.

When it arrived, we stepped inside, and when the doors slid shut, he said what I was thinking. "Mouse. That can only be one person."

"Yeah." Somehow, I wasn't surprised. "Beth Howell."

It was not a last-minute decision to have conference attendees stop at the Button Box on Friday night, so really, no one could accuse me of sucking up for the sake of saving my reputation. I'd included an open invitation to all attendees in the conference booklet (and just so no nasty rumors get started about me taking advantage of my position as conference chair, I did pay for the ad space), and though I knew there were also some other group activities planned that night (the theater, a baseball game, a concert at the House of Blues), I still expected a couple hundred people to be in and out of the shop.

Self-serving?

Not really. In fact, though they were encouraged to browse, I made it clear I wasn't selling that night. Not one single button. If folks wanted to call me once they got home and purchase something they'd seen, that was another story.

"Now, if only I could get Beth Howell to materialize."

I was speaking under my breath, but leave it to Stan not to miss a trick. He was standing near the refreshment tables, which had been set up along the far wall of the shop, and since he was taller than me, it was easier for him to scan the crowd of seventy-five or so who'd gotten there at the stroke of seven and were already munching appetizers and sipping wine and beer and soft drinks.

"What's she look like?" he asked.

"It doesn't matter." Gloria Winston — never one to miss out on free food — came up to the table to grab (another) plateful of cold shrimp, and I greeted her and waited until she was out of earshot. "The way she's been slipping out of sight, it's obvious Beth's too smart to show up here. Especially after she went through Thad's . . . er,

Brad's . . . room this morning. She must know we know."

"She might know you know someone was in there, but there's no way she can know that you know it was her."

I think this made sense. While I was trying to make sure, Kaz strolled over. He was dressed to the nines in his black chauffeur suit and white shirt. For the occasion, he'd added a wild tie, free-form boxes in shades of green and outlined in black. It was the first I realized his tie and my scoop-neck jungle-print dress actually kind of matched. Before I could decide if he'd planned for us to look like twins or if it was some sick twist of fate, Kaz smiled and looked around.

"Nice crowd." He wasn't as tall as Stan, but he had me beat by a whole head. He, too, studied the happy, chatting conference-goers, who were oohing and aahing over the buttons displayed in the glass cases along the opposite wall. Stan had been true to his word; the Button Box shined like a newly minted penny, from tin ceiling, to sage-green walls (Kaz and I matched those, too), to the oak floors.

Stan had even made sure the display cases were cleaned on the insides so that each button in them was shown to perfection.

"And aren't you the smart one," Kaz said.

"Getting all your suspects here in one spot."

Stan perked up. But then, he is a retired cop, and I guess some old habits are hard to break. "Suspects? Really? Give me a rundown."

Before I could, Kaz did the honors.

"That's Langston Whitman," he said, nodding toward the back of the shop, where Langston, Elliot, and a few other people were examining the display of old police-uniform buttons I'd let Stan arrange, partly so he'd have something to do while he was babysitting the shop but mostly because I figured he'd enjoy looking through them. "Langston is a vendor, and Thad stole from his booth."

"Which is hardly a reason for murder." This bit of logic came from me, and Stan nodded in agreement.

"Maybe the stealing part isn't." As if there was any chance Langston and company might actually know what we were talking about, Kaz turned his back on them. "But he's crazy about Elliot, and he respects Elliot's work as an artist. The fact that Thad stole one of Elliot's awls —"

"You think he would take it that personally?" I gave Langston a careful look and was just in time to see him put one hand on Elliot's shoulder. "You're right," I admitted.

"Langston feels things deeply, and he might be offended that Thad took the awl. But if that's the case, he wouldn't have turned around and used the awl as the murder weapon. That would be a worse sacrilege than stealing it."

Kaz raised one shoulder. "It might have been the only weapon around."

"Maybe." It was as much as I was willing to concede.

"Then there's Chase," Kaz told Stan, discreetly glancing toward where Chase and Gloria Winston had their heads together. "Rival Western collector. And he's never had one good thing to say about Thad."

Stan narrowed his eyes and gave Chase the once-over, from the top of his Stetson to the tips of his black pigskin cowboy boots. "Seems a good-enough reason to me. These button collectors, they're a crazy bunch, you know." He elbowed me in the ribs, just so I'd know he was kidding.

"Then how about Daryl?" Since Kaz's eyes were gleaming when he said this, I felt perfectly justified in turning away and pretending I was inspecting the nearby tray of grilled asparagus wrapped in prosciutto. "He lied to the cops, and they sent Jo in to prove it."

"Good work, kiddo." Stan was drinking

seltzer water, and he raised his glass in my direction. "I always said you would have made a good cop."

I made a face. "Not good enough to figure out what's really going on around here."

"You will." Further down the table, a woman scooped up the last of the baked brie, and since Stan took his job as helper seriously, he went to take away the empty platter and get another one from the back room to replace it.

No sooner had he left than Helen took his place. "Lovely, dear." She patted my arm. "Just lovely. With the way things are going for you at this conference, I suppose all we can do is hope no one gets food poisoning."

It wasn't funny. But then, she wasn't trying to be.

"So far, we're doing OK," I told her, and whispered a prayer that our luck would hold. "Now if we could only find those missing buttons."

She gave me another pat. "Not to worry. These things have a way of sorting themselves out."

I hoped she was right.

"Talkin' about the murder investigation?" Chase Cadell joined us. He was drinking a can of beer. "Josie here thinks maybe I'm the one who killed that old rattlesnake Wyant."

"Did you?" Leave it to Kaz not to beat around the bush.

Chase slapped him on the back. "I sure hope you're gonna be the assistant to the chair of the next button conference," he said, throwing his head back and laughing. "You are really somethin'. Helen, you keep this young fella in mind as your number-two man." Apparently, the fact that I was confused by the comment didn't fail to register with Chase. He turned my way. "Ain't you heard, Josie? Since hers went so smoothly last year, and yours has been . . . well, you know . . . There's talk of making Helen the chair of the next conference, no matter where it's held."

"Well, that would just be silly," Helen chirruped. "I'm not the only one who can run a conference."

"They say you're the only one who can run one well. Beggin' your pardon for mentioning it, Josie, but you're a smart woman, and my guess is you've heard the grumblin'. They say Helen here is the best there is, and if we were smart, we should have just stuck with her."

"Silly. That's what it is." Helen's cheeks were as pink as the carnations on her print blouse. "And shame on you for even mentioning it, Chase. Josie's done a wonderful job with the conference. Well, as wonderful as anyone can when so many things have gone wrong."

"There are some people who think she's wonderful, anyway." This comment came from Kaz, and believe me, I knew he wasn't talking about himself. In fact, he was looking toward the back of the shop, where Daryl was standing near a display of tortoiseshell buttons. I was just in time to see him tuck his phone in the pocket of that all-too-familiar plaid sport coat and turn to walk toward the front of the store — directly for me.

"Courage!" His smile told me Kaz didn't take this nearly as seriously as I did. "If this Daryl character gives you a hard time —"

He didn't. In fact, though I could have sworn he was going to come over and talk to me, Daryl zoomed right past and out the front door.

"Thank goodness." I breathed a sigh of relief. That is, until I looked outside and saw that Daryl had walked a little ways down the sidewalk and was talking to someone who stood just outside the mouth of the alley that led back to the tiny courtyard I shared with the building next door.

300

It was nearly dark, and the shadows there were thick. I edged closer to the front display window for a better look, but thanks to the glare of the lights in the shop and the reflections in the window, all I could tell was that whoever Daryl was talking to, it was someone small. Small and gray.

An electric shock shot through my body, and I plopped the glass of wine I hadn't had a chance to drink on the nearest table, excused myself, and headed for the door.

By the time I got out there, Daryl and Beth Howell were nowhere around — and there was only one place they could have gone.

Just after I'd opened the shop, the merchant next door approached me with the idea to put a little courtyard in the small open space between our buildings and the ones on the street behind us. There wasn't much to our little urban oasis, just the red brick walkway I followed to the tiny patio surrounded by a number of potted annuals that were quickly fading in the close-to-autumn weather. That, and a park bench. There was also a single post light, and in its soft glow, I saw Beth Howell, her eyes wide and her mouth open.

Was she going to curse me for finally tracking her down? Or call out a warning?

I never had a chance to find out.

But then, that was because something smashed into the back of my head, and the world went black.

CHAPTER SIXTEEN

I have no idea how long I was out. I only know that when I finally woke up, the first person I saw was Kaz. At least I thought it was Kaz. It was a little hard to tell, thanks to the pyrotechnic display going on inside my head.

"Jo? Are you all right? What happened?"

Yeah, that was Kaz, all right. I'd recognize the voice anywhere, even if the thread of panic in it was unfamiliar. Maybe he realized there were stars shooting across my line of vision because he leaned down until his nose was just a couple inches from mine. In the dim glow of the post light, I saw that his face was drawn with worry.

"Don't move," he said when I tried, and to make sure I stayed put, he put his right hand on my shoulder. "You came outside, and we got worried when you didn't come back in after a while. Damn!" His bit his lower lip to control his anger. "If only I'd checked sooner. Don't worry, though, everything is under control. Helen's in there keeping the cocktail party going like clockwork, and Stan's calling the cops and an ambulance."

"Don't . . . need . . . ambulance." Even to me, my voice sounded like it came from the end of a long, dark tunnel. I squeezed my eyes shut against the pain that racketed through my head, and while I was at it, I grabbed Kaz's left hand and twined my fingers through his.

One.

Two.

Three.

I took a series of slow, deliberate breaths, anchoring myself to consciousness courtesy of the feel of my hand in Kaz's.

"There's no blood." I wasn't thinking clearly enough to wonder about this, but I was grateful for the information anyway. When I opened my eyes, I saw Kaz was leaning over and trying to see as much of the back of my head as he could without actually moving me. "Your pupils aren't dilated, either." He double-checked by staring into my eyes. "They're supposed to be dilated, right? I mean, if you have a concussion?"

If I ever knew, I'd forgotten that particular

bit of trivia in the wake of the clunk on the head.

"Daryl," I squeaked.

Kaz sat back, his face twisted with disbelief. "At a time like this, you're thinking about Daryl? Give me a break! You're not actually attracted to the guy, are you?"

I would have laughed if I had the strength, and if I wasn't convinced that if I did, my head would split open and my brain would go bouncing through the courtyard. "Daryl was here," I said, because I wasn't sure how head injuries affect people and I wanted to be sure to mention it — right then and there — before I forgot. "With Beth Howell."

Of course, this didn't mean a whole bunch to Kaz. I was aware enough to know that. Kaz wasn't in on the details of the case. Not like Nev.

Nev . . .

Did I float off again? I guess so, because the next time I drifted to consciousness, Nev was the first person I saw. As if he'd been tugging at it, his hair stood on end, and he was wearing jeans, a Cubs T-shirt, and sneakers. He was pacing behind two paramedics, who were kneeling on either side of me, and in front of Stan and Kaz, who were standing side by side and peering at me, talking quietly, and looking concerned.

"You probably shouldn't move her, right?" Nev leaned over the shoulder of one of the paramedics. "I mean, it could be dangerous to move a person who's been injured before you know what happened, right? Isn't that true?"

"We're cool, Detective." That same paramedic wasn't just cool; he was cucumber-like, and his even voice and steady tone sent a message Nev obviously didn't get.

He leaned over the other guy's shoulder. "Can you tell if she's OK?" Nev demanded. "Can you tell what happened?"

The first time I tried to speak, the words refused to come, so I ran my tongue over my lips and gave it another go. Success! The words scraped out of me. "You could ask me. Somebody came up behind me . . . hit me over the head."

"Don't talk." Nev wedged his way past one paramedic, and the man had no choice but to give ground. Nev knelt beside me and clutched my hand, but because there was one of those blood-pressure monitors on one of my fingers, that wasn't the best plan. The monitor fell off, the paramedic repositioned it, and while he did, Nev grabbed my other hand.

The paramedic checked the meter. "Her vitals are fine," he said, and backed off. "She's gonna have one heck of a headache and some bruises from hitting the ground, but other than that, she'll be OK. Take it easy, though. Don't push."

Nev turned back to me. In the halo of light, I could see his face, and it didn't reveal the telltale signs of worry. Not like Kaz's had. In fact, if it wasn't for the way he clutched my hand like there was no tomorrow, I wouldn't have known Nev was upset at all. His eyes were unreadable. His expression, stone. When he asked, "What happened?" his voice was as hard-edged as a knife.

I'd told Kaz. At least I had a fuzzy memory of telling Kaz. Something about Daryl. And a mouse. Since Kaz and Stan were busy talking and I didn't have the energy to interrupt them, I knew I'd have to do my best and try to call up the memory again on my own.

"I came outside," I told Nev, "because . . ." There was a very good reason, and I struggled to recall it. "Oh, yeah." When I tried for a smile, it made me wince, and the closest paramedic helped me sit up and held an ice pack to the back of my head.

Before I could lose myself in the wondrous

sensation of lessening pain, I forced myself to stick with my story.

"Daryl," I said.

"You want Daryl here?" Nev's mouth twisted, and he sat back on his heels. "I can try to locate him if that's what you really want. Are you telling me . . . Are you actually attracted to the guy?"

There was a lesson to be learned here. I think it had something to do with guys and ego, but since I wasn't exactly thinking straight, it was kind of hard to know for sure. I promised myself I'd think about it later when my head had cleared and supernovas weren't bursting behind my eyes, and I did my best to make myself understood.

"Daryl was here," I said, and because even with my head pounding, I knew that wasn't enough to satisfy a Chicago detective, I added, "He was here at the shop, at the cocktail party. Ask Stan and Kaz; they'll tell you. He was looking at buttons. Tortoiseshell," I added, because for some reason I could not explain, this seemed particularly important. "But then he got a phone call, and he stepped outside. When I looked out the window — you know, the front display window — he was standing on the sidewalk. He was talking to Beth Howell."

Apparently, even said detective could be caught off guard. Nev's blue eyes went wide, and he whistled low under his breath. "Did it look like they knew each other?"

I tried to nod and found out within a nanosecond that this wasn't the best of plans. My brain was in no mood to appreciate movement. "Definitely," I said instead, holding my head very still. "I went outside to see what they were up to, and I couldn't find them. That's when I realized they must have slipped back here into the courtyard."

"And you followed them?"

A dim memory floated through my head, ill-formed and fuzzy. "I must have," I said. "Or I wouldn't be back here right now." Another thought bubbled to the surface. "Yeah, I remember when I got back here, the only one I saw was Beth. She was —"

"Beth Howell attacked you?"

This time I tried to shake my head, and I discovered soon enough that it was no better a move than nodding. "She never came anywhere near me. In fact . . ." Thinking (no easy feat at that particular moment), I squeezed my eyes shut. "She looked as if she was going to warn me about something."

"The knock on the head?"

"I guess so."

"But you didn't see Daryl?"

I thought back over the scene again. "No. I'm sure of it."

"Which means he was probably the one who attacked you."

"I guess." The paramedic took away the ice pack and replaced it with a fresh one, and once again, I took a few moments to sink into the chilly comfort. It gave me a chance to try to make sense of everything that had happened, and when that ended up being a losing cause, I asked Nev, "But why would Daryl want to hurt me? He said he liked me."

Nev got to his feet. The knees of his jeans were dirty, but he didn't make a move to dust them off. "You can be sure I'm going to find out," he said.

The paramedics had said my vitals were fine, so I got up, too. Or at least I tried. When the world wobbled and I swayed with it, Nev grabbed one arm, and Kaz scrambled over to take hold of the other. Honestly, I'm not sure which one slipped his arm around my shoulders to keep me upright; I was too grateful to care.

"You should go to the hospital," Kaz said.

"You should go home and go to bed," Nev suggested.

I glanced his way. "I'd rather go with you

when you question Daryl."

"Who said anything about questioning Daryl?"

OK, so it wasn't actually a lie, since he never had said anything about interrogating Daryl, but it was borderline. And he wasn't very good at even twisting the truth that much; a muscle jumped at the base of his jaw. "If you think he did this . . ."

"If I find out he did . . ."

"If *I* find out he did . . ."

The impassioned version of that comment came from Kaz.

The other one — more steely and all the more intimidating because of it — was delivered by Nev. "If you find out he did . . ."

Slowly and carefully, I looked Nev's way.

He met my eyes before he finished his sentence. "That will be a good thing. Because then you might find out more about why someone stole the Geronimo button, then threw it away. And who killed Brad."

I don't know how these things work, but I do know that by the time we got back to the hotel and were standing outside Daryl's room, Nev had a warrant in hand. I guess that was just in case Daryl was smart and had hightailed it out of town before the cops caught up to him and then Nev could legally search his room.

Then again, maybe Daryl wasn't all that smart. When Nev rapped on the door and identified himself, we heard the sounds of shuffling from inside.

Have I mentioned that Nev is tall and as sleek as a habitual runner? Maybe so, but let it be noted, he can sure pack a punch. Rather than wait to see if Daryl would man up and answer it, he kicked open the door, and he and the two uniformed cops who'd come along for backup raced into the room, guns drawn.

We'd left Kaz and Stan back at the Button Box to give my excuses, host the tail end of the reception, and close up, and I had strict orders to stay out of the way, so I stood back against a wall in the hallway while all this was going on. Fine by me. Though I wouldn't have admitted it to Nev for a million dollars, my legs were rubbery, and if I moved too fast, the world bounced and blurred in front of my eyes. I might be nosy enough to insist on being in on the interview with Daryl, but I am not dumb, and I'm certainly not a risk taker. I was all for taking it slow and easy.

It wasn't until I heard the cops give the all clear and Nev tell me it was OK that I entered Daryl's room.

I was just in time to see Nev slapping handcuffs on a guy I'd never seen before. He was Daryl's height, Daryl's weight, and in fact, he was wearing the same dorky orange-and brown-plaid sport coat Daryl had worn to the cocktail party at the Button Box earlier in the evening. But believe me when I say that this guy was no Daryl.

He was clean-shaven, blond, and oh, have I mentioned, incredibly gorgeous? His face was all planes and angles. His eyes were green like oak leaves in summer. He had a dimple in his chin that made him look delicious — and dangerous — all at the same time.

My heart skipped a beat at the same time my brain wondered if that whack on the head had shaken lose my ability to think straight.

And not just because I was immediately smitten.

It was Nev, and the handcuffs, and the stranger that had me confused.

"Where . . . ?" Apparently, the man was someone who needed subduing, and now that the cuffs were on him, I dared to take a step closer. "What happened to Daryl?"

"Really?" When he looked my way, Nev raised his eyebrows. "A woman as perceptive as you doesn't get it?"

"A woman as perceptive as me . . ."

Maybe it was because of what happened back at the Button Box. Maybe that's why I couldn't make any sense of what he said.

That is, until the hunk's left eye twitched.

Inside my battered brain, the pieces clicked, and my breath caught in my throat. "Daryl?"

One of the uniformed cops had been digging through a suitcase on the dresser opposite the bed. He came out holding a dark wig, and I bet anything there was a pair of Coke-bottle glasses and colored contact lenses in there, too. He tossed a wallet to Nev, who flipped it open and looked at the driver's license inside.

"You mean Donovan," Nev said.

Chalk one up for post-traumatic stress. My knees gave way, and my breath whooshed out of my lungs. I sank down onto the bed. It was that, or end up nose to floor.

I stared at the handsome hunk in the dorky clothes. "Donovan Tucker the documentary filmmaker?"

I guess now that his cover was blown, Daryl . . . er, Donovan . . . was free to be his real self, and that real self was suave and as cocky as a college athlete. "Boy, do I have one hot film on my hands this time," he crowed. "Crazy button collectors *and* a murder. I'm going to Cannes with this one! Detective . . ." He looked at Nev. "Look this way, OK? And talk really loud. I'd hate to miss one word of this."

I guess he'd have to find another way to immortalize us. But then, that was because Nev reached over and snatched away the tiny video-recording device that had been attached to Donovan's lapel.

The recorder I'd never even noticed all those times he leaned in close and asked me questions about buttons and collectors and . . . gulp . . . told me how much he liked me.

My stomach swooped.

"You lied to us? About being a button collector?" Let's face it, certain things are way more important than Cannes. This was one of them. The button community is close-knit, and there's not a more dependable, honest, and knowledgeable bunch any-where. We help each other out. We trust each other. And to think that this snake in the grass . . .

I swallowed the lump in my throat. "You came to the conference to make fun of us?"

"To get the truth." Gorgeous or not, there was something about the smile on Donovan's face that made me want to smack it off. "If the people who appreciate my films find the truth about button collecting — and button collectors — funny, that's beyond my control." He tried for a nonchalant shrug, but since his hands were cuffed behind his back, he flinched, then made it look as if it was no big deal. "My art is all about honesty," he crooned.

"And you're all about being sneaky and underhanded." I bounded to my feet, then decided sitting was a better option. I dropped back down on the bed. "How could you lie to so many people?"

Apparently, Nev was not as concerned about the button community as I was. "And why did you attack Ms. Giancola?" he asked Donovan.

"Did I?" Another of those sizzling smiles, and this time, I could tell Nev had had enough; his fists clenched, he backed away.

"She saw you outside the Button Box," Nev pointed out.

"But did she see me in the courtyard? Did she see me hit her?" When neither of us answered, Donovan smiled. "No, I didn't think so. In fact —"

One of the cops eyed a big closed suitcase, which was lying near the foot of the bed, and Donovan darted a look his way, then forced his gaze back to Nev. "What was I saying? Oh yes, I was reminding you that anyone could have been in that courtyard."

It was my turn. "How do you even know it happened in the courtyard if you weren't involved? And what do you mean by anyone?" I asked him. "You mean anyone like Beth Howell?"

Anther shrug. Another wince. Another twitch, and a fleeting look toward that same cop, who had now lifted the suitcase and plunked it on the bed.

Donovan forced his gaze away from the cop and back to me. "Who?"

"You're a lousy liar," I told him.

"And it's a good thing you just film movies rather than try to star in them. You're a terrible actor, too." Nev strolled closer to the bed. "What's in the suitcase?" he asked Donovan.

He ran his tongue over his lips. "Just the usual stuff. Clothes and toiletries and nothing."

"You mean something." Nev stepped that way. "Or you wouldn't look so nervous every time you glance that way."

"It's buttons. Go figure." The cop who'd lifted the suitcase had also opened it, and he pulled out two button trays. Each had only one button on it.

Buttons that looked awfully familiar.

This time, I threw caution to the wind, and not caring how much the floor tipped and the walls closed in on me, I got to my feet.

Nev and I got to the suitcase at the same time.

I looked at the white pearl buttons attached to the mat boards, and my breath caught in my throat. "It's —" I pointed. "They're —"

Nev nodded. "They sure are," he said. He had slipped on a pair of latex gloves, so he could take the trays from the cop's hand, and turned to Donovan with them. "You want to explain?"

Donovan blinked, and I swear, the color in that gorgeous face of his didn't fade bit by bit; it washed out in a flash. More blinking, and he trembled. "My goodness!" His smile wasn't any more steady than his shoulders. "How did those get in there?"

"That's a very good question." Nev's voice was steel. So was the look he tossed Donovan's way. "Maybe you can think about your answer when we take you down to the station and book you for attempted murder."

"Murder?" I didn't think he could get any paler, but in a heartbeat, Donovan went waxy. "I didn't —"

"You assaulted Ms. Giancola. And she could have been killed. In my book —"

"But I didn't mean —"

"I don't know that, do I?" Nev narrowed his eyes and stared at Donovan with a look that went right through him. "Now, if you would like to explain yourself . . ."

"There's nothing . . . nothing to tell." Donovan's knees were shaking, and he dropped into the chair next to the desk by the window.

"There obviously is." This was me talking, and not even a look from Nev that told me I was probably better off keeping my mouth shut could have stopped me. Then again, I had already found the Geronimo button in the hotel trash. And now I was looking at two more. That kind of confusion tends to throw a button collector a little off-kilter.

"One and only," I said, talking out loud. "There's only one one and only Geronimo button. And you have two. And if you got them from Brad . . ." My mouth fell open, but then, like I'd told Nev earlier, I never really thought of Daryl/Donovan as a murderer. Yet he had the buttons that should have been the button, and if he got them from Brad, who we'd thought was Thad . . .

Yeah, I know; it confused even me.

"No doubt we'll find Brad Wyant's fingerprints on these cardboard mats," Nev said.

Donovan did a little more blinking. "Who's Brad?"

Leave it to Nev to be cool, calm, and collected. He leaned back against the TV armoire. "Brad Wyant was the man you thought was Thad Wyant. You know, the man you killed down in the laundry room," he said.

"Killed? Me? No!" Tears slipped down Donovan's cheeks, and he gulped in long, shaky breaths. "I never killed anybody. I just . . . I just . . ." He sobbed. "You've got to believe me! I was just trying to protect my mother!"

CHAPTER SEVENTEEN

Nev's a smart cop, and he wasn't taking any chances. Rather than let Donovan Tucker spill the beans right then and there, Nev knew it was wiser to get him to the station, where whatever Donovan was going to say — and however he was going to explain that comment about his mother — could be video recorded.

That explains why, less than an hour after Donovan dropped the bombshell, I was standing on the outside of the one-way mirror that looked into the interrogation room, where Nev sat across a gray metal table from Donovan.

"You're sure you don't want an attorney?" Like I said, Nev was smart. Dotted i's. Crossed t's.

Donovan shook his head. "I haven't done anything wrong."

"What about the assault on Ms. Giancola?"

Donovan's lower lip trembled. "It's not like I've ever hit anybody over the head before. I didn't realize . . ." He sniffed. "I'm sorry. Please, tell her that for me. Since she was at the hotel with you, I'm guessing she wasn't seriously hurt. But I knocked her out." He gulped so hard, I saw his Adam's apple jump. "You see it in movies all the time, but I didn't think I could actually do that. Not with just a bump on the head."

Oh yeah, he sounded plenty sincere. But I could tell Nev wasn't buying it. His gaze never leaving Donovan's face, he sat back and cocked his head.

"Back at the hotel, you mentioned your mother. What's her name?"

Donovan wiped a tear off his cheek. "Jenny Tucker."

Who?

I could see a dim reflection of myself in the glass, and the me looking back at me was clearly confused, nose wrinkled and mouth pulled up at one corner.

Like anybody could blame me? I'd been expecting Donovan to name Beth Howell because . . . Well, because it wouldn't explain everything, but it would at least explain why he'd been outside the Button Box with her and why she wasn't around by the time Stan and Kaz found me in the courtyard.

"Who's Jenny Tucker?" I asked under my breath at the same time Nev voiced the same question to Donovan.

He ran a hand through his golden hair. "You know her as Beth Howell."

"Aha!" This was me, of course, because Nev was way too professional for that kind of response.

He made a note on the legal pad on the table in front of him. "And why is Jenny Tucker going under an assumed name?" he asked.

Donovan shrugged. He was still wearing that goofy orange-and-brown-plaid sport coat, and on a guy as incredibly handsome as he was, it looked like somebody's warped version of a Halloween costume. I suppose in a lot of ways, that's exactly what it was. "Mom wasn't sure if the list of registered attendees would be published before the start of the conference. When she signed up, she didn't want to use her real name and take the chance that Thad Wyant might see it."

Nev tapped his pen against the pad in a sort of Morse code message that told Donovan that although it was a start, that wasn't nearly enough of an explanation.

The rapping got to Donovan in no time

323

flat. He drew in a long breath and let it out slowly. Inside that oh-so-not-chic sport coat, his shoulders sagged. "You see," he said, "Thad Wyant is . . . Well, I guess I should say *was*. Thad Wyant was my father."

Whoa!

I actually jumped back, and though I was sure Nev was just as surprised by this news as I was, I was amazed that he managed to keep his poker face in place. He took a note before he glanced up at Donovan. "Explain."

Donovan's mouth puckered. "There's not much to explain, Detective. Unless you're not familiar with the birds and the bees?"

Something told me he was going for funny. It was the same something that told me he should have known better.

A police interrogation room is the last place for trying out one-liners.

Apparently, Nev felt the same way. As if he was moving in slow motion, he got to his feet, his hands braced against the table. He leaned down so that his nose was even with Donovan's, and though the sound from the speaker in there was crystal clear, I had to strain to hear Nev.

"Attempted murder isn't funny," he growled, and I learned a lesson. Even a guy in a Cubs T-shirt could be intimidating. If it was the right guy. "Neither is the real thing. And right now, Mr. Tucker, you're looking good for both."

Donovan's bravado melted like an iceberg in tropical waters. "M . . . m . . . my mother used to be a button collector," he stammered. "She . . . she met Thad thirty-six years ago at a button conference, and they had a fling. When she told him she was pregnant, he said she must be mistaken, that there was no way the baby — me — that there was no way I could be his son. Like I said, that was thirty-six years ago, and after I was born, well, she says she tried contacting him, but he was such a hermit, she could never find him. Then she heard about this convention and how he was coming to be the guest of honor. She saw this as her opportunity to finally confront Thad, face-to-face."

"Which explains their showdown on the lake cruise," I mumbled at the same time Donovan cried out, "That doesn't mean she killed him."

"Nobody said it did." Nev, the voice of reason. "But you've got to admit, she must have been pretty darned angry."

Donovan shrugged. "Who wouldn't be? The scumbag ran out on her when she needed him the most. He refused to acknowledge me as his kid. All she wanted was what he owed her, what he owed me. You know, back child support. It's not like she wanted that stupid Geronimo button or anything. She just wanted . . . you know . . ."

Nev leaned forward. "I don't."

Another shrug, and by this time, I almost felt sorry for Donovan Tucker. Sure, he was a slimy filmmaker who'd infiltrated our conference for the sole purpose of finding people to poke fun at. And yes, he'd taken a cheap shot (literally) at me that had left me with stars in my eyes and my head feeling as if there were elephants in there doing a Zumba workout. But it was obvious the poor guy was scared to death, and worried about his mom, to boot.

I know . . . I know . . . That didn't mean he wasn't our murderer.

I told myself not to forget it and waited to see what would happen next.

"It was her pride," Donovan said. "Mom just wanted him to admit he was my father so that she could walk away with her pride intact. She wanted what was legally hers. All those payments he'd dodged all these years. On that cruise the first night we were in town, he told her he didn't even remember her. Imagine how that must have hurt her."

Still waters really do run deep, and it turns out Nev had a bit of showman in him. He timed his next comment down to the second. "You know," he said, dropping back into his chair. "You killed the wrong man."

Donovan's mouth dropped open. "What are you talking about? Thad Wyant —"

"Wasn't lying that night on the cruise when he said he didn't know your mother. That's because Thad Wyant — the real Thad Wyant — has been dead for weeks. That was his brother, Brad. He was here in Chicago pretending to be Thad."

"But . . . why?"

"Doesn't much matter, does it?" Nev scribbled another note on his legal pad. Donovan hadn't said anything especially interesting, so I suspected it was a stall tactic.

It worked.

As if the gray plastic padding were on fire, Donovan shifted in his seat. "Whoever he was, I certainly didn't kill him. And my mother didn't, either!"

"She had the perfect motive. Thirty-six years, did you say? Thirty-six years of resentment. And anger. Then we start asking questions, and she lures Ms. Giancola into that courtyard and —"

"No! That was my idea. See . . ." As if

weighing the wisdom of saying anything else, Donovan drew in a long breath and let it out slowly. "I suppose you're going to find out anyway, so I might as well tell you. The night of the banquet, when I went out to the lobby to take that phone call . . . I saw my mom out there."

"Which is why you made up the story about Thad Wyant arguing with a man in a raincoat."

"It is," Donovan admitted. "But that's just because I figured if you were looking for the guy in the raincoat, you'd be too busy to find out about my mom. Just because I lied about that doesn't mean she killed Wyant, though. Just because she was in the lobby the same time he was . . . There were other people in the lobby, too."

His voice was so sincere that even I couldn't fail to catch the drift of what Donovan refused to say. I may not have had the nerve to voice my suspicions. For Nev, it was part of his job description.

"You were trying to divert suspicion because you thought she really had killed Wyant."

Donovan's gaze snapped to Nev. "I may have considered it. Briefly. I mean, it seemed logical. Just for a moment. But then I thought about it and . . . You don't know her. She's not that kind of person."

"But she is the kind of person who's careful to avoid the cops. And who can get talked into leaving town when things start getting hot. That's what she was planning, right?"

"I told you. That was my idea. And she wouldn't have done it at all except . . ." His cheeks got dusky. "You're right. I admit it. I was worried that Mom killed Wyant. She had plenty of reasons. Plenty of good reasons. But it turns out . . ." Donovan looked away. "She couldn't have done it, because it turns out she thought I did."

"Sounds like you had plenty of reason to hate Wyant, too. Did you?"

"Kill him? No. I told you. No. Before that night on the cruise, I didn't even know who my father was. She never told me, see. She said he was a deadbeat. And that she'd met him at some sort of convention. But before I heard them talking on the cruise, I never knew anything more than that."

"So you're innocent. And so is your mother." Nev said it like there was just the vaguest possibility it was true. "So how did you get so wrapped up in this whole thing?"

"Well, there's my film, for one thing." For the first time since they'd walked into the interrogation room, Donovan's eyes glowed with excitement. "I couldn't walk away. Not from something this big. I mean, when I did the brick collectors, sure, that was all like, you've got to be kidding! And it was that way when I made the film about the PEZ collectors, too. But this time, I had the magic combination. Crazy collectors and murder. I had to keep filming. And when Mom called me from outside the Button Box, she told me she was thinking about going to the police. Not to confess or anything. Like I said, she didn't do anything. She just thought she would talk to you guys, you know, and explain about how Thad was my father and . . ." He scraped his hands through his hair.

"I couldn't let that happen," Donovan said. "Not before I finished filming. I had to talk to Mom and convince her to leave town. That's what I was trying to do outside the button shop. Then, when Josie walked into that courtyard, I just reacted. You know? There was a broom nearby; somebody must have been doing cleanup back there. And I just grabbed it and . . . and I clunked Josie over the head. But other than that, honest, I've never hurt another person in my life. I just wanted to help my mother. That's all. I wanted to protect her."

"And before she left, she gave you those

buttons? The ones Brad brought to Chicago with him?"

Donovan nodded.

So did Nev. "She probably figured they were worth a pretty penny, and she could sell them and finally get back some of what she thought Thad owed her."

Donovan fisted his hands and rubbed his eyes. "Maybe. But I don't know how she got those buttons. She didn't tell me. She gave them to me outside the Button Box, said she didn't want the cops to find them, not before she could get them to a lab for testing. There was a little drop of blood on one of the mat boards, see, and my mom, she watches too much TV. She thought she could use it to prove Thad was my father."

Interesting. All of it. But it paled in comparison to Nev's lieutenant walking into the room to join me.

"You're that button expert, right?" He was holding the evidence bags that contained the two sets of buttons and provenance papers we'd also found in Donovan's suitcase. "This ought to be right up your alley. The guys down in the lab, they tell me these babies are phony."

I couldn't sleep that night.

For one thing, Kaz said his nerves were so

shot from being worried about me that he had a couple beers after he and Stan closed up the Button Box. And beer always makes Kaz snore.

Yes, he was on the couch out in the living room of my suite.

Yes, I was in the bedroom, and the door was closed (and just for the record, locked, too).

But there was no way I could sleep with all that noise.

And that didn't even count all the racket inside my head.

Donovan Tucker, his mother, Brad Wyant, phony Geronimo buttons.

If I hadn't had a headache before, I surely would have after Lieutenant Daniel Kane delivered the news.

Not that the buttons themselves were phony. I mean, they were real buttons, obviously, and one look and I knew they were also old.

It was the provenance papers that told the tale.

"The guys at the lab are sure of it." The next morning, Nev and I were talking over coffee in my suite. Unlike Kaz, who'd been up and moving early and had left to go downstairs a half hour before Nev arrived, I hadn't mustered the energy to even get dressed. I'd bet anything I looked like a fright with my hair pulled back in a ponytail and wearing my flannel sleep pants and an old Bears T-shirt. Honestly, I was in no mood to care, and Nev was so intent on discussing the case, I don't think he even noticed.

"The lab techs explained it all had to do with the ink," Nev said, stirring three spoonfuls of sugar into his coffee and downing it fast. "The papers we found in the trash can a couple days ago along with that button, those were the real thing. The paper was old and so was the ink. The other sets — the ones we took out of Donovan Tucker's suitcase last night — are clearly forgeries. Whoever faked them made them look real enough at first glance. But they were printed on paper that's only been manufactured in the last couple years. And the ink is pretty standard stuff for computer printers."

"But the buttons are old." I drummed my fingers against the table. "Of course, that would be no big deal to accomplish. There were millions of MOP shirt buttons made in the nineteenth century. They're a dime a dozen. So we know Jenny Tucker got the buttons and the phony papers — somehow — from Brad."

Nev was just taking a swallow of coffee

when I said this, and with one finger, he signaled me to stop right there. "We picked up Jenny Tucker at the Greyhound station on Harrison Street this morning," he said. "She had a ticket to Omaha in her purse. The guys who found her took her in, so once I get back to the office, I'll question her, and we should be able to get that part of the story straight." This was good news, and both Nev and I knew it. "Even before I take her statement, though, I'm thinking we're on pretty solid ground as to what Brad was up to. Fake buttons and fake papers. That means —"

"He phonied up the provenance papers." I took over the story. "He bought some old buttons to go with them, or found them in Thad's collection, and he came to Chicago to sell as many of the 'real' Geronimo buttons as he could, to as many collectors as he could find who thought they were buying the genuine article."

"But one of them was genuine, or at least the provenance papers were." Nev's reminder made me think about that button and its glorious history and how it had been tossed in the trash, and my stomach soured. "And the others . . . ?"

He was asking for my expert opinion, and I knew it. "There's no way to tell that one old button was on Geronimo's shirt and the others weren't, of course, but Thad Wyant wrote about the Geronimo button in countless articles and in his book on Western buttons. He never said he owned more than one." Looking through everything I could find that Thad Wyant had ever written was one of the things that had kept me from sleeping a wink the night before.

"He was so proud of that button," I told Nev, "that if there was more than one, he would have mentioned it for sure." I'd had a couple sips of my own coffee and — thank goodness — my head was starting to clear. "So there's Thad out in New Mexico, and his brother kills him and assumes his identity. And he must have heard Thad talk about the Geronimo button because it was Thad's claim to fame. And Brad realized he could sell the button and get big bucks for it."

"And that if he had more than one, the bucks would be even bigger."

Nev and I were on the same page, and we signaled it with a look across the table.

"That," I said, warming up my coffee with some from the carafe, "explains the money you found in Brad's room."

"Yup." Finished with his first cup, Nev poured another. When he called to tell me he was stopping by to talk to me this morning, I'd gotten right on the phone with room service and had them bring up some Danish, and he reached for a cherry-cheese pastry with white icing drizzled over it and took a bite. "It might also explain how he ended up dead," he said, while he chewed.

I nodded — slowly, because though my head felt a whole lot better, I wasn't taking any chances. "So Brad checks the list of registered attendees we published, contacts some people, and tells them he's interested in selling the Geronimo button."

"They pay him up front. Cash. As soon as they arrive at the conference. He tells them once he has money in hand, he'll arrange to meet them to deliver the button."

"And that's why he made a note on each of those envelopes. To remind himself where he was supposed to go to deliver each of the buttons. And he delivers two buttons, including, apparently, the real one. But before he can get the other two to the people who bought them, somebody figures out what he's up to."

"And kills him. Over a button!" It wasn't what he said; it was the way he said it, and realizing it, Nev gulped down a mouthful of Danish. "I didn't mean —"

"Sure you did. But don't apologize. I

understand. Unless you've got buttons in your blood, you can't possibly imagine how important the Geronimo button is to collectors. The chance to own that kind of a piece of history . . ." The very thought took my breath away.

While I was trying to get it back, Nev finished off the cherry-cheese Danish and reached for one filled with apricot. Apricot was my favorite; I was glad I'd ordered two. "Notice he didn't ask you if you were interested in buying it."

"I don't specialize in Western buttons."

"Chase Cadell does." We exchanged looks, and I knew Nev would be having a little sit-down with Chase very soon. "I'm also thinking," he said, "that Wyant figured you were too smart to fall for a scheme like his."

Was I? I wondered. If I'd been approached by the man I thought was Thad Wyant and offered the Geronimo button for ten thousand dollars, would I have seen through the scam? Or gone running to my ATM?

"Brad must have made each of his buyers agree to keep the transaction secret," I said, because it was better than trying to get Nev to understand the green-eyed monster of overwhelming button desire. "Otherwise, word of the sale would have gone through the conference like wildfire."

"And he couldn't have let that happen because then he could have only sold to one person."

"So he makes each of them agree to a secret deal, and because he's not taking any chances, he buys a plane ticket to get out of town as soon as the last money's in his hot little hands. Just in case anybody does spill the beans, he'll be long gone, and when the police in Santa Fe come to look for him —"

"They'll find Thad in the freezer, and Brad will be back in California. Only before any of that can happen, somebody kills Brad." Nev was convinced. He pulled out his notebook and clicked open a pen. "Who's that serious about buttons?" he asked.

"Here at the convention? Everybody!"

He scratched the pen against his chin. "That's not very helpful."

"It certainly doesn't narrow down the field."

"Except . . ." Nev's hand hovered over the last apricot Danish, and yeah, I must have flinched or something, because he changed his mind and reached for another cup of coffee instead. "What if you paid ten thousand dollars for something you didn't get?" he asked. "Wouldn't you want your money back?"

"Yeah, if I didn't get a button I was supposed to be buying, and if I bought one, then found out it was a fake."

"Only nobody knows about the fake buttons. Nobody but us. Well, and Brad Wyant, but he's not talking."

I wasn't sure where Nev was headed with this, so I propped my elbows on the table, cupped my chin in my hands, and listened.

"It's like this." Whatever the idea, Nev was warming to it, and he brushed crumbs from his hands and sat up. "We know four people gave Brad ten thousand dollars each. That means that, originally, there must have been four Geronimo buttons he agreed to sell. Or at least what those people thought were Geronimo buttons. One button was found in the trash."

"And you have two more."

Nev nodded. "That means there's one more out there. We might be able to work that angle somehow."

"Except . . ." I was as sure of this as I was that if I didn't move fast on the apricot pastry, I wasn't going to get any, so I grabbed the Danish and took a bite. "The one person who still has the button has no idea that it's not the real Geronimo button. That means that person thinks he — or she — owns a glorious piece of history. So he

— or she — isn't likely to give it up."

"Unless we tell people that all the buttons were phony. And that if they come forward and admit they bought one —"

"They'll get their money back!" This was so brilliant, I almost wished I'd let Nev have the last apricot pastry. Almost. Suddenly, I wasn't feeling so groggy anymore. I got up and hurried into the bedroom to get dressed. I was scheduled to give the remarks at that afternoon's luncheon. And I knew exactly what I was going to talk about.

CHAPTER EIGHTEEN

I got downstairs just as the continental-breakfast crowd was breaking up, and I was headed into the ballroom to check on arrangements for the lunch where I would implement the brilliant plan Nev and I had come up with when Helen hurried over.

"They found them!" I didn't have to ask what she was talking about. It had to be the trays of buttons missing from the contest. I breathed a sigh of relief, but at the same time, I wondered why Helen wasn't beaming. This was good news, indeed, and it sure saved my bacon when it came to my reputation as conference chair. Yet the corners of Helen's mouth were pulled down, and her eyes were narrowed. As if she wasn't quite sure what to make of it.

I guess I could understand. A surprise is a surprise. Even when it's a good one.

In fact, it was the first good news I'd gotten in nearly a week, and I beamed enough for the both of us. "I'm so glad! Who found them? Where were they?"

Baffled, Helen shook her head. "The committee decided the only thing we could do was work with the buttons we had, and we were going to announce the winners at lunch. We were going through the entries one last time, and well . . ." She pressed a hand to her heart. "My goodness, there they were!"

"Right back where they were supposed to be?" OK, I understood now why Helen seemed so confused. I couldn't blame her. This was more than a little weird.

And I wasn't about to question it. I was too grateful.

Helen had always been a stickler for fairness, so I wasn't surprised when she said, "We've got judges looking over the found entries right now. They'll be included in the contest just like they were never gone."

"And you'll announce the winners?" I asked Helen, and I didn't wait for her to answer. She was the judging committee chair, after all, and I was sure by the time lunch was over, she'd be less shocky and more inclined to share the good news.

Feeling (slightly) less worried than I had in days, I headed into the ballroom. There was a tech there from the video company we'd hired to record each of our sessions, and while I had the opportunity, I went over the details of how the DVDs would be available in the vendor room the next morning and how the company would ship a supply to the secretary of our organization for people who wanted to order them via our website. That taken care of, I composed my thoughts and went over in my head what I'd say to the collectors who'd be assembled there for lunch.

The minutes moved like hours. But then, I was anxious to walk up to the podium and make the announcement I knew would galvanize the crowd.

When lunchtime finally rolled around, I was seated at a table at the front of the room, picking my way through a chicken Marsala that was having a hard time getting past the lump in my throat and trying not to look too anxious when I saw Nev slip in through the doors at the back of the room.

I was so on edge, my hands were trembling, and I tucked them in my lap. After all, Kaz was seated there at the committee table with me, and I couldn't let him catch on to what was up. What I had to say had to come as a surprise — to everyone. And all I had to do, I reminded myself, was keep calm and get through the announcement of the button-contest winners.

The moment the thought hit, I cringed. It was no wonder why. The announcement of the winners is usually my favorite part of any button show (well, in addition to the panels, the featured speakers, the vendor room, and the chance to reconnect with friends and customers), and I hated that I was so wrapped up in the investigation that I was wishing the time away.

Buttons.

This was all about the buttons and the dedicated collectors who put so much time and trouble, so much money and sweat equity, in to assembling their most wonderful buttons to show off to their fellow aficionados.

I owed it to those collectors — and to myself — to pay attention and join in the applause as each winner was announced.

"Our next category . . ." Helen was barely taller than the podium. I watched her silvery hair bob behind the microphone. "The next category is ivory buttons. And our winner is . . ." She paused, drawing out the suspense. Or maybe Helen just couldn't find her place in the list of winners on the podium in front of her. That is, until she said, "Gloria Winston."

I sat up like a shot, and dazed and confused, I watched Gloria, shoulders back and head high, march up to the front of the ballroom to receive her prize for first place. Yes, I applauded. Just like everyone else in the ballroom. But all the while, all I could think about was that scene in the ladies' room with Gloria just a couple days earlier and how she'd been so upset about the measle she'd gotten for including a bone button in among her ivory ones.

The measle that had disqualified her tray from the contest.

The tray that had then gone missing.

And was found.

And was now a winner.

Honestly, I didn't know what any of it meant. But I recognize weird when I see it.

And this was weird.

"But how . . ?" I mumbled the words under my breath, then stopped myself. It was bad form to look like I was questioning the results of the contest.

Even though I was questioning the results of the contest.

And apparently, Nev could see that.

Across the ballroom, he gave me a quizzical look that I sloughed off with a (hopefully) casual lift of my shoulders. It was all the time I had to consider the mystery.

345

Helen finished presenting the last of the prizes, and it was my turn to take center stage.

I walked out to the dais, positioned myself behind the microphone, and drew in a breath for courage. "It's been quite an exciting week," I said, and at any other conference, I'm sure the attendees would have smiled at me and nodded and mumbled comments on how much they'd enjoyed this panel or that one, this speaker or that one. But this wasn't any other conference, and nothing about it had been normal. Before they could meet my remark with stony silence, I headed them off at the pass. "That's an understatement," I groaned.

Good move. There was a ripple of laughter from the audience.

"I have to say, when I volunteered to chair this conference, I never thought I'd be dealing with murder. Of course, you all know about that. It's no secret that a horrible event happened here on Monday night. But there are some things about the death of the man you all knew as Thad Wyant that you're not aware of, and before we each go our separate ways tomorrow, I think the least I can do is tell you as much of the truth as I know. I will warn you now: none of it is good news."

Another ripple. This one was more like the rumble of thunder.

"Number one," I said and steeled myself for the reaction I was sure was coming, "Donovan Tucker was here."

The rumble rose to a roar, and I silenced the crowd with a wave of one hand. "There's not much we can do about it now," I told them. "He attended the conference under a false name, he had a hidden camera, and he kept it rolling the whole time. My only consolation is that although he might have been trying to show the world how crazy button collectors are, I don't think he got much of a chance. Our panels have been excellent. Our speakers — every last one of them — were professional and interesting and informative. If Donovan Tucker wants to make fun of that, so be it. My guess is no one who watches his movie — if anyone watches it at all — will agree. What they'll see is some fine, intelligent, and educated people discussing a subject they love, and doing it with style and class."

"You tell 'em, Jo!"

The words of encouragement came form Kaz, who gave me a thumbs-up.

"That's not all," I said, hitting the tough stuff before I lost my momentum. "It's also important that you know something about the death of Thad Wyant. Namely, that the man who was murdered here on Monday was not Thad Wyant."

This time, the roar was a veritable tsunami of noise. Dozens of people called out questions, and the person-to-person murmur lasted so long, I wondered if they'd give me a chance to continue.

I was pretty much assured of it when Kaz put two fingers in his mouth and let out a whistle that broke the sound barrier.

The room fell silent.

"The man who was killed here was actually Brad Wyant, Thad's brother," I told the stunned button collectors. "His murder, like every murder, is a terrible tragedy. But the police tell me the reason he was here in Chicago to begin with . . . Well, it's a pretty ugly story."

I told them how Thad had been killed back in Santa Fe and how Brad had come to our conference with larceny in his heart. Believe me, I had their attention then. One hundred percent.

"Brad Wyant came to Chicago to sell the Geronimo button," I said, and before another cascade of voices could drown me out again, I added quickly, "But the button he was selling as the Geronimo button . . . Well, I'm sorry to report this, but it was all

348

a hoax."

This time I expected the uproar, and I simply waited it out. When it finally ebbed, I got through the rest of what I had to say as quickly as possible.

"The police tell me that four people here at our conference agreed to deal with Brad, thinking they were buying the real Geronimo button. They each paid ten thousand dollars for it. Detective Nevin Riley is in the back of the room." I waved that way, and Nev held up a hand so people could easily identify him. "If you were one of those people who paid Brad Wyant for a button, you can talk to Detective Riley. We're going to be meeting here in the ballroom at four this afternoon, and Detective Riley assures me that if you come forward then and tell him what happened, and if you can prove you paid for what you thought was the Geronimo button, you can get your ten thousand dollars back."

That was it. All I had to say.

I stepped away from the podium and headed right into the service entrance just as the waitstaff was coming the other way, carrying dessert. It was that, or get swallowed up in the crowd that surged forward to ask questions.

I didn't need questions, I needed answers.

And at four o'clock, I intended to find them.

Great plan, right?

Too bad four o'clock came and went — and nobody showed up in the ballroom but me and Nev.

I held out hope. Honest, I did. At least until four thirty. That's when I leaned back in my chair and groaned, "Is police work always this discouraging?"

"Hey, at least we've got nice, comfy chairs to sit in. And iced tea!" The catering manager had brought up a pitcher when we got to the ballroom, and Nev poured himself another glass and topped off mine. "You should see some of the stakeouts I get involved in. Long hours sitting in a police car tend to make me crabby."

I have seen Nev crabby. Which means he's also short-tempered, abrupt, and bristly. I was grateful for the ballroom and the comfy chairs, too.

Except . . .

"Iced tea or no iced tea, we're not getting anywhere." Any more iced tea and I'd burst. I had another sip, anyway.

"After that offer we made to get them their money back, I thought your collectors would come running," Nev commented.

"Button people never do what I expect them to do."

"That's because a lot of collectors care more about their buttons than they do about the money. And yes," I added when I knew he was going to tell me that was just crazy, "it does sound odd. But a collector's reputation . . . Well, that might be more important to that person than getting his or her money back."

He cocked his head, considering this. "Who?" he asked.

I shrugged and let out a laugh. "Everybody. I've told you that before. Everybody who comes to a conference —"

"But who fits that bill and had the opportunity to kill Brad Wyant?"

I knew what he was getting at and considered the possibilities. "Donovan Tucker and his mother were out in the lobby at the right time," I said. "And Helen was late for the banquet, and Langston was in the vendor room. I know that, because I ran into him when I went after Helen. Chase was in the ballroom, and talk about somebody who would care more about his reputation than about money!"

"Anybody else?"

"Well . . ." Something had been niggling at the back of my mind since lunchtime,

351

and I'd hesitated to mention it because it seemed so silly. "It's probably nothing," I told Nev.

"It could be something."

"But it doesn't have anything to do with Brad's murder."

"Anything that we know of."

I gave in with a sigh. "It's the contest. And Gloria's ivory buttons. She got a measle, see." Nev's eyebrows rose, and I explained how Gloria had been disqualified and why. "So how did that button get changed on her tray?" I asked.

"And why?"

I waved away Nev's question. "The why is the easy part. If Gloria's the one who did it."

His eyes lit. "We could ask her."

Apparently, button dealers aren't made for stakeouts, even ones that include comfy chairs and iced tea. Just the thought of getting out of the ballroom and on to something where we were actually doing something other than just sitting around and waiting cheered me no end. I jumped out of my chair at the same time Nev stood. "It's the last full day of the conference, and like all serious collectors, I'd bet Gloria is in the vendor room."

We got there in record time, and I glanced

around at the three dozen or so vendor tables and the hustle and bustle going on all around us. The last day of any button show is always busy with people wheeling and dealing and hoping the buttons they've been coveting since early in the week are still there, and maybe available now at a better price.

Before I had a chance to spot Gloria Winston, Langston caught my eye. He gave Elliot instructions before he walked away from his booth and strolled over. "Any luck?" he asked.

"With getting people in to get their money back?" Of course it was what he was talking about. Langston is one of the most intelligent people I know, and that means he's naturally curious. "You'd think it was an offer they couldn't refuse," I said.

He lifted his shoulders in an elegant gesture. "You'd think."

"Have you seen Gloria?"

Langston is taller than me, and he glanced around the room. "A while ago. She was at the booth next to mine, saying something to the dealer there about getting more ivory buttons. But I don't think he was interested in dealing. Not for the price she wanted to pay."

"And now?"

Langston looked around again. "It's too crowded in here to see clearly, but you could try near the far doors. There are a couple big women standing over there." He craned his neck. "I can't tell if one of them is Gloria."

I thanked him and headed that way. I'd just dodged around a woman carrying two shopping bags when I bumped into Helen and nearly bowled her over.

"I'm so sorry." When she jumped back and swayed, I put a hand on her shoulder to steady her. "I was looking for Gloria and —"

"No problem. Really." Helen glanced away. She'd been digging through a poke box, and she tucked her hands in the pockets of her white jacket. Definition time: at shows, vendors usually put out a box of miscellaneous odds and ends of inexpensive buttons for collectors to poke through. Poke-box buttons usually sell for less than a dollar each and are generally worth about that much or less. Sure, it's fun to poke, especially for a new collector, who isn't sure yet which buttons to specialize in. For experienced collectors like Helen —

I couldn't help myself. I took a long, hard look at the top layer of the buttons in that poke box. If Helen was looking through it, she might have heard a rumor about some valuable button having inadvertently been dropped in there. Like button collectors everywhere, it was hard for me to ignore the siren's call of an overlooked treasure.

"You're holding out on me." I was teasing — and fishing for information just in case there was something in that box I would love to get my hands on. "What are you up to, Helen?"

"Nothing. Really. Just looking around one last time. I really need to get back to my room and pack and . . . and I'll see you later, Josie."

Who would have thought a senior citizen could walk away that fast?

"What?" I asked a couple minutes later when Nev found me looking through that poke box.

He leaned over my shoulder. "You're supposed to be looking for Gloria Winston."

It was my turn to look as mortified as Helen had when I found her midpoke. "Oh, yeah, Gloria . . ." There was nothing unusual in the box after all — a whole lot of MOPs, some black-glass buttons that were pretty but hardly valuable, a couple realistics that I knew I already owned — nothing I could turn around and sell at the Button Box, and nothing I couldn't live without in my own collection, so I walked away.

That was when my phone rang.

I checked caller ID and gave Nev a questioning look. "Daryl? I mean Donovan. Why isn't he —"

"Out on bail," Nev said, just as I answered and listened to the words that rushed out of Daryl.

"Now?" I said in response. "You need me to come up to your room now?"

"I think it's important," Donovan said. "I caught something one day when I was filming, and I don't know if it's important or not, but I think you should see it. Of course . . ." Now that he was out of police custody, the edge of cockiness was back in his words. "If you're not comfortable coming here, I could always come to your room."

Yeah, like that was going to help.

Or make me forget that this was the same guy who'd whacked me over the head with a broom handle.

What was that about a siren's call?

I guess the chance of learning more about the mystery that had all our brains in a muddle was just as strong as button desire.

I signaled to Nev that he needed to come along with me and told Donovan I'd be right there.

CHAPTER NINETEEN

I wanted all the answers, and by the time we were done in Donovan's room, I still didn't have them. Oh, I had another piece of the puzzle, all right. But the picture still wasn't in focus.

There was only one way I could think to make things come clear.

I made some phone calls and issued a few special invitations. That evening at the Button Box, I said. Seven o'clock. I told my guests I wanted to thank each of them personally for helping me out at the conference.

I was there at six thirty, and though Stan had already closed the shop for the day, I'd called to tell him what I was up to, and he insisted on staying around. Just in case Nev needed backup, he said. I invited Kaz, too, and yes, it was against my better judgment, but he had just about as much stake in the results of this investigation as I did. After all, he'd picked up the slack as my assistant when I'd been forced to concentrate on the case.

A few minutes before seven, we were ready. As we'd done at the end of the last case I'd helped Nev investigate, we arranged chairs in a loose circle in the center of the shop. Nev and I talked about the things I was going to tell my guests — including the huge surprise I hadn't revealed at the luncheon that day — and he took up his position in the back room, the better to let the folks I'd invited think they could speak freely, without a law-enforcement official there to listen. Or slap on the cuffs.

Deep breaths.

One last look to make sure everything was in order.

And my guests arrived.

Donovan and Jenny Tucker showed up first, and I hoped that when the button collectors got there and realized who he was, I could keep them from wringing Donovan's neck. Then again, if he opened his mouth and said stupid things about film and honesty and how he was immortalizing button collectors so people could laugh at us, I decided he was on his own.

Langston, Chase, Helen, and Gloria shared a cab and showed up together.

As one, they stopped just inside the door and aimed death looks at Donovan. How did they know Mr. Hunk was the nerd from our convention? It was that same, damned sport coat, of course. Apparently, good looks and a sense of style do not go hand in hand.

"You can deal with him later," I promised, ushering them to their seats. "After I'm done talking to all of you."

"Talking?" Helen glanced around the shop. Stan had done a great job of getting everything cleaned up from the cocktail party the night before. The shelves and displays were back in order and back in place. The appetizer tables and the make-shift bar were gone.

"But I thought this was a kind of party," Helen said. "When you called, you said you wanted to —"

"Thank you. Yes. That's exactly what I said, and it's what I want to do." I took my place at the portion of the circle nearest the front door. It wasn't like I expected them to make a break for it, and I certainly didn't think I could stop them if they tried. It just seemed like the best place to stand.

There was no use beating around the bush, so I got right down to business. "I want to thank you by offering you the truth," I said. "And the truth begins with the fact that you're all suspects in Brad Wyant's death."

"Don't be ridiculous!" Gloria sniffed.

"You're plum out of yer mind," Chase hollered.

"I didn't do it." Jenny Tucker clutched her hands over her heart. "I wish I did. I swear, I wish I'd had the nerve. But I didn't kill him."

I shushed them by holding out my hands. "I kind of figured you'd all say that. But if we look at this thing objectively . . . well . . . there's been a whole lot happening this week, and it's taken me a while to figure out that some of it is related to Brad's death and some of it isn't. The trick has been getting everything sorted out. What it comes down to, of course, are those phony Geronimo buttons."

"Told you the guy was a no-good snake in the grass," Chase rumbled.

"You did," I admitted. "But let's not forget that the man who tried to swindle people here at the conference wasn't Thad Wyant. I didn't know him, but I've been rereading everything he ever wrote about the Geronimo button, and I think I can say this — Thad loved that button too much to ever part with it. No, it was Brad's idea to sell phony buttons, start to finish. What I couldn't figure out, though, is why no one who paid him would come forward to ask for their money back. It didn't click right away. Not until . . ." I swung around to face Gloria. "Not until this afternoon, when you accepted the first-place prize in the ivory-button category."

Gloria's shoulders shot back. "I don't see what that has to do with —"

"Everything," I said, interrupting because I was in no mood for more deception and lies. "You said it yourself, Gloria, that afternoon when you were so upset about getting a measle on your tray. You said if people found out you'd been careless, that you hadn't done your research and you weren't the expert you pretended to be, you said they'd think less of you, that they'd stop inviting you to speak at meetings and conferences. That's why you did it, Gloria. That's why you stole the trays from the contest."

Her jaw dropped. Her mouth opened and closed. "You can't possibly know —" Gloria bit off the rest of what she was going to say.

But that was enough to confirm my suspicion. "You did it so you could switch out the bone button on your tray for an ivory button, so you wouldn't be disqualified. You couldn't stand the thought that anyone would see a measle on your tray."

"Honestly!" This was Helen, so filled with outrage that her voice was shrill. "Cheating in a button contest. It's unheard of!"

"It's not like I hurt anyone." Gloria folded her beefy arms over her ample chest. Her chins wobbled. "If anyone found out I'd made such a stupid mistake . . . I couldn't let that happen." She was not an attractive woman, and the gaze she leveled at the people gathered in the Button Box was anything but friendly. "If any one of you opens your mouth and word of this gets out —"

"What are you going to do, Gloria?" Langston demanded. "Kill all of us, just like you killed Brad Wyant?"

"I never did." Gloria leaped from her chair. She was nearly as tall as Langston and had at least a good sixty pounds on him, and I didn't even like to think what would happen if things got to the smackdown stage. Good thing Kaz kept a level head and got up, gently putting a hand on Gloria's arm and guiding her back to where she belonged.

"Well, I certainly didn't kill him." Langston picked a piece of lint from his impeccable gray pants and flicked it away.

"Though I will admit . . ." When he reached into the breast pocket of his houndstooth jacket, his lips were as puckered as if he'd just bit into a lemon. He brought out his checkbook. "I've got the receipt for the bank withdrawal here. I'll admit it, Josie. I was one of the people who agreed to buy the Geronimo button."

I breathed a silent prayer of thanksgiving. Finally, we were getting somewhere!

Rather than let anyone know how relieved I was that my little scheme was working, I kept my voice even. "I thought so," I said. "But then, that's because I know how smart you are, Langston. You knew a good business deal when you saw one."

"That's exactly what it was." The look Langston threw around the circle wasn't exactly condescending. After all, he depended on button collectors for his livelihood. It was more perceptive and just a little sympathetic. "I wasn't as enamored of that button as the rest of you. But then, I don't have buttons in my blood. When the man I thought was Thad Wyant contacted me and asked if I was interested, I said I was. I gave him my money, but I never got the button. He was supposed to show it at the banquet on Monday night, and he didn't want anyone to be suspicious. We were going to meet on Tuesday morning, and he was going to turn the button over to me then."

"And you were going to sell it to the first person you found who would up the ante."

In response to my comment, Langston gave me one of his sleek smiles. "Like you said, Josie, it was business. I might have been angry at the man for ripping off my booth, but I wasn't going to let that stand in the way of turning a pretty profit." He sat back and crossed one leg over the other. "That doesn't mean I killed him."

"I'm guessing you didn't." Yeah, I was laying my cards on the table. At least some of them. When it comes to strategy, I'm not as hopeless as Stan thinks I am when he beats me at his monthly poker games. Maybe that's why Stan sat up and gave me an eagle-eye look. "Langston wouldn't have killed Brad on Monday," I said, not so much for Stan's benefit (because I was sure he'd already figured it out), but for that of the rest of my guests. "For him, it was all about business, and he wanted the button. Langston was the buyer Brad had listed as number two, and you heard what he said; he was supposed to meet Brad on Tuesday morning. He wouldn't have killed Brad before he had the button."

"Can I get my money back now?" Langston asked. "Tonight?"

I put him off with a smile. "We've got a couple more things to take care of first. Like how Jenny here had every reason in the world to hate Thad Wyant."

"Jenny?" Her eyes squinched for a better look at the woman sitting across the circle from her, Helen leaned forward. "You're Beth Howell."

"She was registered for the conference as Beth Howell," I explained. "Her real name is Jenny Tucker. She's Donovan's mother. Thad Wyant was Donovan's father."

Just as I expected, there was a collective gasp from those seated around me. "Jenny was outside the ballroom the night of the banquet because she was following the man she thought was Thad. She wanted him to admit that he was Donovan's father. And Donovan . . ." I glanced his way. "When he saw his mother out in the lobby, he was curious. Then the next day, he heard the news about the murder, and put two and two together. He thought she actually might be the killer."

"Well, that explains it then, doesn't it?" Helen slapped her hands on her thighs. "We know who did it, and we can be on our way. It's a busy night, Josie. You know that. There are a lot of people to say good-bye to and a lot of plans that need to be made for next year. You know . . ." Helen sat up a little straighter. "I've been asked to chair the conference in Phoenix. I'm sorry, Josie, but the truth is the truth, and there are people here at the conference who are convinced I'm the only one who can handle a conference this size. You know, without so many . . ." She chose her words carefully. "Without so many mistakes being made."

"The mistakes, yeah, we'll get to those. For now, though, I think it's important to point out why I don't think Jenny did it."

Jenny's hands curled into tight little fists. "I didn't. I wish I did. But I didn't."

"Of course you didn't. If he was going to pay you for all those years of missed child support, you needed Thad to be alive and kicking. Once you found out he was dead . . ."

She hung her head. "I hoped there would be an estate. That Donovan could get part of it. Thad owed him, after all. He was Donovan's father, and he owed him."

"That's why you pretended to be part of the housekeeping staff and searched Brad's room." Of course, Jenny knew this, but I mentioned it for the benefit of everyone else. "What were you hoping to find?"

Her shoulders were so slim that when she

lifted them, it was barely noticeable. "DNA," she said. "You know, so I could get it tested." When she looked up at me, Jenny's gray eyes sparkled. "I hit the jackpot. You know, those cardboard cards with the buttons on them."

"Yeah, the cards." This had confused me from the moment we found the cards in Donovan's suitcase. "If they were in Brad's suite —"

"Why didn't the cops find them?" Jenny laughed. "Sometimes, the cops don't know everything. Back when I first met Thad, back when things were going . . . you know, when they were going well for us . . . we were at a button conference, and we went back to his room one night. The first thing he did was go over to the air conditioner and start fussing with the carpet right under it. The day he checked in, see, he'd made a slit in it, and that's where he kept his extra money. He told me it was something his mama always did when the family traveled together. Said it was one place nobody would ever look if they came to rob the room."

"Which explains how Brad knew the hiding place, too." I nodded. "And that's where —"

"Where he hid those button cards. Sure."

367

Jenny laughed. "At first, I thought I could sell those buttons, but then I realized there was something even more valuable on one of those cards. A little spot of Thad's blood."

"Only if you'd had it tested, you would have found out it wasn't Thad after all," I reminded her.

Jenny frowned. "Son of a bitch cheated me, even after he was dead. Cheated my son out of everything that should be his."

"And if Jenny had killed Brad . . ." Like I said, Langston was smart. He'd already figured out exactly what I was going to mention next. "If she was after DNA and she killed him, she could have had all the blood she wanted. I mean, she could have soaked up some of his blood with one of those hand towels that must have been in the linen room where they found the body. She wouldn't have needed to go through his room, looking for DNA."

"Exactly!" I acknowledged his shrewdness with a smile.

"I still don't see . . ." Helen made a move to stand up and head for the door.

"About the mistakes, yeah." Since I planted myself right in front of her, there was really no place she could go, and she plopped back in her seat.

"Everything that went wrong at the conference — that's what got me thinking. That is, after Donovan here showed me what he'd caught on camera the night of the banquet."

"Not the killer!" Chase shot up like a shot.

"You don't actually believe anything a man like that filmed." Helen tsked.

Gloria narrowed her eyes and sent a death look in Donovan's direction.

"Actually, what Donovan showed me has nothing to do with Brad's murder. Not directly, anyway. It has everything to do with what's been going on at this conference to discredit me."

"You mean purposely?" Helen's cheeks paled, then shot through with color. "No one would ever do a thing like that! We love you, Josie. You know that."

"I know there was only one person dressed in pink the Monday of the conference." I gave Helen a level look. "It's clear," I said. "Or at least it was once I took a really good look. There you are, Helen, in the background of the shot Donovan took right before the opening ceremony. You're unplugging the microphone, and my guess is you did it for the same reason you called and cancelled the salads and the milkshakes. The same reason you misplaced some of the nametags the night of the cruise. You wanted to go down in the history of the

International Society of Antique and Vintage Button Collectors as the best conference chair ever. You wanted to be invited to head next year's event. And you couldn't do that, not if you didn't make me look incompetent."

"Well, I never!" Indignant as all get-out, Helen got to her feet and headed for the door, and when Kaz made a move to stop her, I signaled him to back off. "After all I've done for this group," Helen wailed. "After all I've done for you, Josie. To think that you'd think I was that kind of person!" She sniffled, pulled a lace-edged hankie from her purse, and touched it to her nose. "I'm leaving."

"Yes, of course. You're free to go." I made sure I stayed as calm as I was able. This was the big moment, and I didn't want to give anything away. "You can all go now," I said, glancing around the circle at my guests. "Only there's one thing you need to know before you do. Brad Wyant was a creep who'd come to rip off as many people as he could, and he found four people to sell the phony Geronimo button to. Only what you don't know . . ." I drew in a breath. "What you all need to know," I told them, "was that one of those buttons was the real thing."

CHAPTER TWENTY

"It didn't work." Nev and I were back at the hotel, in that alcove with the soda and the ice machines, and I leaned my head against the wall. It was nearly two hours after we'd left the Button Box and nearly an hour and a half since we'd been standing in the alcove, and I wasn't feeling any more upbeat about what happened back at the shop now than I was when my guests walked out. "We didn't get anywhere. I accused Helen of the most awful things and —"

"And we don't know yet." Remember how Nev told me about stakeouts? Well, that's pretty much what we were up to. We were on a stakeout, right between the vendor room and that trash can where we'd found the Geronimo button a couple days earlier. Being a veteran of these sorts of cloak-and-dagger operations, Nev knew to keep his voice down. "Telling them one of the buttons was real is bound to bring out our perp," he reminded me, the way he'd been reminding me since we got back to the hotel. "All we have to do is be patient."

"Yeah, but this is a stakeout, remember, and you're going to get crabby."

Was that a smile that lit Nev's eyes? It was kind of hard to tell since it was late and the hotel had agreed to help us out by turning down the lights in the corridor and in the little alcove where we were hiding. He stepped closer. "I said I get crabby on regular stakeouts," he crooned. "I didn't say anything about getting crabby when you're around."

That actually wasn't true, because, like I said, I'd seen him crabby a time or two. Then again, that was back when we didn't know each other very well. These days . . . I thought about all we'd been through together, and I found myself smiling, too.

I mirrored Nev and moved a step closer to him. "So when I'm around, you're in a good mood?"

"The best." He put his hands on my arms and bent his head toward mine. "In fact, I'm hoping when we get this case wrapped up —"

"Somebody's coming!"

We'd stationed Kaz out near the hotel registration desk to keep an eye on things, and didn't it figure, he picked this exact moment to scoot by and warn us.

My sigh and Nev's overlapped.

"Who is it?" Nev whispered.

"Couldn't tell." Oh yeah, I felt the touch of Kaz's gaze just at the place where Nev's hands were on my arms, but when we heard the sound of footsteps from out in the hallway, he didn't have the luxury of commenting. Just as we planned, he quickly and carefully opened a nearby service door and ducked into the stairwell there.

Nev and I backed away from each other and listened. A minute later, what we heard was the sound of somebody rattling through the nearest trash can. With a nod, Nev indicated it was time to move forward. We did —

And found Chase Cadell with his head down in the trash.

"Too late, Mr. Cadell," Nev said, and when Chase flinched and stood up, Nev shone his flashlight in his face. "We found the button days ago. It's been in the police evidence room ever since."

"Button?" Chase let go a nervous laugh. "I swear, I don't have a clue what in the tarnation —"

I leaned in close to him. "It was the real one," I said.

Chase's face fell like a badly baked cake. "Goldarnit!" he moaned. "I had the real one? The real Geronimo button? And I tossed it? I mean —" It was too late to take back the confession, and Chase knew it.

"Let me guess," I said. "You were either buyer number one, scheduled to meet Brad after the cruise on Sunday, or buyer number four. Did you meet him in the laundry room? Before the banquet?"

"That might be true." Chase's gaze darted between me and Nev. "But that doesn't mean I killed him. Why would I? I had the button. And I only got rid of it . . ." As if he could call back time and get his hands on the precious button again, Chase looked longingly at the trash can. "I got rid of it on account of I figured if you found it on me, you'd think it was evidence, that I killed Wyant."

"Which we do." Nev flicked his flashlight off and on three times, a signal to the uniformed cop waiting nearby that he could come and escort Chase to the security office.

"I didn't kill him," Chase said as he walked away. "I paid him, right enough. And I got that there button, and I'd put my hand to it and swear if it was here. I didn't kill him."

"Maybe," Nev conceded once Chase was gone. "Maybe not. Once we find the person who has the second button —"

He didn't finish, but then, that was because I poked him in the ribs with my elbow. "Shh," I hissed. "Listen."

We did, and we heard the small sounds of shuffling from inside the vendor room. This time, Nev took the lead. Together, we walked to the closed door, and on the count of three, he pushed the door open, and I flicked on the lights.

Was I surprised to see Helen digging through the poke box I'd found her at that afternoon?

I wanted to be. Honest to gosh, I tried. Instead, all I could do was close in on her, my heart as heavy as my voice.

"I was hoping it would be Gloria," I said.

"Gloria? Really?" She sparkled. But then, Helen always did. Too bad that smile of hers wavered around the edges. "I don't know . . . I don't know what you mean, dear."

"Sure you do. And it all comes back to what I said earlier, doesn't it? You couldn't stand to let anyone think you weren't the best. You sabotaged everything you could so that folks would think I was a loser and you were the best conference chair ever. And you . . ." My voice clogged, and I coughed away the pain. "Gloria was buyer number three. She was supposed to meet Brad in the bar after the banquet, but by then, he was dead. You were buyer number one, the person who got the button from Brad on Sunday night. You've kept it hidden all this time, but when I announced this afternoon that the buttons were phony, you figured you could get rid of it. That's why you were digging through the poke box, not to find a button, to lose one. Once I let the cat out of the bag that there was more than one phony button and that the buyers could get their money back, you figured people would start coming forward, and somehow, the cops would find out you were one of the suckers Brad preyed on. You couldn't be found with a button that might make you look guilty, either of being taken in by Brad or of his murder."

Even as I said this, Nev put up a hand, a signal to the waiting crime-scene tech to come retrieve the poke box and take it away.

"It was all about your reputation." I should have been mad, but I couldn't muster the energy. I studied the woman who I'd always looked up to as a friend and a mentor. "That's why you had to make me look bad, and that's why you killed Brad.

You couldn't let anyone know what he'd done to you."

Helen lifted her chin, but it says something about how she felt that she refused to meet my eyes. Instead, she glanced at Nev. "If I cooperate . . . ?"

He didn't say what would happen, he only gave her a nod as a way of telling her to keep talking.

"You're right, Josie." She looked at my shoes instead of my face. "I was buyer number one. You heard Brad say that yourself —"

"Room 842 tonight at eleven." Brad's words from the night of the cruise washed over me like ice water. "He wasn't just making casual conversation; he was telling you where to meet him to get the button. And you . . ." I would allow myself a good swift kick in the pants later. For now, I needed to sound as confident as I could. "You weren't drinking that night. That's not why you were all hopped up. You were excited about getting your hands on the button."

"And that next evening, when I saw the man I thought was Thad come through the lobby, and then Chase follow him —"

"You figured something was up."

Helen nodded. "I followed Chase down to the laundry room, and I slipped into that room across the hallway from the one Brad and Chase were in. I heard them talking. I heard Brad tell Chase that he was selling him the real Geronimo button, and I thought . . . My goodness!" Helen pressed a hand to her heart. "I thought it was impossible. How could Brad sell the button to Chase when he'd already sold it to me? And that's when I figured out what he was doing. I assumed all the buttons were fakes, and I knew he was playing us for suckers. I was so angry . . ."

Helen's hands curled into fists. "I waited for Chase to leave and then . . . Then I went into that linen room and I confronted Brad. When I first walked in, well, he was startled. He pulled that beautiful awl out of his pocket, like he thought he had to defend himself or something. But then he saw it was me, and he put it down there on a pile of towels. I told him he was a bad person and that I was going to tell everyone at the conference what he was up to. And he . . ."

Helen wiped a tear from her cheek. "He laughed at me, Josie. The man I thought was Thad Wyant, the greatest Western button expert on the planet, laughed in my face. He told me he knew I'd never tell anyone what he was up to because if I did, he said it would be like admitting that I was a fool. An old fool, that's what he said, an old fool who didn't know her buttons anymore. I don't know what happened, not exactly. I only know I was so angry, I couldn't see straight. I grabbed the awl —" Reliving the scene, Helen clutched an imaginary awl in one trembling hand. "And I lashed out at Thad. It wasn't until . . ." She looked down at her empty hands, and her shoulders bent beneath the weight of the truth. "When I finally realized what I'd done, he was already dead. You don't think I'm an old fool, do you, Josie?" Helen held out a hand to me. "You believe me when I say I was out of my mind, that I didn't know what I was doing?"

The pull of friendship is strong, especially when a friend is in trouble. I could no more have resisted taking Helen's hand than I could not take my next breath.

She timed it perfectly.

As soon as Helen had ahold of my hand, she pulled me close, then shoved me as hard as she could. I hit the nearest vendor table with a bang. The table skidded and tipped, I slammed into Nev, and we both hit the floor. Buttons flew everywhere. In the chaos, Helen took off running.

But remember what I said about Stan and backup.

He had her by the shoulders before she ever made it to the door. A second later, Nev was up off the floor. He put his handcuffs on her and led Helen away.

CHAPTER TWENTY-ONE

"And what's wrong with being a button collector?"

On the giant movie screen at the front of the theater, the woman with the chestnut hair and bowed lips — me — lifted her head and stuck out her chin.

"Defensive," I whispered to Nev, who was seated next to me and not listening to a word I said. "I was getting way too defensive."

He shushed me by patting my arm.

"Some of my best friends are button collectors," I said on-screen. "I'm a button collector."

Terrified that someone might recognize me, I glanced from left to right. No worries. It wasn't like *Buttoned Up,* Donovan Tucker's latest opus, was attracting crowds, in spite of the fact that it was billed as the unlikely convergence of buttons and murder. Still, I wasn't taking any chances; I sank down in my seat.

"As a whole, button collectors are educated, interesting, well read, and a heck of a lot better company than a lot of the non-button collectors I've met. If you think being a button collector means being boring —"

"Doesn't it?" That was Donovan's voice, and I pictured that day in the coffee shop and the way he'd leaned closer to me, eager to catch everything I had to say on video.

On-screen, the camera zoomed in on my face.

I put my head in my hands and groaned.

"I can't believe you talked me into this." Since we were just about the only people in the theater, I didn't feel bad about saying this out loud. "I don't think I can take another minute."

"Really?" Nev had just finished the buttered popcorn he was munching, and he brushed his hands together and took my arm. "Then let's get out of here."

Outside the Landmark Century Centre Cinema, he looped an arm around my shoulders. "We always had fun seeing movies before."

"Yeah, but not movies that I'm in."

He gave me a squeeze. "They're my favorites."

OK, yes, I admit it, the smile he gave me made me forget how mortified I was to see my face on the big screen. Almost.

"So . . ." He glanced up and down North Clark. "It's early. You want to go for dinner?"

I said I did, and we headed for the nearest burger joint. We were almost there when Nev glanced at me out of the corner of his eye. "So, you heard from Kaz?"

"No." It wasn't like I was trying to spare his feelings or anything; it was just the truth. "Ever since Amber went back to wherever Amber came from, Kaz doesn't need me anymore. He doesn't need to hide out."

"At least not for now."

"Look . . ." I stopped, and because the sidewalk was crowded, I stepped closer to the front display window of a men's clothing store. "I think we need to talk."

Nev made a face. "Not about Kaz, I hope. You don't think I think —"

"It doesn't matter what you think. What matters is what's real. And what's real is that I'm over him. He's over me. He only comes around when he needs something."

"Yeah, but he keeps coming around."

It wasn't jealousy. Not exactly. It was more like Nev was just stating the truth, and that meant I couldn't deny it.

383

"No doubt, the next time he needs to hide or he's low on money . . . Yeah, he'll show up again," I said. "But even if he does . . ."

"Even if he does?" Nev asked.

And honestly, I couldn't think of the right words to explain.

Instead, I showed him. I kissed him.

Right there.

Right on the sidewalk.

Right on the lips.

"Wow!" When I was finished, Nev said what I was thinking. "So now it looks like we have something else to talk about right? First it was murder, then Kaz, now —"

I wasn't ready for the L word, so I didn't let him say it. Instead, I slipped my arm around Nev's waist. "Not to worry. If we run out of things to say, we can always talk about buttons!"

MOTHER OF PEARL BUTTONS

Billions of mother of pearl (MOP) buttons were manufactured in the late nineteenth and early twentieth centuries, many of them stamped from the shells of mussels taken from the Mississippi River. In fact, Muscatine, Iowa, once reigned as Pearl Button Capital of the World.

Of course, since they were so common, MOP buttons are not especially valuable. They are, though, quite pretty, with a nice shine and a shimmer of color.

To determine if a button is made of shell, hold it to your cheek. Mother of pearl is cooler than plastic. You can also look for striations on the back of the button.

For more information on vintage buttons and button collecting, contact the National Button Society at www.nationalbutton society.org.

CPSIA information can be obtained
at www.ICGtesting.com
Printed in the USA
FFOW051224180213